Praise for *Everyone Is Still Alive*

'The characters are sharply drawn and the author has a knack for wry phrases . . . If you like *Motherland*, you'll love this funny, tender book' *Sunday Times*

'One of the most honest, poignant and well-observed books about family life we've ever read . . . Full of wisdom, you'll be clutching your heart for a long time'
Woman & Home, Book of the Month

'A touching drama about the minutiae of family life . . . An impressive debut from an accomplished memoirist'
The *i*, 40 Best Books for Summer

'This is a book about going to new places and the fear of new people, but also about the comfort of community, the way that a place like Magnolia Road can be a source of the kind of friendship and support that gets you through even the darkest times' *Observer*

'Rentzenbrink takes you by the hand and reassures you that you're not alone . . . Full of wisdom' *Woman*

'A compassionate and insightful look at relationships and friendships in a wonderfully well-observed novel that is tender, sharp and, at times, very funny'
Sunday Express

'Warm-hear⸻ *The Times*

D0452290

'One of the most honest, poignant and well-observed books about family life we've ever read'
WOMAN & HOME

'Touching, tender and profound'
DAISY BUCHANAN

'Wonderfully well-observed . . . very funny'
SUNDAY EXPRESS

'Brilliantly caustic'
GUARDIAN

'I devoured it'
PATRICK GALE

'If you like *Motherland*, you'll love this funny, tender book'
SUNDAY TIMES

'Sharply observed and utterly compelling'
PAULA HAWKINS

'Hilarious and moving'
DAILY MAIL

'I can't stop thinking about it' ELIZABETH DAY

'Wonderful' KATE MOSSE

'Sharply observed and utterly compelling, *Everyone Is Still Alive* had me cackling on one page and crying the next; Cathy Rentzenbrink's warmth and wisdom are evident in every line'   Paula Hawkins

'Unputdownable – brilliant, beautiful, moving and so funny and well-observed. If you want to know what Happily Ever After looks like, read this' Philippa Perry

'An anti-romantic comedy of Lego and disenchantment, shot through with clear-eyed compassion . . . I devoured it'   Patrick Gale

'I love this book. Funny, wise and clever and full of honesty and kindness. It's a page-turner that makes you look at yourself and your relationships anew. A unique and generous novel about love, loss and friendship'
                    Kit de Waal

'A wonderful novel . . . I loved it. Gorgeous and tender, fabulous at capturing time, place and atmosphere. An utter treat'   Kate Mosse

'Such a beautiful, delicate book'   Jenny Colgan

'A soothing, tender story with loveable characters who pull you in from the very first pages. In a world of chaos, reading this novel was a reminder to slow down, zoom in and look around'   Emma Gannon

EVERYONE
IS
STILL
ALIVE

Cathy
Rentzenbrink

PHOENIX

First published in Great Britain in 2021 by Phoenix Books,
This paperback edition first published in Great Britain in 2022
by Phoenix Books,
an imprint of The Orion Publishing Group Ltd
Carmelite House, 50 Victoria Embankment
London EC4Y 0DZ

An Hachette UK Company

1 3 5 7 9 10 8 6 4 2

A CIP catalogue record for this book is
available from the British Library.

ISBN (Mass Market Paperback) 978 1 4746 2114 4
ISBN (eBook) 978 1 4746 2115 1
ISBN (Audio) 978 1 4746 2116 8

Typeset by Input Data Services Ltd, Somerset

Printed in Great Britain by Clays Ltd, Elcograf S.p.A.

MIX
Paper from
responsible sources
FSC® C104740

www.orionbooks.co.uk
www.phoenix-books.co.uk

To Erwyn

Author's Note

Many years ago, I visited a friend who lived on the real-life Magnolia Road by the Thames. I sat in her garden watching the trains go by and wondering what it would be like to live in one of those beautiful houses. My friend has long since moved away and I have enjoyed letting my imagination run wild in writing this novel. If there are any similarities to real people or circumstances, these are purely coincidental.

We must love one another or die.

W. H. Auden

Literature is mostly about having sex and not much about having children. Life is the other way around.

David Lodge

Magnolia Road
Liam Quinn

We were obsessed with external threats that year. That's how it seems to me now. We worried about this politician and that dictator, about laws and tariffs and refugees and recessions. Every time we looked at a screen it delivered evidence of peril. We feared the worst and had no idea what we could do about it. Were we fiddling as Rome burnt? Were we rearranging the deckchairs on the Titanic? Were we failing to sufficiently check our privilege? Had we lost perspective in allowing news about trade deals to perturb us as much as the possibility of nuclear war? We took the children to school and drank coffee at the cafe. We picked them up and drank wine at each other's houses. Sometimes we asked ourselves why we had ever thought it was a good idea to bring these little lives into this broken and damaged world. In between conversations about phonics and nits and the next PTA fundraiser, we wondered how to find any point and purpose in our tiny endeavours when

1

the planet felt like it might explode at any moment.

We were looking in the wrong place. I see that now. The danger, when it came, had nothing to do with politics and global events. There was no cause and effect. We could not have seen it coming. It was not modern. What happened in Magnolia Road was as old as time.

Chapter One

Juliet runs her fingers over the rack of silk scarves and chooses a blue one covered with little silver birds. She ties up her hair with it, then walks up the stairs to the attic. She has decided to approach this task with brutal efficiency. She does not allow herself to read any letters, or dwell on the stationery that will now never be used. Nor does she open any of the photo albums. She just gathers any official correspondence into a folder marked 'Mum' and packs everything else into plastic containers. It is not a big job. Her mother was a methodical and orderly woman who disliked clutter and had little interest in accumulating material possessions. Everything nonessential she owned was a gift. Juliet considers the photo hanging on the wall of her and Liam on their wedding day, basking in the sunshine outside the registry office. She is pregnant and Liam has his hand on her bump. They look happy. She leaves it where it is and does the same with the heavy serpentine vase on the windowsill. The noticeboard, too, can stay. It has a vintage look about it. Liam will enjoy pinning things to the green baize.

Once the surfaces are clear, Juliet mops and wipes until all is pristine. She is dry-eyed throughout. Maybe this will be the day that the tears stop. She tries it out in her head: *The week after my mother's funeral we moved into her house and I stopped crying every day.*

A spritz of polish catches in the back of her throat. She opens the window and takes a few deep breaths of the sultry air, hearing the noise of an approaching train. They come every few minutes, whizzing by on the built-up embankment at the end of the garden. She can almost see the passengers as individuals but not quite; they go by in a blur.

Down in the garden, Charlie is playing on the grass and Liam is sitting at the long stone table reading a book. That was a thing her mother loved, that huge table. The people who sold her the house nearly thirty years ago asked if they could leave it in place until they worked out how to transport it. But they never made any arrangements, so Juliet's mother became its owner. She said it made her think of Narnia, that when she looked out of the window in the dusk she could almost imagine animals sitting and feasting, a squirrel arguing with a robin, a badger clinking tankards with a horse. Juliet looks down at her husband and son, solid, real, one a tiny facsimile of the other. *This is my family now,* she thinks. *This is what I have.*

She picks up the last box, carries it down the stairs and adds it to the pile by the front door. As she straightens, she catches a glimpse of herself in the mirror. A bit of hair is trying to escape from the scarf. As she tucks it back in, she smooths her finger over the streaks of grey at her temple. There are more every day.

She walks into the kitchen. Here, too, the window gives onto the garden. Charlie is looking intently at something in his hand. She can't see what it is. She fills a jug with water and ice, puts it on a tray with three glasses and takes it out.

'Look,' says Charlie, 'I met a very friendly beetle.'

'That's lovely.'

'Can I show him my bedroom?'

'You're not allowed any creatures inside, remember. Come and have some water.'

Charlie gulps it down quickly so he can get back to his new pal. Liam doesn't look up from his book.

Juliet presses the cool glass against her forehead. 'I've finished,' she says. 'I've packed everything up and given the room a good clean. Not that it was dirty but, you know. The boxes are stacked by the door. Will you drive them over to the storage place if I do Charlie's tea?'

Liam nods.

'So, it's all yours now.'

He nods again.

'You can arrange your stuff when you get back.'

He picks up his glass. 'I'll go as soon as I've had this.'

'Sorry. I didn't mean to rush you.'

Another train is coming, drowning out any possibility of conversation. When Charlie was a toddler, he would point and say, 'Rain, rain, see rain.' Juliet would lift him into her arms and he'd chortle with glee at the

5

magic of the metal monster. Now he doesn't even look up. He only has eyes for his beetle.

Liam has finished his water but is still engrossed in the book. It is his new thing, to have periods where he leaves his phone alone and communes with literature instead. He has explained to Juliet that this will aid his concentration and help him to focus. Maybe it will. He is also expecting to reap creative benefits from having a room of his own. That's what swung it for him, when they were discussing what to do, whether to move. 'You can have the study all to yourself,' she had said. She knows he thinks Magnolia Road is a bit square, a bit posh, a bit heteronormative, not the sort of place he imagines a hip young writer should live. If hip is even the right word. It probably isn't.

Juliet hopes that having a room of his own will help him to be happy and productive. Her mother always referred to it as the study but Liam thinks that sounds twattish, so they have rebranded it as the attic. She watches Charlie whispering to the beetle. It will be good for him to have a garden. It will be good for them all to have a bit more space than they had in the flat. No wonder things were tense when they were continually on top of each other. She is sure it is the right thing to do, to cross London, move from east to west, to live in her dead mother's house.

Charlie tucks into his fish fingers, though most of the peas end up on the floor.

'I miss Granny.'

'I know, darling. So do I.'

'Why did she die?'

He has asked this question many times.

'She had cancer.'

'Why did she get cancer?'

'I don't know. Some people do. It isn't a fair thing.'

'Why didn't she live with Grandad?'

'She and Grandad stopped living together years ago.'

'Will you and Daddy ever stop living together?'

'I don't think so, darling. I hope not.'

'Aren't you sure?'

She hesitates. 'Well, it isn't only up to me, is it? But I hope we will carry on living together. It's nice, isn't it, us all living together?'

'Very nice.' He eats his last bite of fish finger. 'I will marry you when I grow up, Mummy.'

'That's very sweet, but you won't want to. You'll have lots of friends and you won't want to hang out with me any more.'

'Mummy!' His voice is full of outrage. 'I will always want to hang out with you.'

Later that night she closes the book on Robin Hood and his adventures. 'OK, little man. Sleepy time.'

'Is it my birthday tomorrow?'

'No, not until the next day. Tomorrow we'll settle in a bit more and go to the park.'

'I'm settled in.'

He does indeed look at home. Her mother used to have him to stay for several days at a time and had enjoyed making her spare room into a little boy's paradise. There is a mural of a steam train across one wall and his curtains – which black out the sun to help him sleep – are dotted with luminous fish.

Juliet turns off the main light and presses the button on the turtle nightlight that casts an array of little green stars onto the walls and ceiling.

'Where's that naughty Froggy?'

Charlie holds his cuddly toy and giggles.

Juliet lies down with Charlie for a last cuddle. As she admires the stars she sees something else glowing on the ceiling.

'What's that?' she asks.

'The solar system,' Charlie says, carefully. 'Mars and Jupiter and Saturn and some other ones. Granny put it there so I can look at it before I go to sleep.'

This is not going to be a day without tears, after all.

'Granny loves us a lot,' says Charlie.

Juliet doesn't correct the tense. She swallows hard and whispers goodnight. Charlie holds on as she tries to slide off the bed.

'Another story.'

'You've had two stories. The light is switched off.'

'Can I have an apple?'

'No. It's sleepy time now.'

'I'm thirsty.'

'No, you're not. Go to dozy land. I love you very much. Cuddle Froggy until you go to sleep.'

She tucks his blanket around him. It is blue with silver stars. Her mother brought it to the hospital on the day of his birth. Then she has to prise his fingers off her arm. It is always like this. Whatever she does is never enough.

Juliet stands and weeps by the window in her mother's bedroom – now hers. Theirs. Tomorrow she'll pack up the clothes and take them to a charity shop. The alcove is still full of her mother's books. She sees a copy of *How to Stay Married* by Jilly Cooper and opens it. She knows what she'll find. There, on the flyleaf, a dedication from her father to her mother. 'Let's give it our best shot, sweetheart.' It doesn't sound all that optimistic. Maybe he knew all along that he was not the faithful type. He is on his third marriage now and Juliet hardly sees him. He came to the funeral and ruffled Charlie's hair whilst his wife, dressed all in black and even a hat with a little veil, pressed Juliet's hand and said to be sure to tell them if she needed anything, anything at all.

Juliet flips through the book. She's read it before. Always be in a good mood, is the key; be cheerful and tolerant and don't ever refuse sex. Don't be a bore or a martyr. Be sure to serve up delicious dinners when he comes home exhausted from the office. But what if you are the one coming home from the office, she wonders; what if you are the one who has to bring home the bacon and then cook it, too?

She looks out of the window. They are right down at the bottom of Magnolia Road, in a cul-de-sac bounded by railway lines, the M4, the Thames and under the flight path to Heathrow. Her mother didn't mind the noise of the trains and the planes, said she liked to have evidence that life was happening around her.

The house opposite – Brian and Jim – are having building work done. Brian came over when they arrived with a pot of tea on a tray. 'You won't have unpacked the kettle yet,' he said, and Juliet smiled and thanked him, though they are using her mother's kettle along with everything else so they barely need to unpack anything. 'Lovely service, last week. You picked my favourite hymn. Isn't that what we all need, for our foolish ways to be forgiven? You did your mum proud. We're happy to have you here. A family! So nice for us old 'uns to be surrounded by young life. Shame you missed the street party. Hope you don't find our building work too annoying. We're having a loft conversion done. A wet room. Imagine! I won't keep you. So many jobs. It takes a year, they say, the grief, you know, to get over it, to move on. Just leave the tray on the pavement. I'll pop back later.'

Juliet has heard this theory from lots of people. When she told her assistant they were moving house, Adi said, 'Oh, but are you sure that's a good idea? My mum says you shouldn't make any decisions until a year has passed. That's how long it takes. To function again and see things clearly.'

'I don't have that much time,' Juliet said, gently, because she loves Adi with her youthful enthusiasm and fierce competence. 'I can't wait to feel better. I have a child who needs to know where he is going to school and can't have his mother lying on the sofa crying for the next twelve months.'

It was mad, surely, to leave her mother's house empty but she didn't like the thought of strangers living there. That doesn't bother her with the flat. They have let it furnished to one of her colleagues' daughters. Juliet hopes she will be happy. She was, when she first bought it. She loved the sari shops and the fruit and veg sellers with their unfamiliar produce, and the Portuguese cafe where she used to eat fish on toast. It is different over here in West London. Staider, less multicultural. They don't have to stay, she told Liam, if they don't like it. But they should try it out. They should give it a year.

It is certainly quieter. She wouldn't be able to look out of the window of the flat for so long and not see anything happen. A couple she doesn't recognise come out of the house a few doors up. They are both beautiful. He is tall and black, she has red hair and a slightly worried expression. He opens the gate for her. There is something solicitous in the way he is with her. *They are in love*, Juliet thinks. They are young and in love. She watches them walk up the street holding hands. They might be going out for dinner. Or to the pub. She would bet money they have no children. They look too unblemished, too self-contained. They are in thrall to each other, perhaps, but not to the demands of tiny hands, of insistent infant appetites. There are no children down at this end, but she has seen families further up the street. She hopes Charlie will find it easy to make friends – she has told him he will. He was sad about leaving Tyler and Mahir behind, but she has promised him that in this new life he will make lots of friends. The way she has spun it, kindred spirits grow on trees, and he will find boon companions in the blink of an eye. She hopes she has been telling the truth.

There is a tread behind her. Liam puts his hand on her shoulder. 'Looking for tips?'

She is still holding the Jilly Cooper. 'I was thinking about Mum.'

'Shall we christen our bedroom tonight?'

For a moment she doesn't know what he means. And then she remembers – yes, that was what they used to do, that was their shorthand for sex in a new place. It feels the wrong thing to say about her dead mother's room.

'Sure,' she says, 'let's wait until Charlie is sound asleep. And I need a shower.'

'Don't sound too enthusiastic,' he says.

She puts the book back on the shelf. If you refuse your husband, Jilly says, you only have yourself to blame if he strays. Strays. The word echoes in her head. Like a dog.

'Just a bit tired,' she says. It has been a long day, not helped by Liam hiring a van that was too small so they had to make two trips across the sweltering city. She feels the irritation rise in her again, tries to push it down. 'And I feel a bit grubby.'

He slips his fingers under her scarf and pulls out a few curls. 'I like this thing,' he says, 'very World War Two. You look like a sexy munitions girl.'

She feels the rasp of his damaged finger against her neck. It was one of the first things she'd noticed about him, that the tip of the forefinger of his right hand was missing. He'd lost it to a woodturning lathe when he was seventeen and working in a factory. She liked that he was different from her previous boyfriends, all of whom were university-educated professionals. She thought it would mean he was strong and practical and good at fixing things, though none of that turned out to be true.

'Munitions must have been dirty work,' says Juliet, trying to keep her tone light. 'I bet those girls needed a wash when they came off duty.'

Liam kisses her neck. She stops talking.

'Is it my birthday?'

Juliet squints at her alarm clock. It is 5.30 a.m.

'No, darling. Not until tomorrow. Go back to sleep.'

'Too noisy.'

'That's just the planes. Lie in bed and think about where they've come from.'

'I'm not sleepy.'

She is awake now. She goes back to Charlie's room with him.

'Play with me, Mummy.'

'It's too early. You can play quietly but I need to lie down.'

She lies in his bed and listens to the planes and the trains. She hopes they will get used to the sound, be able to sleep through it. Or maybe she will become one of those hyper productive types who get up in the early hours to meditate or exercise.

Juliet runs through her list of jobs for the day. She has to wrap Charlie's presents and buy a cake. And candles. And some party food. Last year her mother organised it. Now it is down to her. More sorting. Packing up Mum's belongings and putting them into storage so that there is room for her family to expand into their new space. And making a list of all the admin she has to do. She has to cancel Mum's mobile phone and get the names changed on the utility bills. She has to phone the bank. And she has to apply for probate, which she still doesn't fully understand and everyone tells her will be a nightmare. There is so much to do when someone dies and it is the raw and grieving who have to do it. *I wish you were here, Mum*, she thinks. *For every reason, and also so you could help me with all these tasks.*

'Is it my birthday?'

It is 3.30 a.m.

'It's not morning time yet. Go back to bed.'

'Am I having a party?'

'No, you know that. We were too busy with the exciting move. We'll have a lovely day just the three of us.'

'Are my friends coming?'

'Just us. It's a bit far. You'll have lots of new friends soon.'

'Am I getting a pet?'

'We don't have space for a pet.'

14

He stands and stares at her.

'Come on. I'll tuck you back in.'

In his room she smooths the duvet over him.

'Lie down with me, Mummy.'

She weighs her options. He is more likely to go back to sleep if she agrees. And it is his birthday. She slides in and puts her arms around him, rubs her nose against his cheek. As she drifts off to sleep she can smell that Froggy needs a wash.

'Wake up, you stinky pleasants. It's time to pay your taxes.'

Juliet opens her eyes. Charlie stands poised with his plastic bow and arrow. He is misquoting the Sheriff of Nottingham, just before Robin Hood saves the day and makes sure all the peasants get to keep their money for themselves.

'Happy birthday,' she says.

They go next door and wake Liam. The gifts go down well. Charlie puts on his Darth Vader costume immediately and runs around waving his lightsaber. Then he looks through his encyclopaedia of beetles. Juliet tries to encourage him to read some of the words but he is only interested in the pictures. Then he wants to put the Star Wars stickers from his new book all over the wardrobe.

'Do you know,' says Juliet, 'we should go downstairs for some breakfast, and I think Froggy needs a special birthday wash now he's five.'

Charlie is resistant but Juliet says he can push the

button himself and watch him go round in the washing machine, so he agrees and they sit on the kitchen floor together as he spins in a blur of yellow and green.

'Froggy is as old as me,' Charlie says.

'Yes,' says Juliet, 'your very first friend. Granny brought him to the hospital.'

'When I'm grown up, I'll have a real frog.'

'When you are grown up you can do whatever you like.'

Charlie spends the rest of the morning in the garden. Liam helps him put together his Playmobil Noah's Ark and then sits and reads while Charlie arranges all the animals around it. Then the Lego mini figures get involved. When Juliet takes him some carrot sticks, Noah has been sidelined and Han Solo is in charge of directing the animals onto the Ark.

Liam closes his book with an air of finality.

'Good?' asks Juliet.

'Very good.'

'What was it about?'

'Marriage. Children. Art.'

He stares into space and Juliet goes back inside to get lunch ready.

The stormtrooper cake is a triumph. Julie forgot to buy candles but finds some in the kitchen drawer. They are gold and surprisingly hard to blow out, so Liam has to help Charlie to prevent the cake from being drowned in spit. They sing 'Happy Birthday' and clap. Charlie doesn't want them to cut the cake at first, but they compromise by lifting off the stormtrooper's iced face intact and carving up the sponge underneath. She hasn't eaten sugar for a while – Adi told her it is bad for her skin, something to do with collagen – but it feels odd to refuse a bit of her son's birthday cake. She has one piece and then another. It is delicious.

After lunch Liam takes Charlie to the park. Juliet looks at the cake and thinks it might be a nice gesture to take some round to the neighbours, but with the icing gone it doesn't quite look good enough so she eats another slice herself. When the others get back, they put *Star Wars* on the telly and Liam and Charlie watch it while Juliet dozes on the sofa. She hears Liam telling Charlie he has the force and Charlie almost believing him. They order a Chinese takeaway for tea as it is Charlie's favourite food, but none of them are that hungry. By the end of the day Juliet feels full and a bit sick but pleased they have given Charlie a good time. He goes to bed surrounded by Froggy, his new Darth Vader cushion and the giraffe from Noah's Ark.

'Happy, Mummy?' he asks, as she tucks him in.

'Yes, darling,' she says. 'I'm always happy when you're happy.'

'But still sad because Granny is dead.'

'Well, yes. I'm both. That's the thing with feelings. You can have more than one at the same time.'

Later she investigates the kitchen. She is used to being in there when she visits but everything feels different now it is hers. Her mother enjoyed cooking. There is a row of chef's knives on a magnetic rack on the wall, several different-coloured chopping boards, and a whole cupboard full of baking trays arranged in a neat stack. The big mixing bowl sits in the corner of the worktop.

Juliet could play a grief-themed version of *Ready Steady Cook* with all the food. Several tins of anchovies and packets of ginger nuts. Various flavoured cooking oils. Pine nuts, sesame seeds, dates, rose water. She has no idea what she will do with most of it but can't bring herself to throw it all away. Lots of oats – her mother was a great believer in the restorative power of porridge. Packs of red, green and yellow jelly and tins of fruit. Juliet picks up a tin of mandarin oranges. Her mother will have touched this as she put it in her trolley, buying it so she could make fruit jellies with Charlie. She can see her mother, then, standing in her apron, behind Charlie up on a stool, helping him divide the cubes, guiding him to stir the water so they dissolve. Juliet feels the tears come. She sinks down onto the floor. Is she really going to feel like this for a whole year? Flicking between numbly experiencing the world though a sheet of perspex and crying her eyes out? Still, she might as well get it all out of her system. She has to go back to work the next day.

And all the articles she has read about grief suggest that it is dangerous to suppress it.

'Mummy.'

It is 2 a.m.

'What is it, darling?'

'I've accidentally wet the bed by accident.'

'Oh, sweetheart.'

Juliet strips the bed and wipes down the plastic under-sheet. She dries Charlie off and helps him into clean pyjamas. Then she remakes the bed and throws the sodden Star Wars linen down the stairs to go in the wash the next morning. Froggy is a bit damp, too, but Charlie doesn't want to let him go. 'I need him.'

'He's too wet,' says Juliet in a hard, cross voice, chucking Froggy over the bannister. 'You'll have to make do with one of your other toys.'

He cries and she pats him for a bit, feeling mean. Liam sleeps like the dead so it is always up to her when Charlie needs attention in the night.

In the morning, as she gets dressed for work, she snaps at Liam. 'Charlie wet the bed again last night. We'll have to do something about it. I can't go on losing sleep.'

'He's worried about starting school. Just stick him in a night nappy again until it sorts itself out. It's not a big deal, is it? We just need to not make him feel like it's a big deal.'

She feels wrong-footed. Like she is the bad parent traumatising her child by making a fuss. In the kitchen she tries to put Charlie's bedding in the washing machine but it is full and so is the tumble dryer, so she gives up and leaves it in a pile on the floor, Froggy sitting on top, for Liam to deal with.

At lunchtime she phones the school and asks if

19

Charlie can come in and see the building and meet his teacher before the start of term.

'He's a bit nervous,' she explains.

'Bless him,' says the school secretary. 'Pop in tomorrow afternoon. Mrs Karigi will be in then, setting up her classroom. She's very keen.'

Juliet feels a sense of achievement. Then she goes out to buy night nappies. In the queue, she checks her personal email. Her mother's ashes are ready for collection from the crematorium. She feels the familiar twist in her belly and can't really believe her mother has been turned into ash. She looks around her at all the flesh-and-blood bodies buying painkillers and deodorant and cosmetics. How are these people still alive when her mother is dead?

She takes a breath, reads through the rest of the email. The ashes must be collected within two weeks or they will be scattered in the garden of remembrance. Because she has not chosen anything from the range of urns, the ashes will be in a plastic bag within a grey box. If she wants to make other arrangements she can let them know. They have attached the catalogue. She remembers being at the crematorium and Liam nudging her in front of the display cabinet which showcased the urns and scatter tubes. 'That one looks like an ice bucket,' he whispered. They were all rather ornate or sentimental. She can't imagine her mother – what is left of her – reposing in any sort of container with angels or love hearts or teddy bears. The box will have to do.

Back at home, Juliet bathes Charlie and casually produces the pull-ups.

'Pop these on just in case you don't wake up when you need a wee.'

'But I'm a big boy. I don't need a nappy.'

'Yes, you are. Of course you are. This is just in case. And they're not nappies. They're night-time pants. And guess what? Tomorrow, you and Daddy are going to see your new school and meet your teacher.'

The next day Juliet goes straight to the crematorium after work. She is planning to walk home but the box is heavier than she expected so she orders an Uber. The driver is chatty and asks about her day, what she's been up to. She wants to tell him about the ashes but worries she might cry so is non-committal as she keeps her hand on the box. Almost she feels a tingle, a warmth. Maybe she is imagining it.

When she gets home she stows the box at the back of the cupboard under the stairs. Charlie is in bed. He shows Juliet a piece of paper that Mrs Karigi has given him. The Golden Rules. Juliet reads them out. *We are gentle, we are kind and helpful, we listen, we work hard, we look after property.*

'Well, they sound sensible,' she says, 'and you are gentle and kind and helpful. I think you'll be brilliant at following the Golden Rules.'

'If we don't,' says Charlie, 'we need to go and sit on the thinking chair.'

'Golly,' says Juliet.

After lights out she goes downstairs.

Liam says, 'You'll never guess who Mrs Karigi is.'

'Who?'

'The beautiful redhead from up the road. Who lives with the tall, black dude.'

'Oh.'

'She looks like you, don't you think?'

Juliet considers. 'It's just the hair, isn't it? She must be a couple of decades younger than me.'

'She looks like your little sister, then.'

She's not convinced.

'God loves us, Mummy.'

'Does he?'

'He made all our fingers and all our toes and he knows all our names.'

'That's nice.'

It was Liam's idea. He noticed the posters for a summer camp in the last week before Charlie went back to school. Only £45 for 10–4, Tuesday to Friday. Liam doesn't seem worried that it all happens in a church and Charlie is getting some hardcore indoctrination. When Juliet queried it, Liam said that kids had to learn to make up their own minds, though Juliet is sure he was fed up of being on solo childcare and wanted to have some time to himself.

'And all rock is Jesus.'

'Is it?'

'Every stone and every pebble.'

'Lovely. Do you want a story?'

'I've got to say my prayers. If we need help, we can ask God and He will answer.'

'Go on then.'

Charlie closes his eyes. Opens them again.

'I can't remember what to say.'

'What do you need help with?'

'I don't know.'

'I think I remember a prayer for bedtime, hang on.' Juliet racks her brains. '"Now I lay me down to sleep, I pray the Lord my soul to keep. And if I die before I wake, I pray the Lord my soul to take."'

She feels proud of herself for dragging that up from somewhere deep in her memory, then notices Charlie's worried face.

'Am I going to die?'

'No, darling. That's a silly prayer, actually. Very old-fashioned. You're not going to die.'

'Ever?'

'Well, one day. But not until you are very old.'

When Juliet wakes to feel Charlie's hand on her arm, she thinks he has wet the bed again. She looks at the clock. It is 3.45 a.m.

'Is everyone still alive?'

'Oh, darling. Yes, everyone is still alive.'

'Even Granny?'

Juliet swallows. 'Granny is dead but everyone else is still alive.'

'You won't die, will you, Mummy?'

'I'll try very hard not to.'

'Promise me.'

His little face illuminated by the streetlight is so earnest. Juliet thinks back to those far-off days when she had abstract opinions on the sort of mother she wanted to be. She remembers splaying her fingers over her bump and pledging that she would never lie.

'I promise.'

She takes him back to his bed.

'Get into bed with me, Mummy. Make the bad dreams go away.'

She lies next to him. 'Shall I tell you what I do when I have a nightmare?'

'What?'

'I pinch myself on the arm. In the dream. And that wakes me up.'

'Does it?'

'Yes. Try it next time.'

Juliet waits until Charlie is asleep. Then she gets out of his bed. She is wide awake now. She walks downstairs, gets a glass of water, looks out of the sitting room window at the street. All is quiet. The residents of Magnolia Road do not come and go in the middle of the night. *Everyone is still alive*, she thinks. *That's what I have to think about. Liam and Charlie and me. We are all still alive.*

Chapter Two

The porridge is burnt. Juliet pokes it with a spatula. Definitely ruined in the time it took to answer two work emails. Fuck. She wanted to give Charlie the best possible start to his first day at school. She stares into the fridge. There is no more milk. Eggs! Juliet chucks a knob of butter into a pan, cracks two eggs on top of it, and stirs it all together. She puts a slice of bread into the toaster.

'Charlie,' she shouts up the stairs. 'Breakfast.'

She hears his lolloping footsteps. No longer the patter of tiny feet but still not yet a grown-up sound. Charlie comes into the kitchen. Why is he still in his pyjamas? Liam was supposed to be getting him dressed. Hadn't they agreed that? Where is he? Still asleep? Or has he gone straight up to the attic, leaving everything to her?

'Look, Mummy, I've done you a surprise,' Charlie says. He holds out her laptop. It is covered in Star Wars Lego stickers.

'That's lovely,' she says, hoping they'll peel off easily.

'You like Princess Leia.'

'I do, darling. Thank you.'

She takes the laptop from him and glances at the clock. She has forty-five minutes to feed him, wash him, dress him, sort herself out and get them all out of the door.

She sniffs. Smoke is rising from the toaster. Juliet pulls up the lever. She is still not used to it. Liam was always amused that the highly expensive toaster doesn't pop itself and used to tease her mother about it, 'The more you pay, the less you get.' Mum would say she just wanted something that would last. Juliet examines the toast. Still edible. She scrapes some butter onto it and puts the plate down next to Charlie.

'I don't like the black bits,' he says, looking down at where burnt specks have mingled with the butter.

'They are extra tasty,' says Juliet, cringing at herself. Her own long-dead granny used to say things like that to get her to consume food. Crusts would give her curly hair, carrots would make her see in the dark, something would give her hairs on her chest.

'Can I have messy cheese?'

Juliet gets a bag of grated mozzarella out of the fridge and shovels a bit onto Charlie's plate. He looks down at it. She can see it doesn't look appetising. A slab of burnt toast, a bit of runny egg, a pile of cheese.

'I miss Granny,' says Charlie.

'I do, too,' says Juliet. Her mother would have provided a nourishing bowl of porridge, or would not have burnt the toast. She would have made a face or an animal out of the egg and cheese.

'Why did Granny die?'

Juliet doesn't want to explain about the cancer for the millionth time.

'She just did. It's not fair and there is no logic. She just died.'

Leaving us to fuck up her house, Juliet thinks. They've only lived here for a couple of weeks, but since she went back to work the laundry basket overflows, and the dishwasher is always half full of clean stuff as she and Liam face off over whose turn it is to empty it and just take out what they need, letting the dirty dishes accumulate in piles on the worktop.

'Who is taking me to school?'

'Daddy will take you and pick you up. Except today where we'll both take you as a treat.'

Charlie looks grumpy, as though that doesn't sound like much of a treat to him.

'Who will play with me?'

'Well, I will. Or Daddy. And there will be lots of new friends to make at school.'

'You don't really like playing, Mummy.'

'Don't I?' It's like a dagger to the heart. She has always tried to scrabble around on the floor and join in with Charlie's games. Dressing up his teddies. Racing his cars. Doing mending with his play tools. Building towers of bricks and knocking them down with a plastic hammer. And now Noah's Ark and all the bastard Lego. Endless Star Wars. Again and again. She does find it all boring, but she didn't know that Charlie knew it.

'Granny liked playing. She liked cars and building.

You like reading and chatting but you don't like play-ing.'

'Reading and chatting are good, too, aren't they?'

'Yes.'

'Eat up.'

Liam comes in. He is showered and dressed. 'Any breakfast for me?'

Juliet could stove his head in. 'I burnt the porridge, I'm afraid. There's bread. Can you make sure Charlie fin-ishes? I have to get ready. I'll bring his clothes down.'

Juliet runs upstairs and slathers on a bit of face cream. There's no time for make-up, she'll have to do it on the train. She walks into Charlie's bedroom. The floor is a sea of Lego, Playmobil, jigsaw pieces, Top Trumps and trading cards. Juliet opens the cupboard. She spent last weekend labelling Charlie's uniform. She takes an item from each pile and picks up his shoes.

Downstairs, the breakfast is finished and Liam is looking at his phone. No digital detox today, then.

'What's going on in the world?' asks Juliet.

'Nothing good,' says Liam, putting his phone down on the table and ruffling Charlie's hair. They've stopped discussing news in front of him since he asked if there was going to be a war. 'Just a load of Cabs behaving badly.'

Cabs is their child-friendly shorthand for Cunts and Bastards.

'They dominate the news cycle in increasingly des-perate attempts to compete for the title of least appeal-ing politician of all time,' says Liam. The line sounds rather rehearsed to Juliet; perhaps he has already used it somewhere.

'Out of your pyjamas, darling,' Juliet says, but Charlie goes too slowly so she whips his top off and throws it in the direction of the washing machine. She helps him out of the bottoms and into his dinosaur pants and then the grey shorts. She undoes the buttons on the polo shirt and eases it over his head. Shit, she's forgotten socks. She runs upstairs and back down. Socks on. He is very wriggly. Shoes. She pushes them onto his feet and fastens the Velcro strap. He has crumbs around his mouth. She gives his face a quick wipe with the dishcloth, flattens his hair with it. He tries to break away.

'Stop wiping me, Mummy.'

'That's it. Are we all ready?'

Liam looks up from his phone. 'Am I coming, too?'

'That's the idea,' says Juliet, brightly. 'That we are all together for Charlie's first day.'

They walk out of the front door into the sunshine. Juliet gets Charlie to pose by the gate. She takes a few photos, then bobs down to be in one with him.

'Let's have a family picture.'

Liam scoops Charlie into one arm and then puts the other around Juliet. She takes the photo and lingers in the embrace.

They walk up Magnolia Road.

'First day at school,' says Juliet. 'It's exciting, isn't it?

She looks at Charlie. His nose is running.

Juliet pats her pockets and rummages in her bag. Nothing.

'Have you got any tissues?' she asks Liam.

'No.'

'Look at Charlie's nose.'

'They'll have toilet paper at school.'

'We don't want to deliver him dripping with snot on his first day. I'll have to go home and get some.'

Liam looks at her, then pulls the sleeve of his sweater down over his hand and wipes Charlie's nose.

'There you go, mate,' he says.

They arrive at the entrance. The children are cute in their new clothes and lots of them have two parents along. Clearly it is a thing to show a united front on the first day of term.

Some older children are scooting across the playground. One of them is wearing a helmet studded with dinosaur spikes. He looks like a punk with a Mohican. They are massive, some of these kids. Is she really going to leave her precious son in this mayhem?

'What do we do now?' says Juliet.

'We line Charlie up outside the class,' says Liam. 'Blue class. Come on, mate.'

They join the line. Juliet scans it. Brown, blonde and ginger heads all jostle together. There is a little boy with a topknot, a little girl with a headscarf. The boys are all in shorts. Most of the girls are in checked summer dresses; a few are wearing trousers and polo shirts. Lots of the parents seems to know each other and are happily chatting. She sees a woman with identical twin sons who lives a few doors up from them on Magnolia Road. Juliet waves, but she has looked the other way and is talking to a tiny blonde who looks like a doll and a woman who has a baby in a sling. Juliet feels foolish and tries to turn the wave into scratching her nose.

Mrs Karigi comes and opens the gate. Juliet notices how all the dads perk up at the sight of her, hold themselves straighter, suck in their beer bellies.

'OK, darling.' Juliet bends down and gives Charlie a hug. 'Have a good day. I love you.'

'Good luck, mate,' says Liam, patting his shoulder. 'I'll see you later.'

Charlie trots in.

Juliet sees the small blonde woman tell her small blonde daughter to be awesome.

The woman with the baby is trying to detach her son from her leg. 'I don't want to,' he is crying. 'I don't want to.'

'Come on,' says Liam.

They leave the school and walk back up to the main road.

'Nit spray,' Juliet says, 'I forgot to douse him with nit spray.'

Liam doesn't respond.

'And teeth. I forgot his teeth.'

At least Charlie has agreed to have school dinners. Organising a packed lunch every day might be the final straw.

'You've got to pick him up at three fifteen,' says Juliet.

'I know.'

'Charlie said this morning that I don't like playing with him.'

'You don't.'

'Is it that obvious?'

'Yes.'

Juliet looks at her watch. 'I'd better get a move on. Do you want to walk me to the station?'

'I need to get cracking.'

'What are you working on today?'

'The novel,' he says, as if it is obvious and she is stupid to ask.

'Good luck,' she says. She moves in for a kiss and catches his scent. He does smell good. She rests her cheek against the rough knit of his sweater. She feels as though there should be something more in this moment, that she wants something else from him but that she doesn't know what it is, or how to ask for it.

She's walking away when he calls her name.

Her heart lifts. She turns around. She expects some type of loving gesture, something that acknowledges they have done a good job in getting their child into his new school. That life may be difficult sometimes but they are in it together.

'We've got mice.'

'What?'

'Mice. A mouse. I saw one this morning.'

'Where?'

'The kitchen. Next to the bin.'

'Fuck.' Juliet says it louder than she meant and gets a look from the mothers she saw in the playground earlier.

The woman with the baby in a sling makes a protective gesture towards it. *Oh, come the fuck on,* Juliet wants to shout, *it's not like the baby understands.* She gives them an apologetic smile.

'What do we need to do about it?'

Liam shrugs.

'Traps?' Juliet thinks of Tom and Jerry, of a cartoon-like chunk of cheese tied to a piece of string. 'Rentokil, is it? Is that what they're called?'

'Yeah, maybe.'

'I have to go,' she says, 'or I'll miss the train.'

Juliet misses the train. She runs across the bridge, but it pulls out while she is still on the stairs fumbling for her Oyster card. She sits on a bench and gets out her phone. Social media is flooded with first-day-at-school pictures. She looks at the photos she has taken and chooses the one of the three of them outside their house. They look so alike, her menfolk, with their blue eyes and dark hair. Charlie has a smattering of freckles over his nose, just like Liam did when he was a boy, according to his mother. She checks that neither the house number nor the logo on Charlie's polo shirt are decipherable, then posts it. They all look happy. They are happy. Though it's never like she thinks it will be, real life. She was expecting to feel momentous.

She googles Rentokil, then calls and arranges for a home visit. What else? She needs to make friends with those women in the playground. She cringes at the thought. She has never been at her best at the school gates. All the social confidence that she employs so well professionally deserts her and she doesn't know how to speak the language of child-related small talk. Maybe that is something Liam can do. He's good with women.

She calls him but it goes to voicemail. 'Rentokil are coming between four and six. Just a thought, but make sure you're friendly to all those mums. Get to know them. We don't want Charlie to be left out. Maybe you can put them in a novel. Love you.' God, she wishes Liam would do a bit more around the house. Every time she tries to have a discussion with him about their respective roles he looks so bored that she can't bring herself to carry on. Will he sort out the kitchen today, or will she have to load the dishwasher when she gets back? Will Charlie's pyjamas still be lying inside out on the floor and the pan of burnt porridge sitting next to the sink? She hates being such a pushover but the only alternative is to nag and that doesn't feel great either. Still, she doesn't have time to think about it now. Charlie is safely at school. Liam can look after himself.

Juliet flicks to her work email. Adi warns that the car project is going tits-up. They need to find five famous people who would like a car for a year in return for one photo shoot with it. They need to convince the client that the famous people who are willing to do it create the right message for their brand and manage their expectations about who they will be able to get. No, they won't be able to get a royal or Victoria Beckham. They might be able to get one of the other Spice Girls. That's her life. Giving more stuff to people who already have too much, as Liam likes to say. Still, it pays the bills, and someone has to do that. She scans her email. Problems, problems. The client is restive and unconvinced by the only former pop star they've so far found who is willing to be seen with the free car. She'll have to jump on a call with him and calm him down. He is a vain man who likes to be flattered. Most of her working life is about figuring out how her clients want to feel and then delivering that to them so they will carry on ponying up the huge fees. And finding new clients. That's what she'll be on today after sorting Car-gate. She's chasing new business. After all that time off to be with her mum, she needs to show that she can bring in the deals. She's got to make it rain.

The train pulls in. Not too busy. She sits next to a man in a suit reading the *Metro*, gets her laptop out and peels off the Star Wars stickers. Then she opens her make-up bag and squirts a bit of concealer onto her fingertips. She feels the thrill of transformation, a surge of adrenaline. By the time she gets to work she will look and feel the part.

When she gets home that night, Charlie is asleep and Liam has laid the table. He sits her down with a glass of wine. 'Charlie had a good time at school. And guess where I was when you left me a message about making friends with those mothers?'

'I don't know.'

'I was busy making friends with them.'

'Really?'

'Yep.'

'How did you manage that?'

'I went to the Coffee Traveller and they were all at that big table at the front. I sat down at the end of it and we got chatting.'

'Well done you.'

'I know. Sarah, Lucy and Helen. Mothers of Bella, Max and Leo, and Freddie, all in Charlie's class. Sarah has an older daughter called Alice and Helen has an ugly baby called Daisy. They were all in the same antenatal class and have been friends since. Their kids went to a Montessori nursery together. Sarah's idea. She's the Queen Bee. Bosses the others around. She's very short and full of energy and bustle.'

'Sounds fascinating.'

'It was. I learnt loads of stuff. Mrs Karigi is new to the school and the street. They were all calling her and her husband the beautiful couple when they moved in, but they've stopped now they know she is the kids' teacher. Helen said she has a kind face, that she will be kind to the children. When Helen left – she had to take Daisy to the doctor's about her cough – Lucy told me that her son, Freddie, is a total nightmare and once gave Max a nosebleed by chucking his toy trumpet right in his face. Then Sarah shushed her.'

'Gosh,' says Juliet, realising that when Liam said he didn't have time to walk her to the train station because he had to get on with his novel, he was actually planning to go and sit in a coffee shop.

'All the kids are turning six in the next few weeks.

Sarah is transforming her house into a witch's palace for a select few, and Helen is throwing a whole class party, which they all agreed is the only polite option if you're not hosting in your own home. Lucy says she can't be arsed and will run the risk of social ruin, but hopes everyone will remember all the effort she went to last year with the piñata.'

'Well—' Juliet holds up her glass in a toast '—here's to you. Making friends in Magnolia Road. What did Rentokil say?'

'Odd geezer. Looked a bit like a rat. He put down all these little white boxes. Chaz got upset. He thinks it's good we've got mice, that we should be grateful about it. He said lots of people would be jealous if they knew about our lovely mice.'

'Oh God.'

'I know. I distracted him by letting him watch *Blue Planet* on your iPad. The rat man says it will work quickly and that we need to keep everywhere clean. Especially the floor. They like crumbs.'

Juliet sips her wine, waiting for more. Will Liam say, *So I washed it*, or, *So I decided I'll mop on Mondays and Thursdays*? He doesn't.

She gets up. 'I'd better clean the floor then.'

'What, now?'

'Unless you want to do it tomorrow.'

Liam shrugs. Juliet goes to the cupboard under the stairs, and retrieves her mother's broom and the mop and bucket. She hasn't used them since the day they moved in, when she cleared the attic.

Liam is leaning in the doorway, looking at his phone. 'I'll order food. Curry? The usual?'

'Yes,' says Juliet, as she wields the broom. She decides she might as well try to lead by example.

She empties the dustpan into the bin, then fills the bucket with hot water and measures out a cup of floor cleaner.

'It doesn't actually take long,' she says. 'It's getting started that's the problem. Once you're away it's quite satisfying.'

'Sounds like writing,' says Liam.

'How did it go today?' asks Juliet, as she tackles a stubborn mark. She tries to keep her tone light. Sometimes he wants to talk about it, sometimes he doesn't.

'I've decided to follow your advice.'

She feels a pleasant flutter. 'How? I can't remember giving you any.'

'Novel-wise. I thought I might write about this street.'

'Really?' She squeezes out the mop. It wasn't a serious suggestion. 'What about *Home Front*?'

'I'll stick it on the back burner for a while. I need a rest from it. I've known for ages that I've got to change tack. And you gave me the idea. If I need to be friends with these women for Charlie's sake, I might as well put them in a novel. It's the same as *The Human Experiment*, really. I had to be there, behind the bar, listening to all those people, so I made a book out of them. I can do the same thing now. I might weave in a bit of history. There was a pearl-stringing factory, Sarah says. And it used to be called Dead Donkey Lane. And did you know there are no magnolia trees on the street? That's because it was named for the nearby wharf. But I'll start with the here and now. These women and their husbands. They talk a lot about their husbands. It's like they're from another planet. Planet Privilege. Stephen and Bas both own their own companies. Sarah has a cleaner. Lucy has a French au pair.'

Juliet nods. 'Bas?'

'Short for Bastiaan. Dutch. He's lived here for years. Lucy says he hardly has an accent and is very miserable about Brexit, which I said was understandable and then Sarah said she was blowing the Brexit klaxon, which they had to invent because no one ever talked about anything else and only got pointlessly wound up, so now they have a no-politics rule. And Lucy said, "Just let me tell him about Sofia's dad," and Sarah gave permission – honestly, it was like that – and she told me about how this one British dude who has a German wife accidentally voted to leave because he got confused and hadn't worked out it would have implications for his family. I said, "Are you sure he doesn't want rid of his wife?" Anyway, it's good they don't talk about it because I don't want to get bogged down in all that. There will be enough boring Brexit novels in the next few years without me adding to the pile. Working title *Magnolia Road*. What do you think?'

'I like the title,' says Juliet.

'I'll write it in real time. So by next summer I'll have finished my difficult second novel at last. Something will have to happen. Something big. A reveal. Maybe someone is shagging someone, maybe two people go off together. Maybe there is some kind of accident or Perfect Sarah is revealed as a criminal or a dominatrix. Or maybe it doesn't have to be a big thing. Maybe the point is that nothing happens. Everyone gets a year older and that's it. The world doesn't get better or worse, it just is.'

The water in the bucket is black. Juliet opens the back door and pours it down the drain. They might mind, she wants to say, these neighbours, the mothers of the children who will become Charlie's friends. They might not like being exposed. But she doesn't want to be a killjoy. She doesn't want Liam to give her that look like she is his jailer or his teacher. She knows that if she objects to him storifying their neighbours then she'll end up feeling at fault. And it's nice to see him enthusiastic about something.

'How exciting,' she says, as she fills the bucket again. 'I might as well do the bathroom floor quickly.'

Not before time, too, she thinks as she picks up two empty loo rolls and then mops around the base of the toilet, trying not to breathe in the stale urine. They could afford a cleaner but Liam doesn't approve of taking advantage of people in lower socio-economic groups. Not that he ever does much of it himself.

She looks in at Charlie. He is curled up with his arms around Froggy, his cheeks slightly flushed. Her heart fills up. It is so easy to love him when he is asleep. She gathers his uniform and a damp towel from the floor, and puts them in the laundry basket.

The curry arrives. They eat it and drink more wine, and Liam continues to expand on his idea. Stories about people who all live in the same street, who are phenomenally, ludicrously lucky but don't see it, who are buried in doubt and fear and worry about their kids and what their spouses are up to, and are too busy comparing themselves to others and drowning in envy to see their own good fortune. A stag night, maybe, someone being made redundant, a porn addiction, though he had that in his first novel. Privileged people at work and play. No politics, no global events. He wants to dwell in the domestic, to capture a slice of life as it is lived. First world problems, that's what he is going to lay bare. Magnolia Road. It is a good title, isn't it? Magnolia. Like wallpaper. Boring. White. Like most of the people in this street.

Chapter Three

Dan is having lunch at his desk when Helen rings to tell him he needs to be home by 6.30 p.m.

'Why so early? I thought we were heading out at eight.'

'Yes, but you need to spend some time with the babysitter.'

'Do I? Why?'

Dan takes the last bite of his sandwich as Helen explains. She says 'obviously' a lot, though nothing is. He makes the occasional affirmative and supportive sound as he allows his mind to wander over the calls he has to make as soon as Helen gets off the phone. Month end is approaching and he is nowhere near his target. He needs something major to come in but can't see where he'll find it. Leaving the office early will not send the right signal.

'I still don't understand,' Dan says. 'Why can't the babysitter bathe Daisy or do Freddie's story? Or amuse herself while you do it. Aren't we paying her a tenner an hour? Don't we get a bit of self-sufficiency for that?'

'Some of that goes to the agency. Sarah said she was great. And Lucy. They've both used her.'

Ah, thinks Dan. Sarah and Lucy. The women who have been ruling his life since Helen met them at antenatal classes. If they have ordained child-related best practice then there is no point in him questioning it. He'd learnt that over the affair of the secondary window bars.

'I'll see you at six thirty,' he says and hangs up. Dan closes his eyes for a moment, then stands and throws his sandwich wrapper in the bin. Lacing his fingers together, he stretches his arms out. Where has his mojo gone? He sits again and picks up the phone.

After an averagely shitty afternoon, Dan trundles home on the District Line with some geezer's briefcase rammed into his arse. The benefit of starting work early and leaving late is that usually he misses the peak of the rush hour. He gets off the tube and trudges on towards home. His phone pings; a text from Helen telling him to buy dishwasher tablets, so he pops into the shop. He looks at the chocolates. Roses, Matchmakers, Ferrero Rocher. His anniversary present for Helen hasn't arrived yet. He has bought her a subscription to The Goddess Box, and for a year she will get beautiful lingerie delivered every month. But maybe he should get something to give her now. Something small. Just a gesture. He decides on a box of Green & Black's miniatures as it looks the most upmarket. She'd turn up her nose at Black Magic or Milk Tray.

At home, he walks up the stairs, trips over the

43

recycling box, pushes past Daisy's buggy and Freddie's scooter, and finds Helen in the sitting room giving the children their tea. There's a blue plastic sheet under the table to catch the spatters and spillages. Daisy is gumming on a breadstick, and Freddie has baked bean juice all round his mouth and down his school shirt. Dan pats his head and gets some on his hand.

'Hello, young man.'

Freddie stares at him, and then twirls his fidget spinner with a menace that makes Dan thinks of triads and Chinese stars.

'Look at Daisy's cheeks,' says Helen, dodging away from the kiss Dan tries to give her and handing him a wipe for the bean juice. 'They're so red, aren't they, you poor little duck.'

She lifts Daisy out of the highchair and coos at her. Daisy dribbles back.

'Just something small,' says Dan, giving her the chocolates. 'Your real present hasn't arrived yet.'

Freddie snatches at the box before Helen can take it. He tears at it.

'Don't,' snaps Dan, snatching it back. 'It's for Mummy.'

'You can have one, sweetie,' says Helen. 'What colour would you like?'

'Green,' says Freddie, giving Dan a triumphant look.

Dan runs a bath for Freddie and asks him questions about school, but Freddie doesn't answer. He won't get in the bath unless he can bring the fidget spinner, refuses to have his hair washed, is cross about having his mouth

44

wiped and then doesn't want to get out. Dan wrestles him into his pyjamas and into bed, then reads him a story about a rabbit who wants to go to sleep. Freddie yawns. Dan pulls the blinds and turns on the nightlight and the music. Freddie will only go to sleep if played out by the same CD of Baby Classics that he's been listening to before he was even born. It is also essential that he must be clutching Blue Bear, his dilapidated cuddly toy who needs to come everywhere with them.

Sometimes, and they never understand why, all the usual rituals will lose their power and Freddie will stay up screaming for what feels like hours, until Helen succumbs and gets into bed with him. This is looking good, though. Dan gives Freddie a last pat on the head and then remembers he has forgotten to get Freddie to do his teeth. Fuck. With all that chocolate, too, though that's Helen's fault not his. He can't face getting him up again so leaves him, closing the door gently as he goes out.

Dan takes a deep breath and leans against the door for a moment. He feels he deserves a round of applause every time he manages to get Freddie through bath and bedtime without a major meltdown. Last Sunday Freddie bit him hard on the shoulder; the week before it was a sharp kick to the bollocks. Freddie inflicts pain and then laughs. Apparently, Helen says, this is normal behaviour for a five-year-old boy. Though he's nearly six. Is he normal? Dan isn't sure. He's a destructive little fucker, likes stamping on snails and slugs. He whines and whinges all the time, still sucks his thumb and sometimes wets the bed. Some of Dan's colleagues make a big show of getting home for bathtime a couple of evenings a week. They claim to find it enjoyable. They must be lying. Or maybe they have different kids. He'd avoid it if he could.

Helen comes up with Daisy in her arms. Dan hardly ever sees his wife without one of their children attached to her.

'All done?' she says.

'Yes,' he says.

'Did you remember his teeth?'

'Yes,' says Dan, and is saved from further questioning by the doorbell.

Dan lets the babysitter in and makes her a cup of tea as she tells him about the many younger cousins she looked after growing up in Toronto. She has long blonde hair, very white teeth, and exudes youth and health. Dan tries to keep his eyes on hers, and not let his gaze drift down to where the gap in her white blouse shows an occasional flash of pink bra.

Helen comes out of their bedroom. Dan can't tell if she is ready or not. She's not dressed up in any way. She's wearing some type of sack over a pair of leggings. She hasn't bothered with make-up. Or if she has, it's that pretend stuff. Make-up to make women look like they are not wearing make-up.

'They're both asleep,' Helen says, then shows the babysitter round and runs through all the information she needs to maintain these two little lives for the next three hours.

46

Outside in the street Helen looks up at Dan. 'Do you think the babysitter seems OK?'

'Seems fine. She is agency vetted and double recommended, after all. Where are we going?'

'To the Pilot,' says Helen. 'Sarah said they're doing good food these days. And I wanted to go somewhere different but not far away, as it's the first time.'

'The first time?'

'It's the first time we've left Daisy with a stranger.'

'So it is.'

Dan holds open the pub door for Helen. The air is full of chat and laughter and he feels instantly old. He wishes he'd changed out of his suit into a pair of jeans. They find a table, sit down and pick up the menus.

'You have to order at the bar,' says Helen. 'I'll have the chorizo and sweet potato salad with no dressing and a sparkling mineral water.'

The girls at the next table are sharing a jug of Pimm's. Dan envies the cucumber, the mint sprigs.

'You don't fancy a Pimm's?' he asks. 'Or a celebratory cocktail?'

He doesn't understand Helen's rules about what she can drink while breastfeeding. They change all the time depending on her mood.

'No, thanks.'

'Wine? A glass of Prosecco? Champagne, if they have it?'

'No.'

At the bar, Dan relays Helen's requests and orders a rib-eye with triple-cooked chips and a large glass of

47

Shiraz for himself. He wonders what they are going to talk about.

They spent their first wedding anniversary in Budapest, the second in Barcelona.

'Boston next year?' he'd said. 'Bangor, Berlin, Birmingham?'

Now, he puts the glasses down on the table. 'Happy anniversary,' he says.

Helen looks up from her phone to flash him a tiny, tight smile.

'Are you guys quizzing?' The waitress is holding a pint pot with money and some pens in it, a sheaf of papers.

'Sorry?'

'The quiz is about to start. Do you guys want to take part?' She is Australian, or a New Zealander. Dan can never tell the difference. She is wearing very low-cut denim shorts, has a silver ring through her navel. Dan imagines licking it, pushing his tongue into her belly button.

'It's only a pound each,' she says. 'It's for charity.'

'No, thanks,' says Dan.

She shrugs.

Another Antipodean accent booms out over the loudspeakers. Four rounds of ten questions each, a ball-achingly tedious explanation of when and how to play the Joker.

Dan looks at Helen, who is taking a sip of water. She does not seem to be registering that they are about to eat their anniversary dinner in the middle of a pub quiz.

He gets out his phone. Not that he has any interest in learning more about what is happening in the outside world, not that he wants to check work emails and see pointless, irritating communications from his colleagues or clients.

'I hope you're not going to be on that thing all night.'

He looks up. Helen has somehow whisked her own phone out of sight and is looking at him like he's the worst shit in the world. He turns it off and slips it into his inside pocket.

'Tell me about your day,' he says. One of the women at work, herself just back from maternity leave, has told all the married men that this is a killer thing to say when you get home. It shows willing yet puts the burden of effort onto the other person. Just say that, she said, then all you have to do is nod and smile.

Helen tells him that Freddie was better about school this morning and hardly cried at all. He went into class more or less happily and has agreed to abide by the Golden Rules. And Mrs Karigi completely understands that he is sensitive and needs time to adjust and is letting him spend lots of time at the free choice table. Then she went to the Coffee Traveller with Sarah, Lucy and Liam. They have all agreed to help at Freddie's party, Helen says, but she still can't decide whether to go for Snakes and Ladders or the Heathrow Gym or Brentford Leisure Centre, which is closest, of course, but a bit scruffy and not as good as the other two, though Sarah says she should make up her mind because the popular venues do all get booked up early and she should get the invitations out as soon as she can to avoid any conflicts as it can all get competitive, and Sarah has recommended a designer who will make bespoke party invitations and bags so that will be good. And Dan wants to say, hang on, isn't his birthday still a couple of months away, but Helen is off on the subject of what will go in the bespoke party bags and the difficulties of choosing little gifts that are original and will be liked by both boys and girls, and how individual cupcakes are a better idea than a whole cake and how Sarah has sent her the link to the place that did them for Alice and how she might get an 'F' iced onto them all, and Dan thinks blood might start pouring out of his ears but then the food arrives and Helen's salad has come with dressing all over it.

'I did tell them not to,' says Dan, and sees from her expression that she doesn't believe him. 'Do you want me to take it back?'

'Don't bother,' she says, with a sour look on her face. *Vinegar tits*, he thinks. It's not a nice way to think about his wife. He eats his rib-eye and watches her munch through her lettuce.

'Help yourself to my chips,' he says, 'they're triple cooked.'

'No, thanks.'

The quiz starts. Every answer to the first round is a number. How many Doctor Whos have there been? How many of Henry VIII's wives were beheaded? How many MPs sit in the House of Commons? How many chemical elements are liquid at room temperature?

'Two,' Dan mouths to Helen. Bromine and mercury. She looks unimpressed. She's never been keen on quizzes, and long ago Dan realised she was insecure about her general knowledge. The only time she seems to approve of him these days is when Sarah makes them play Trivial Pursuit. He can always put in a strong showing.

When Round One has finished, Helen tells him that after Freddie's birthday he'll be able to go to Beavers.

'Beavers?'

'Yes, they don't let them start until they've turned six.'

'Beavers?'

'Yes, you know, a bit like Cubs. Girls can go, too. Alice goes to Brownies but Bella wants Beavers.'

Dan laughs just as the quizmaster comes back to the mic again. The subject is Women in History. He knows that Lady Godiva rode naked through Coventry in the eleventh century, that Cleopatra bathed in asses' milk to make herself beautiful, that *La Gioconda* is better known as the *Mona Lisa*, and that Sylvia Plath was the poet and author of *The Bell Jar* who was married to Ted Hughes.

'That's literature, isn't it, rather than history?' he asks Helen, who ignores him until the round is finished, and then tells him that Max and Bella have been chosen for school council and will have various duties and privileges, including an occasional lunch with the headmaster and a trip to the Poppy Factory in Richmond to deliver the fundraising money and see how poppies are made.

51

'It's so nice for Max,' Helen says, 'so confidence building.' Dan can see she is gutted that Freddie hasn't been chosen instead.

'Shall we go somewhere else?' Dan asks, in the break before the third round. 'What about heading down to the river? It would be nice to be outside.'

'The babysitter knows we're here.'

'The babysitter has both our mobile numbers. I doubt she's going to turn up here looking for us.'

'Still, I'd rather stay put.'

'OK.' *Suit yourself*, is what he wants to say. *Suit yourself*. He goes to the bar instead.

Round Three is about Film and TV, and Dan thinks he knows seven of the answers. There was a time when he didn't watch much telly but now it's all he does. Work, kids, telly, sleep. Netflix and chill. He'd thought that meant what he did, to sit in front of Netflix until your brain turns to mush, but it means sex, apparently, one of his younger colleagues told him. That made him feel old, too. There's an occasional obligatory work thing he has to go to, which means he cops it both ends as he has to hang out with people he doesn't like and then put up with Helen behaving like he's skived off his home duties. He has no solo social life. Helen runs everything so it is her friends they see, all of whom have kids the same age as Freddie. He doesn't like any of them. Bossy Sarah and Posh Lucy, married to smug Stephen and boring Bas. At least Bas is always in the bad books for being away too much. Stephen works hard all week long, then spends his weekend hanging

out with the kids or training for marathons or triath-
lons or doing family-protecting DIY. And now this
Liam. Liam from Leeds. The women are all over him
because he's a writer, but as far as Dan can work out
he has only written one book and that was a few
years ago, and he lives off his wife who has a big job
in PR. Helen has his novel on her bedside table and
picks it up every so often, but Dan can tell she isn't
enjoying it.

It is impossible to talk over the questions. Dan decides he might as well get hammered.

'Another drink?'

Helen looks at her watch. *She wants to go home*,
thinks Dan, *but Sarah will have told her there is some
optimum time we're supposed to spend here on this anniversary date night.*

'Or a pudding?' Dan asks.

'Yes, OK,' she says, 'I'll have some profiteroles.'

'Why don't you have a glass of Prosecco to go with
them?'

'OK then.'

The Prosecco comes in a little screw-top bottle and is
two glasses' worth. Dan pours some into the flute with
a flourish and pushes it towards her.

An enormous bowl of profiteroles arrives and Helen
scoffs it all down quickly with no apparent pleasure.
She doesn't offer any to Dan. Not that he's bothered, but
he's sure there was a time when they'd get one pudding
with two spoons and laugh together as they shared it.

I'm drunk, thinks Dan, halfway through Round Four

when he can't remember what the unit of currency in Hungary is.

'We've been there,' he says to Helen. 'What were we spending on our first wedding anniversary?'

'You're shouting,' she says. 'Shut up. I can't remember.'

He sits back in his chair. Yes, Budapest then Barcelona. Then the next year Helen had been pregnant with Freddie and they'd been in the process of buying the flat, so they went for a walk along the river and she told him how great life was going to be when they lived just off Magnolia Road. Perfect, she kept saying, as she patted her bump and they sat outside the City Barge and ate fish and chips and giggled, and then went home and had gentle pregnancy sex. They still liked each other then, before Freddie was born, the wrecking ball that crashed into their marriage. He'll be six in a few weeks, and Helen will work herself into a massive state about his party and it will cost a fucking fortune and none of the kids will eat anything and Freddie will be overwhelmed and kick off, like he did last year when they took his whole Montessori class to the pottery cafe in Kew. A crap choice, but Sarah had done it for Alice so Helen wanted the same. It was a rainy day so all the parents and kids were stressed, and as soon as they got there Freddie cried because he wanted to paint a teapot, not the little plate that was included in the party price.

'No,' Dan said, knowing it wouldn't just be Freddie who ended up daubing paint on a twenty-quid teapot if he caved. 'Just do the plate.'

'It's his birthday,' said Helen.

'He's not having the teapot,' said Dan, trying to keep his voice down. 'Just make him be happy with the plate.'

It was too cramped and hot in the cafe. The windows were all steamed up. The children were bored and restless because they'd done it before.

'I want a teapot,' said one of the twins.

'I want a teapot,' said Bella.

It had been Sarah who saved the day, suggesting to Helen that she take Freddie outside for five minutes and then getting all the other children started with the plates. Dan had been grateful, though it was always odd to see the way Helen trusted and obeyed Sarah and did what she said without question. Freddie painted his plate when he came back in but then got upset because Bella's effort was much better than his. He burst into tears, bit one of the twins and, when the woman at the till asked if he'd had a good time, said, 'This is the worst birthday ever.'

It will be the same again, no doubt, whichever softplay hell-zone Helen decides on. They'll have tantrumming children, will have to clear away thirty uneaten lunches, then take home sacks of presents, and the only thing that will make Freddie happy is to open them all in a frenzy, not looking at or appreciating anything, until there is a massive pile of torn paper and a smaller pile of toys. It is obscene. Helen, though, thinks Freddie will be scarred for life if he doesn't spend his birthday coked out of his head on sugar and with more stimulation than even a normal kid could cope with in the company of thirty of his closest friends. She doesn't admit it, but Dan knows she thinks that throwing a whole class party is the way to make sure that Freddie gets invited to everything in return, so Dan is stuck with it, like everything else, caught in this life where Helen is always trying to emulate Sarah and Lucy. 'Sarah says' are the two words most frequently heard in their house. That was how they'd ended up spending a fucking fortune on the Montessori nursery. And the Vitamix. 'Six hundred quid for a blender?' he'd said to Helen. 'That's insane.' But she seemed to think their children's lives would be ruined if she was deprived of the means to furnish them with homemade nut butter and hummus. She claimed it would be economical in the long run because she would be able to turn leftovers into soup. She never uses it now. To be fair, it was a relief when she stopped making him a green smoothie to take to work, like Sarah does for Stephen. It was a disgusting sludge that tasted of kale and lemon. He used to pour it down the drain before he got to the tube. When he couldn't find a cotton bud the other day, Helen said she isn't buying them any more because Sarah says they are bad for the environment. She didn't tell him what he is supposed to do instead and can't imagine she'll be chuffed when wax starts cascading out of his ears.

He drew the line at the 10 per cent: 'Sarah says Stephen gives ten per cent of his net profits to charity.' Dan knew what was coming next. 'We can't do that,' he said. 'We don't have enough to give ten per cent of it away.'

Dan gets most of the answers right. Queen of the South is the only football team to get a mention in the Bible. Expiry dates on crisps are always on a Saturday. A cross woman at the next table is disputing whether or not *The Mikado* is an opera. She says it's an operetta and doesn't count. Finally it is over, the charity money is raised, and the quizmaster tells everyone to come back the following week.

'Not fucking likely,' says Dan, draining his glass. 'Why do people even do this shit? Hasn't Google made it all pointless?'

Helen is fiddling with her phone. 'Sarah was surprised you made such a fuss about meeting the babysitter.'

'What?'

'I told Sarah you made a fuss about meeting the babysitter. She was surprised. She thought you'd appreciate that I was asking for your involvement with the kids.'

Fuss. What a spiteful little word. Dan stares at Helen and thinks of his day at work. Times are tough and every day Dan thinks he might get made redundant. He's started to long for it. At least then he wouldn't have to turn up the next day and do the same shit all over again. He's started to wonder how much money he'd get, how long it would last, what sort of freedoms it might fund. Escape, that's what it would mean.

He tries to speak slowly and calmly. 'I still don't understand why you wanted me to meet the babysitter. I trusted you to find the babysitter. I knew you wouldn't leave the kids in an unsafe situation. I don't understand why you needed me to sign off on it.'

'Sarah says Stephen always wants to meet the babysitter. He likes to be involved in the welfare of his kids.'

Does she? he wants to say. *Does she? What else does Sarah say? Does Sarah know we haven't had sex since Daisy was born? What does she think about that? Does she factor that in when she talks about us? Cor blimey, what a cunt, he didn't want to meet the babysitter. He's a bit distracted, mind, what with his imminent redundancy and the fact he thinks he's never getting laid again but still, you'd think he'd get his priorities right.*

'Let's go,' is all Dan says. 'Let's go.'

They walk home in silence. He can't get his head around the way Helen must have put the phone down on him and then rung Sarah to slag him off. Fuss.

The children have not woken up. Helen goes to stand over them and Dan says goodbye to the babysitter.

'Can you take the recycling out?' Helen says.

'Now?'

'It's overflowing.'

'I'll do it in the morning.'

Helen purses her lips. Another black mark against him, obviously.

'OK, I'll do it now.'

He carries the crate down the stairs to the rubbish area outside. Once their recycling was full of wine bottles; now it's all jars of expensive organic baby food.

Dan takes off his suit and hangs it over the edge of his chair. He puts his shirt in the laundry basket and gets

into bed in boxers and a T-shirt. As usual, Helen undresses in the bathroom and comes to bed in pyjamas.
She has lots of different sets and all of them look like
Daisy's clothes, little-girl colours with dots or hearts
or teddy bears. They lie side by side, not touching. He
remembers Budapest, giggling in the restaurant, kissing in the lift at the hotel. He can't remember what she
wore then. Nothing, probably. He reaches out a hand,
rests it on her shoulder.

She pushes him away. 'I have these dreams.'

'You have a dream?' For a moment he thinks she
might tell him she wants to leave London. He's only
here for her. He hates this poky, expensive flat that
eats all their money. He hates their pretentious friends.
They could move back home, nearer to his parents, get
a bit of help with the kids. They could live a different, easier life. Maybe he wouldn't feel so skint if they
weren't living near so many people who have so much
more than they do. They could live in a nice suburb of
Leicester, in a house with stairs and a garden. London
money goes quite far in the Midlands. He could take
Freddie to the football, have a kick about with him in
the street.

'I dream terrible things, Dan. The end of the world.
Apocalypse. Bombs. Fires. Floods. Buildings are burning. Bodies everywhere. I have to keep the children
safe. We are hiding and hungry. You are gone. You were
too . . . You couldn't . . .'

She peters out and Dan takes a deep breath. *You were
too . . . what?* he thinks. *Useless? Ill-equipped for the end*

of the world? You couldn't . . . what? Protect us? Look after us?

He remembers the secondary window bars. Fiddly fuckers that took him a whole Saturday to put up. Why do we need them, he'd said, I thought we chose this flat because it's a really safe area. Sarah, Helen told him, thought they were essential. Stephen, she said, had put them up on their windows with no bother. You couldn't be too careful. Someone on Thames Road had been broken into last week. Better safe than sorry.

Helen talks through her sobs. 'I'm alone with Freddie and Daisy. I need to keep them safe. My phone doesn't work. Nothing works any more. I'm scared of what I might have to do to keep the children alive. To get food for them. I'm so frightened.'

She is snivelling, funny little gasps. *She needs some help*, Dan thinks. *Or I do. Or we do. This can't be normal.* She is curled into a tight ball, facing away from him. He pats her shoulder awkwardly, and listens as she cries herself to sleep.

Dan wakes. He has been fucking the babysitter. Or was it the waitress? She was bucking on top of him, tits falling out of her pink bra. He is nearly there. He slides out of bed and into the bathroom, and wanks into the toilet. Babysitter, waitress, babysitter, waitress. He comes, hears it splat against the bowl, reaches for the toilet paper.

He wipes himself off, sits down, pisses. The night-light from the hallway casts a shadowy glow. They all deserve better than this. If he earnt more money, Helen might worry less about the future. If she worried less about the future, she might occasionally agree to have sex with him and then he wouldn't be tossing off over every woman he meets.

As Dan walks past Daisy's room he feels something under his foot. He leans down. It is a wooden letter 'A' and has fallen from the door. D ISY. It doesn't look any sillier with the missing letter. If he'd been more assertive he'd have held out for a normal name. Kate or Louise, maybe. Daisy Delilah, for fuck's sake. By then they were arguing about everything. By then, Helen had decided that naming Freddie had been Dan's choice and now it was her turn. He hadn't known that, couldn't even remember having a strong view about it. He's not sure he likes the name Freddie. Is it a bit posh?

When did it all become about fuss and turns anyway? He looks down at the letter in his hand. It is pink with little yellow hats. He has an urge to snap it in half, but doesn't. A is for anniversary, he thinks, A is for apocalypse.

The floorboards creak under his bare feet as he walks down the corridor. He eases open the bedroom door. There is enough streetlight coming through the blinds for him to see Helen's untroubled, sleeping face.

It isn't just the sex: he wants to touch a woman again, one who wants to touch him back. He wants a proper kiss and some kindness. Fuck the apocalypse: this is what scares him in the night. He is scared of what thirteen or fourteen years without sex might do to him. He is scared of what might happen when Daisy hits puberty and brings home friends with breasts. He can't keep his eyes off any woman at the moment.

Dan can't face getting into bed. He fetches a glass of water from the kitchen and slumps onto the sofa. He sees his jacket, fishes his phone out of the pocket, turns it on. The screen lights up. It's 2.30 a.m. His thumb hovers over the mail icon, the news icon, but he stops himself with the simple realisation that anything he looks at will only make him feel worse. Though, as he turns the phone off and looks up at the window, at the two sets of window bars and the dark world behind them, he thinks that at least if the apocalypse happened in the night he wouldn't have to go to work tomorrow. He wouldn't have to find a way to tell Helen that he thinks she needs to see someone, or that Freddie needs to see someone or that there's just something wrong. That it shouldn't be like this.

He has a maximum of four hours before Freddie wakes up. He'd better try to get some sleep.

Chapter Four

Helen is woken by Daisy's crying and looks at the bedside clock. It's 3 a.m. *Not bad,* she thinks, walking down the corridor, *not bad*. Some nights Daisy wakes at midnight and will hardly go back to sleep. Her little cheeks are bright red. She must be cutting another tooth. Helen lifts her out of the cot, strokes her tangled curls away from her flushed face. She is hot.

'There there, my love, there there.'

She carries Daisy into the kitchen and puts her in the highchair.

Daisy screams in outrage.

'It's just for a moment, sweetness, just so I can get the Calpol.'

Helen unscrews the bottle. 'Here you are, this will make you feel better.'

Daisy lets Helen put the spoon into her mouth and swallows.

'And look,' says Helen, unwrapping a sachet of teething powder. 'Something for your poor little gums.'

Daisy stares at her.

'That's all it is. Your little mouth is hurting because your teeth are coming through.'

Daisy tugs at her pyjama top.

'OK, my lovely.'

She carries Daisy back to her bedroom, then sits and rocks gently on the nursing chair and hums her usual medley of tunes from *The Sound of Music* as she watches Daisy suckle. She heard Freddie singing it the other day, when he was playing with his Lego, except he was singing 'rainbows on roses'. It was one of those moments when her heart felt so full of love for him it might burst. 'That's so lovely,' she said to him, but then he glared at her and stopped.

The angry red of Daisy's cheeks is subsiding. Hopefully this feed will settle her back to sleep but it might not. This is what Helen loathes about the sleep deprivation that comes with having small children. Not so much that it exists – she expects to have to minister to them during the night – but the unpredictability. She'd almost rather know that she was never getting more than four hours again than be taunted by the possibility of occasional unbroken nights.

At least she doesn't have to worry about going to work. She decided not to go back after having Daisy. She'd wanted to stay home with Freddie but Dan guilted her into it, saying they needed the money, so she worked Tuesday to Thursday and pretty much hated every second. At one time she'd enjoyed her job. She was the office manager of a law firm and she'd liked organising things and sorting everyone out. Her bosses and colleagues had been grateful and appreciative, and a bit of flirtation oiled the wheels, but as soon as she was visibly pregnant she felt like an eyesore. Returning to work had been horrible, too, so with Daisy she held firm. Most of her salary would have been swallowed up by childcare costs anyway. She has friends who work full-time, though she hardly sees them now. She can't see how it all fits together unless you are rich enough to outsource everything. Childcare, cleaning, laundry. One of the many things no one tells you about being a mother is how much time you'll spend with your head in the washing machine. If you could afford lots of help then it would be OK, but you'd have to be doing something pretty high status. It would be no fun being bossed around at work for not much money and then coming home to small children and housework. Helen is glad to be focusing on her children, her home.

'I wouldn't want to leave you, would I, my darling?' she whispers. 'Why would I ever want to leave you?'

Daisy is asleep. Helen gently, ever so gently, lays her down in the cot and tiptoes out of the room.

She looks in on Freddie. In the peachy glow of the nightlight, he looks very handsome, with his little hand curled around Blue Bear. He was a beautiful baby and is an attractive though rather combative child. He was gentle and happy for the first few years of his life, and she'd been misled by that phrase 'the terrible twos' into thinking that he wasn't going to have tantrums. He was almost four when he made up for lost time with a vengeance, screaming and shouting and hitting. He used to aim blows at her bump when she was pregnant with Daisy and this animosity has continued. He was livid that Daisy got to sleep in their room and furious that he then had to change bedrooms so Daisy could move into the nursery when she was six months old. No amount of chat about him getting a big-boy bedroom, that he was too old for the yellow elephants, no amount of Star Wars wallpaper and Pokémon bedding made Freddie feel less usurped. She has to keep a good eye on him when he is around Daisy. He has a jealous look when he watches her and is quick to take any opportunity to give her a pinch or a slap. The age gap between them isn't ideal. She's always been envious of Lucy having twins and getting a whole family in one go. Their plan was to have another child straight away, but Helen miscarried her second pregnancy and then it took a while before she felt ready to try again. Then nothing happened. She'd fallen pregnant very quickly the first two times, and thought it would be the same, but month after month went by with no baby. She'd needed to get an ovulation kit in the end, had to pee on a stick every day to know when it was worth the effort of having sex.

Back in her own bedroom Helen registers that Dan is not in bed. She pokes her head around the sitting room door. He is on the sofa, snoring. He always snores when he drinks too much. She looks at his rash. It started at the top of his cheekbone and has now spread to his forehead. He says he doesn't have time to go to the doctor's.

She's suggested he try a bit of nappy rash cream, that would probably do the trick, but he hasn't, so far as she knows. He probably would if she brought the tub and offered to put it on, but she is so fed up of having to mother him as well as their children that she can't bring herself to do it. *Where's my phone, have you seen my iPad, where's my wallet?* It doesn't seem to occur to him that she might not want to spend her life locating his possessions for him. He never even says thank you. He's incapable of getting out of the door without instructions and often forgets his keys or just doesn't bother to take them, so when he comes home he rings the buzzer, which means she has to stop whatever she's doing to go and let him in, like a servant welcoming the master home for the day. He's forgotten how to shop and cook. He never makes a cup of tea and when she offers he says, 'If there's one going,' as if they have an invisible tea-making elf who is ready to jump into action. He leaves his empties scattered around the flat for her to clear. At the very most, he sometimes picks up a mug and puts it next to the sink, counting on her to put it in the dishwasher. If, rarely, he feeds one of the children, he leaves everything out all over the place. He's not much use with Daisy and he bickers with Freddie, who is more likely to have a tantrum when Dan is looking after him. And he forgets everything. Never remembers that Freddie will need a snack and doesn't know how to pack Daisy's bag. He changes the occasional nappy but always with the air that he deserves a standing ovation. And he lied about doing Freddie's teeth earlier. She knows he did. She felt the head of Freddie's toothbrush and it was dry.

In some ways she feels the rash justifies her not wanting to be close to him. At her six-week post-natal check-up, the midwife said they could have sex again and Helen confessed that she didn't want to.

'You've got to get back on the horse,' the midwife had said, a revolting thing to say to someone who has been butchered to get her children out of her. She feels like the horse, that's the problem. Like a mule, a donkey, a heifer. She's had enough of her body being the property of other people, of having to stick her legs up in the air or whip out a breast when told to by a medic, a man, or a baby. She doesn't want someone pulling at her, poking at her, feeling entitled to take something from her body. She most definitely does not want to be ridden.

She doesn't miss sex. She has the occasional erotic dream that always involves someone massaging her gently with love and care. Usually this person is a professional, a doctor, a nurse, or perhaps a beautician. Always the person arousing her is a woman. She has never before been attracted to women and isn't now, really, but she can imagine curling up peacefully with a woman. A woman would understand that her body feels assaulted and bruised. A woman would cherish and nourish her, soothe and comfort and take care of her. A woman would do her own laundry and go to the doctor's if she had a rash. A woman would not think that everything is about her, in that way that all men seem to do. Helen sees it in the playground every day. The girls are compliant and obedient and line up as they are supposed to. The boys are a rabble, pushing and shoving and all trying to be first. She's glad that at least one of her children is a girl. She's sure Daisy is more co-operative than Freddie was. She already senses that she will be a support rather than a drain. It will be nice when there is one person in her family that doesn't just take from her and think of her as a machine that dispenses drinks, makes meals and always knows where everything is.

She's sick of the sight of Dan moping around, clearly thinking he's entitled to a use of her body, to have a go on her, as though she is a fairground ride or a treadmill or a moped. There's this joke she remembers the boys at school telling. 'What have a fat bird and a moped got in common?' 'They're both a good ride but you don't want your mates to see you on one.' Riding, again. She hates the way men talk about women.

She wishes it could be an agreed thing, that they could be open about the fact that sex isn't happening any more. She dresses and undresses in the bathroom and has thrown away any clothes and underwear that could be interpreted as inviting. None of it fitted her anyway. She can think of few things more depressing than having to truss herself up in too-tight fancy frillies, of trying to cram her massive, veined breasts into tiny, silken cups. She purposely doesn't pay much attention to her personal hygiene. She knows her nursing tops are tatty and unflattering and she doesn't care. She drags a brush through her hair and puts on a bit of perfume, face powder and tinted lip balm for school drop-off and pick-up but doesn't bother for Dan. She covers herself with the children so he can't get near her. Daisy is always in her arms, quite often latched on, and Freddie is an ally in this. 'I don't like you, Daddy,' he'll say, 'go away. Mummy belongs to me.'

Often Freddie will refuse to sleep unless she lies down next to him. Sometimes he wants to breast-feed — 'Don't tell anyone,' she says — and then, even after Freddie's breathing has slowed and he is doing cute, baby snores, she'll stay there, curled up with him and Blue Bear. She'll have to stop that, she supposes, the sneaky feeds. She doesn't want to trauma-tise him, to do anything that leaves him open to being teased. She wants him to be normal, that's the thing. A normal kid. Not an outsider. Not a weirdo. Just a normal kid.

Dan sorts himself out in the shower, she supposes, and she is careful to give him plenty of time, space and privacy to do so. Anniversaries, birthdays and Christmas are more difficult to navigate as Dan feels more than usually entitled. Probably because that's what he thinks normal couples do, have sex as part of celebrations. She can't stand the way he creeps his hand across the bed as though he's a child trying to get her attention. If she had apron strings, he'd pull them. If she could have any birthday present she wanted, it would be a night alone in an uncluttered hotel room. White, maybe, with wooden furniture and linen bed sheets. No plastic, no colours, no mess, no noise. She'd have a bath and wrap herself in white towels, and then have a delicious and enormous room-service dinner with a huge pudding and settle in for a long sleep.

She's a bit hungry now, actually. She goes into the kitchen and looks in the cupboards and the fridge. Kid-friendly low-sugar yoghurt isn't going to do the trick. She wants something thick and sweet. Doughnuts, crusted with sugar and oozing with jam. Or a slab of chocolate. Cake! Treacle sponge. Custard. Sticky toffee pudding. Fudge. Tablet. Salted caramel Häagen-Dazs. Cookie dough.

The freezer yields nothing exciting, not even that low-calorie Halo Top stuff. It's her own fault. If she buys sugary food she eats it, so she tries not to. She opens the snack drawer she keeps for Freddie. If only she was the sort of mum who let her son eat sweets, she could be having a feast right now.

She tucks into a bag of carrot and banana oaty bites. They are better than nothing but only just. 'I'm organic!' it says on the pack. 'There's nothing artificial about me!' Helen chews. 'I wish you were a Mars bar,' she whispers. She is too heavy, but there is no point in trying to do anything about it until she stops breast-feeding. Then she is going to try the Keto diet. She has been reading about it online. Lots of eggs and meat, and the weight will just fall off and she'll have more energy and clearer skin.

She walks back into the sitting room and looks down at Dan. *I was so in love with you*, she thinks. She can't remember what that felt like, though she knows it is a truth. There was a time she loved this man, was crazy about him, would have done anything for him, but she can't summon the emotion. She can see the memory, can play herself a little slideshow of their first dates drinking cold bottles of beer in the swelteringly hot bars of Lan Kwai Fong, of their life in Hong Kong, of their wedding day, of moving back to London together, but it is as though she is watching a film of someone else's life.

Where has all that love gone? She doesn't know. Perhaps she is just too changed by having children, by having them ripped out of her, and if there was any love left after that it was elbowed out of the way by their kids. It occurs to her for the first time that Dan's rash looks the same as the one on Daisy's cheeks. Her children don't revolt her – she can deal with anything that comes out of their bodies – but Dan does.

The other day Freddie asked why they didn't have a garden. 'Max and Leo have a garden, Charlie has a garden, Alice and Bella have a garden,' he'd said. 'Why don't we?'

'Because Daddy doesn't earn as much money as the other daddies,' she'd said, knowing it was shitty and mean of her, but not being able to help it.

As she turns to leave, she sees the box of Green & Black's on the sideboard. She'd forgotten all about it. Organic tasting collection. She takes it back to bed. She has always loved eating chocolate in the night. She sees Liam's novel on her bedside table. They are doing it for their next book club. She was excited about reading something written by someone she knew but it is hard going, full of miserable men with depressing problems. There's a lot about football, which she doesn't understand and finds boring. She's not sure she can face any more of it. She has read all about it and him online, so she knows what it is supposed to be about and will be able to find something to say at book club. Hopefully the next choice will be something a bit more cheerful.

She opens the chocolates. There is a booklet of tasting notes and recipes. She'll read that instead, have a private session, ticket only admits one. Milk with sea salt is pretty good. And so is butterscotch. Maybe she could make truffles with Freddie. White chocolate is a bit sickly. She finishes off with hazelnut. Her secret shame is that she much prefers cheap chocolate to all this high-cocoa ethically sourced organic stuff. She'd prefer to be eating a bumper pack of Maltesers or Milky Ways. She'd sell her soul for a Curly Wurly or a Fry's Turkish Delight or a tube of Smarties.

Helen folds up all the empty wrappers and puts the box in the drawer of her bedside table. She stretches out. Then she remembers the gratitude thing that Sarah keeps going on about. You have to make a list of five things to be grateful for and write them down every day in a special notebook. What could she choose? *I am grateful that Daisy went back to sleep. I am grateful for my midnight feast.* That was nice of Dan, to buy the chocolates. She could reciprocate.

Helen gets out of bed and pads gently into Daisy's bedroom. She finds the nappy rash cream and takes it into the sitting room. She kneels by Dan and smooths it over his forehead.

'Sleep tight,' she whispers, and goes back to bed.

Chapter Five

Juliet wakes with a start, knowing that there is something on her mind. Is it work? Home? What day is it? Friday. *Oh yes*, she thinks, sinking back onto the pillow. *It's my birthday*. She is forty-five. She lies there listening to Liam's breathing. Her birthday is also the anniversary of the first time they woke up together. Liam used to make a fuss of her on both accounts but those sorts of celebrations have fizzled out. She doesn't want to do anything this year anyway. She feels too raw, too orphaned, to celebrate the day of her birth now that the woman who brought her into the world is no longer here. Since having Charlie, she has thought birthday celebrations are the wrong way round, that it should be mothers rather than their offspring who are feted and given treats. She used to text her mother to say thank you. Last year she took her out for lunch in Soho. Afterwards they strolled arm in arm through the bustling streets. They didn't know anything was wrong then; they thought they had years of lunches and walks and celebrations ahead of them. A sad little noise escapes her. She gets up.

Juliet is out of the door, as usual, before either Liam or Charlie are awake. Through the gloom she sees Mrs Karigi on the other side of the road and slows her pace to avoid any awkwardness about whether they might walk together as far as the school. She walks past Lucy's and then Sarah's. She knows so much about these women now. Every night when she comes home Liam tells her snippets from their lives. He refers to them as the Magnolia Wives, though only Lucy and Sarah live on their road. Helen has a first-floor flat on one of the less smart streets.

'It's like Monopoly,' Liam says. 'Sarah would be Regent Street. Her house is much bigger. It's not a terrace. It was built in one of the gaps left by the bombing. And it's smarter because Stephen loves home improvements and gadgets. They've just finished converting the loft and he yearns for an underground extension, but Sarah won't let him. Helen is Old Kent Road. She and Dan were about to move out of London when she met Sarah and Lucy, and forced him into staying and getting a bigger mortgage than they could really afford. Though house prices have gone up so much it turned into a financially astute move.'

'Where are we in this game of Monopoly?' Juliet asked him.

'Oranges or reds, I guess, with Lucy. But we're not playing. Or maybe we are, but at least we know it's a game. Helen doesn't.'

Usually when Liam gets fixated with a new idea, he goes to a bookshop and buys himself a stack of background reading and starts talking wistfully about research trips. This time the material is under his nose. Juliet can't complain as she did tell him to get to know the mothers, and he is less grumpy than he was before the move and seems quite content with the daily routine he shares with the Magnolia Wives. They go out for coffee most mornings after drop-off, and often take the children to the park after school. Last weekend, Lucy drove Liam and Charlie to Freddie's birthday party in her enormous 4x4. Liam said it was the oddest feeling to sit so high above the rest of the traffic. 'That must be why rich people like them,' he said, 'the feeling of superiority. I did tell her that I hoped the revolution didn't happen while I was in her passenger seat, that I didn't want to end up on the sharp spike of a pitchfork for accepting a lift.'

'How did she take that?' asked Juliet.

'Thought it was funny. She's a good laugh, actually.'

Sometimes Juliet feels a bit envious of Liam's life in the street, but mostly she is glad that she gets to head out into the world. Even today, on her birthday, she is looking forward to presenting the final campaign deck to one of her largest clients. She's proud of the work.

Everything goes well with the presentation, and towards the end of the day Adi beckons her into the boardroom where her team has gathered with cake and champagne.

'It's a macaron drip cake,' says Adi. 'Pretty, isn't it? Vegan. I've kept the box so you can take a chunk home for Charlie.'

Juliet drinks her champagne, smiles through the rather excruciating rendition of 'Happy Birthday', and bats off all the questions about where Liam is taking her to celebrate and what they have planned for the weekend. She encourages the others to talk and it is all about weddings. Adi's best friend is getting married and Adi is in charge of the hen night, which she is finding a burdensome challenge because the bride craves – and deserves – an enormous hoopla but also doesn't want any of her poorer friends to feel excluded, so Adi is trapped between a rock and a hard place with an undeliverable brief. The bride has also said she doesn't want any vulgarity, no matching T-shirts, no penis earrings, no L-plates or veils, but Adi is worried that the other hens will expect all that and think that any absences are her fault. There is a horrible fascination to it and, as ever, Juliet is amazed by the way that intelligent young women bleed IQ points when they discuss men and marriage. She drains her glass, thanks them all, blows Adi a kiss, and heads off with the rest of the cake, feeling slightly self-conscious on the tube and hoping she will be in time to read Charlie's bedtime story.

The house is silent. There are toys all over the sitting room floor but no signs of life. She runs upstairs. Charlie isn't in bed. She calls Liam.

'Sorry, meant to text. Hadn't realised it was so late. We're at Lucy's. Come over.'

She crosses the street and walks up to Lucy's house. It is painted a delicate shade of yellow and has a rose trellis by the front door.

'The boys are all upstairs with Magalie,' says Lucy. 'Charlie's such a duck. He fits right in. Go through, go through, Liam's in the garden. We have to be outside because my husband hates cigarette smoke. I'll get you a glass.'

Lucy's garden is smarter than theirs. A rather grand shed sits in one corner and a neglected-looking pond in the other. Liam is sitting at a glass-topped table. It looks like they've been drinking for a while, and the ashtray contains several butts stained with Lucy's lipstick. Liam has a large, knitted octopus on his lap. It has green-and-blue stripes and a huge smile.

'Look,' says Liam, 'say hello to Otto.'

'Hello, Otto,' says Juliet.

'He's the class mascot,' says Lucy.

Juliet is none the wiser.

'Did you not have one at your last school? We had Percy the Penguin in reception. They're trialling extending it to Year One as all the kids love it so much.'

She hands Juliet a scrapbook. There are four entries. Marzana took Otto to the London Aquarium to show him sea creatures. Dylan took him to the zoo and rescued him from a bear. He played piano with Kavari and went to the National Gallery with Sam. There is a photo of Sam holding him in front of Van Gogh's *Sunflowers*.

'It's a spying activity, really,' says Lucy. 'We have to fill the book in so they know we are doing lots of enriching middle-class activities. But the boys are so pleased to get him. Well, it's Leo's turn. A different

79

name gets pulled out every Friday. Nothing too outrageous so far. Last year someone took Percy to Florida.'

Juliet asks Liam whether Charlie had a good day at school.

'He did,' says Liam, playing with Otto's tentacles. 'He invented a new Golden Rule and Mrs Karigi liked it and has added it to the poster.'

'What is it?'

'Guess.'

Juliet sips her wine. She feels put on the spot. 'I don't know. Something about Star Wars? We are careful with our lightsabers?'

'We are kind to mini beasts,' says Liam.

'I should have been able to get that,' says Juliet.

'Freddie massacred some worms,' says Lucy. 'And Charlie was very upset but now he's happy with the new rule.'

After a glass of wine, Juliet says they should be getting Charlie to bed.

'Don't go,' says Lucy. 'Charlie can stay here. I've already agreed the boys can camp in the playroom tonight. Magalie will sort them out. It will be no bother to add Charlie to the mix. Go up and see him, just go to the stairs and then all the way to the top.'

Juliet hopes Liam will decline the offer – surely he has done something for her birthday even if it is just cards and a cake. He says nothing so she finds her way to the stairs and follows the noise. Charlie does seem happily at home in the big playroom at the top of the house. They have been having a cuddly toy fight, he says. He asks if she's seen Otto, and says one day Otto will come to stay at their house. 'Red class have Larry the Lobster' – he pronounces it 'lomster' – 'and yellow class have Sammy the Seahorse, but Otto is best.'

'I hope he isn't too much work for you,' says Juliet to Magalie.

'It's better,' says Magalie, 'when he is here. The boys fight less with each other. We like having him.'

'Shall I fetch his pyjamas? His toothbrush?'

'No need. I can sort him out.'

There seems to be no ceremony to this first sleepover. Juliet pulls Charlie away and takes him over to the other side of the room. There are French windows leading out to a balcony with high rails that looks over the garden.

She picks Charlie up. He is getting so big. She won't be able to lift him for much longer.

'Well done on making up a new Golden Rule.'

'We must always be kind to mini beasts, Mummy,' he says, as though if he doesn't police her she will go out and stamp on a centipede.

She strokes his hair and kisses his cheek. She loves the softness of him. She can see Liam and Lucy in the garden below.

'Look,' Charlie points, 'Daddy's laughing. He's not grumpy here.'

'Daddy is having a nice time,' Juliet agrees. 'Are you having a nice time? Do you want to sleep here?'

'Yes.' He looks fierce and proud. 'Stay with Max and Leo.'

'Shall I get Froggy?'

He screws up his face. 'You can sleep with Froggy to-night.'

She kisses him again and he wriggles away from her.

Juliet smiles at Magalie and says, quietly, 'You will make sure he has a last wee, won't you?'

'Of course.'

Back downstairs, Lucy is laying out packets and pots from M&S and is talking about Bas and how boring he is. Bas is only interested in his work and politics and thinks about nothing else. And he only cares about politics because of the impact on his work, not because he is interested in the planet or the people who live on it. He's obsessed with Brexit and endlessly reads about it in the English, Dutch and German papers. She agrees with him, of course, that it is all pointless and stupid and that all politicians are terrible, but there is a limit to how many times she wants to hear him say the same things. He has no appreciation of art and culture and never wants to do anything or go anywhere. His idea of relaxing is reading *The Economist* on the bog.

'How did you meet?' asks Liam.

'I did a few weeks of temping at his company. He was always a bit monosyllabic but I had the feeling he fancied me. A week after I finished, I bumped into him in Soho one evening and he asked me out for a drink. I'd just split up with a serial shagger and I thought, why not? And I do like tall men. We went to Ceviche and had lots of pisco sours. He couldn't believe his luck at first, though I doubt he feels like that now.'

Juliet doesn't know how to respond so says she is getting cold. She hopes they might leave, but Lucy goes inside and brings out a beautiful cashmere wrap and another bottle of wine.

'Sorry we can't go in, but Bas hates fag smoke. He's a very disapproving husband,' she says, pouring more wine. 'He's hardly here at all, and when he is, he disapproves. Mainly of me. I thought he'd be more easy-going, being Dutch, but he's very straight-laced. And he's not even tall, for a Dutchman. Did you know that? They're all giants. The first time we went over there I realised he is only average height. I felt missold.'

'I like your shed,' says Juliet.

'Lovely, isn't it? It's the same as Sarah's. I couldn't resist.'

'What do you do in it?'

Lucy shrugs. 'I've a few ideas. I used to make bags from found material and I'd like to do that again, but it needs time and energy and I've not much left over from the boys. I don't have a sense of purpose like Sarah. Or you.'

Juliet is surprised at Lucy's impression of her when she feels so directionless and adrift. She can't work out how to communicate any of that so asks why Sarah got her shed.

'Stephen bought it for her when the girls were little so that she could have her own space. He calls it her lady cave. Sounds a bit rude, no? Now she studies in it. She's training to be a therapist. She'll be really good at that. Loves giving advice. She's virtually Helen's full-time counsellor already and she doesn't seem to get bored, which I find amazing.'

They gossip about Freddie's birthday party and how stressed Helen was about it.

'You dodged a bullet there,' Liam says.

'It was awful,' says Lucy. 'Freddie told the other children that the bread was diseased — it had seeds on it — and that pigs had to die to make the sausages, so they all started crying.'

'And Bella asked if anything had to die to make the cucumber,' says Liam, 'and then Dan hissed at Helen, "Just make him eat the fucking hummus." Chaos.'

'Sarah calmed everyone down,' says Lucy, 'but it's all her fault, really, because Helen is always trying to copy her and then fucking it all up. Like when Sarah encouraged Helen to make a fuss over their anniversary and said that she and Stephen go out to dinner all the time and don't talk about the kids, and this keeps them bonded. Of course, when Helen tried, it all went wrong.'

'What happened?'

'There was a quiz on in the pub. He got drunk and started shouting the answers. She was embarrassed. I would have told him to shut up but she's the repressed type. She broods.'

'I've not met Dan yet,' says Juliet. 'What's he like?'

'Stressed,' says Lucy. 'I feel a bit sorry for him. I'm fond of Helen but she is a bit of a buzzkill and obsessed with her kids. She's got the opposite of the Midas touch. She lets life get on top of her.'

'Don't you?' Liam asks.

'I try very hard not to,' says Lucy. 'Admittedly, I've got Magalie who is a cheerful presence. She helps out a fair bit, fitting us in around college two or three days a week.'

'She doesn't live in?' asks Juliet.

'God, no,' says Lucy, 'there's no space. And we've only got one bathroom. Have you seen Sarah and Stephen's loft conversion? They've put in a lovely en-suite for when his mum comes to stay. That's what you need for live-in help.'

It is after eleven when they get home and Juliet is freezing.

'Nightcap?' says Liam, getting out a bottle of Laphroaig.

'I'm knackered.'

'Just one,' he says, as he pours her a glass. 'It's all fascinating stuff, isn't it? The minutiae of their little lives. I think I'll just write them as they are. I'll need to change all the names eventually but it's fun to speculate about them. Maybe I'll imagine an affair for Bas. Or Lucy. Is it less of a cliché if she's the one who starts screwing around? Or maybe a character who has a loft extension done just so they can get a nanny.'

Juliet takes a sip of the whisky, feels the burn in her throat. She doesn't want to put Liam off his stride but she can't help thinking he seems a bit confused. In his last project he was desperate to have lots of strong female characters. Has he abandoned that now? Or are women not worthy of being depicted as strong if their circumstances are too fortunate? Is he Liam Quinn, feminist, friend to all women, or is he Liam Quinn, eaten up with class rage and desperate to expose white privilege?

Juliet takes another sip of the whisky. She is so tired. She's confused, too. Does Liam genuinely enjoy Lucy's company or is it research? Is she freezing cold because she has been putting up with one of her husband's friends or because she has been helping him with his novel?

Liam points at the box on the table. 'What's that?'

'The rest of my birthday cake from work. I brought it home for Charlie. Would you like a piece?'

He opens the box. 'Very posh,' he says. 'What are those things called?'

'Macarons.'

He lets the lid drop and puts his arms around her.

'And the anniversary of the first time we woke up together,' he says.

She stands awkwardly in his embrace. She waits for him to apologise for forgetting but he doesn't.

'Good to have the house to ourselves, isn't it?' he says, as he pulls her towards the sofa.

As she spends more time with the women, Juliet enjoys matching them up to Liam's descriptions. Sarah is the lynchpin around whom everything revolves. She was an HR director in the City before having her kids and now pours all her people skills into her studies and managing her family and friends. She is the class PTA rep, is on the street party committee – 'Such a shame you just missed it this year. I'll sign you both up to the WhatsApp group' – and is the founding member of the Magnolia Road book club. She convenes a special meeting for *The Human Experiment* and invites Liam along to discuss it. He comes home slightly pissed and hyped up and blissed out on the flattery.

'Who was there?' Juliet asks, as she closes her laptop on her work email.

'All women, apart from Brian and Jim. Lucy and Helen. Some mums from school; Sandeep and Suzannah. They all said they loved the book but I think Helen was bemused by it.'

'Any good questions?'

'The usual. Where do I get my ideas from? Is it depressing to write about hard stuff? Do I know what really happened? Why is Jason's dad such a cunt? Sarah asked about how it felt to have left Leeds and whether being taken away from my roots had made it tricky to know what to write about, which was interesting.'

'What's their house like?'

'Full of gadgets. Stephen likes to have the best and newest of everything. Enormous TV. Sarah says she wouldn't bother but he likes watching sport in high definition. I did say they are going against the trend, as one thing I have observed through my social climb is that the TVs get smaller the posher you get.'

Juliet laughs.

'They have a tap that dispenses boiling hot water. And the dishwasher shines a light on the floor to say how much time it has left to run. And has an anti-bacterial blue light. Like the green light at the end of Gatsby's dock. Though you couldn't say Stephen and Sarah are careless people, could you? Loads of chat about the street party. Apparently your mother didn't like it.'

'No, she wasn't one for organised fun. She used to make sure she was on holiday. It was the drunken hymn singing she couldn't bear. That's what they do at the end.'

'They didn't talk about hymns. But Sarah got every-one to agree to make individual bits of bunting so she can sew it all up and they can run it from house to house down the whole length of the road. It's straight-forward to do, she said, and kids love getting involved. She'll send round a link to a useful article and is happy to provide the cardboard templates. Then they can get it out every year. Isn't that great? I can put that straight in my novel. They have a cash bar and a rota for who works it. I've volunteered.'

It doesn't seem to occur to Liam that now he's made all these women his super fans, they'll be reading his next book pretty closely and won't be blinded by a bit of name changing from seeing that he has stolen their lives.

'Can you take Chaz to Bella's party?' says Liam, after lunch on Saturday. 'I feel like heading into town to look at some art.'

'Of course,' says Juliet. 'Won't it be good material, though?'

'I got all the kids' party stuff I will ever need from Freddie's shindig at Snakes and Ladders. I've heard all about it anyway. Face painting and apple bobbing. You can tell me if anything interesting happens.'

'What time is it?'

'Drop-off at four. Pick-up from six. They're encouraged to dress up. He'll want to go as Darth Vader.'

'Present?'

'Fuck, sorry, forgot about that.'

'Don't worry. We can do it.'

'Ta. And then I'll do the Wetland Centre with the twins tomorrow.'

'What's that?'

'It's their birthday. They're not having a party, but Lucy has booked them in for geese feeding or fondling or something and invited Charlie along.'

They wave Liam off and then walk over Kew Bridge to the retail park and head to TK Maxx.

The toy section is upstairs and is divided by gender. Charlie pulls Juliet into the girls' section, which is full of pink.

'That!' He points at an enormous plastic cooker.

'It's a bit big,' says Juliet.

He picks up a till and jabs at the buttons. 'This!'

From everything Liam has said about Stephen, Juliet can't believe he would want his daughter playing with a toy that might encourage her towards a career in retail.

Juliet tries to interest Charlie in a more gender-neutral box of paints but he isn't having any of it. He darts towards a collection of brightly coloured packets. 'Slime,' he says, 'Bella loves slime.'

Juliet picks up the packet. Scented slime, it says, collect all four colours. She tries to read the instructions but the font is too small. She needs to go to an optician. She wishes she were better at this sort of thing.

It costs eight pounds, which feels about right. Is it too plasticky? Too vulgar? Is it the child equivalent of penis earrings? Should she try to pressure Charlie into the paint box or is that too dull?

'Are you sure?' she asks him.

'Yes,' he says. 'And this.' He holds up a cuddly pink unicorn with a stubby golden horn and enormous eyes. Juliet feels almost hypnotised by the huge black pupils and silver irises.

'You need to choose one or the other.'

He finds a smaller pack of slime and a smaller unicorn and Juliet agrees although the combined cost is more, and then she caves in and lets him add a small pink box of something called kinetic sand in the shape of a castle. They choose gift wrap – more unicorns – and a gift bag and go to the tills. The bill comes to nearly twenty pounds.

Then they go and look at the goldfish in the ponds of the apartment blocks next door.

'I used to come here with Granny,' says Charlie.

'I know,' says Juliet.

'Granny liked looking at the fish.'

'Granny liked looking at fish with you.'

'Can we have a pond?'

'They're quite a lot of work.'

'I could make one.'

'That's a good idea,' Juliet says, hoping he'll forget about it.

'Bella has a lizard.'

'Does she?'

'It lives in the attic with the stick insects.'

'That's nice.'

Back at home Juliet takes off the price stickers – they are fiddly and it takes ages – and wraps the presents. They forgot the card. She has spent twenty quid on pink, sparkly crap and doesn't even have a birthday card to go with it. Luckily the gift bag comes with a tag. She tries to get Charlie to write on it but he won't, so she does it for him in pink felt tip.

When they ring the bell at Sarah's house, Bella opens the door. She is dressed all in black and is wearing a tall, pointy hat.

'Hello,' she says. 'I'm six.'

'My,' says Juliet. 'You're practically a lady.'

'I can go to Beavers now.'

'How lovely.'

Charlie runs off with Bella and Juliet steps into the hall. There are cobwebs and strings of tiny orange pumpkins everywhere. Can she just leave or should she find someone? She's still got Bella's present. She walks further in, holding the bag in front of her to justify her presence. Sarah comes out of a door dressed in black. A pair of gold trainers poke out from under her long skirt. She makes a very short, blonde witch.

Juliet holds out the bag.

'Thanks so much,' says Sarah.

'I like your trainers.'

Sarah points out her foot like a ballet dancer. 'Kickers. Aren't they great? The only good thing about being pocket-sized is that I can wear kids' shoes. Now, you are welcome to stay but you can head for the hills if you like.'

'Do you need any help?'

'No, we're all sorted.'

Back in the street Juliet wonders what to do. She has two hours to herself with no plan. She could do anything. She thinks of Liam going to see art. She hasn't time to go into town but she does that every weekday anyway. She hesitates. Should she turn left and go home, or turn right and head out? She could go for a coffee or a walk. She is paralysed by choice. Then she sees other partygoers coming down the street and doesn't want to be caught dithering so she turns and heads for home. She waves at Magalie and the twins – little wizards – on the other side of the street.

She makes a cup of tea and lies on the sofa. She could read a book. Or do some work. Or carry on with the seemingly endless admin resulting from her mother's death. In the end she does nothing. She doesn't read or sleep or make any decisions, she just lies on the sofa and stares at the wall.

*

It is dark when Juliet goes to pick Charlie up so she sees the full splendour of the illuminated decorations.

Bella opens the door again. 'Hello, Charlie's mum. I survived the Tunnel of Terror.'

'Well done you.'

'Go through to the kitchen and have a spicy drink,' Bella says. 'It's only for grown-ups because it has alcohol in it.'

'Thanks very much,' says Juliet.

Helen is in the kitchen stirring a vat of mulled wine. She gives Juliet a cup.

Juliet looks around. The kitchen is part of a large open-plan area that leads onto a playroom that looks out onto the garden, which is dimly lit. She does a double take when a child's head appears from out of the ground.

Helen laughs. 'You're not going mad. There's an underground trampoline. Clever, isn't it? This is such a beautiful house.'

Juliet can hear the envy in Helen's voice. She feels it, too. Even in the midst of a party there is an atmosphere of calm.

She sips her wine and looks at the huge double-fronted fridge covered with paintings and certificates. Bella has won a 'Star of the Week' award. Alice has been awarded her pen licence.

'What's a pen licence?' Juliet asks Helen.

'They get it when their handwriting is good enough. We don't have to worry about it for a while yet.'

There is a Gruffalo family planner that shows what

they are all doing on any given day. The girls have swimming lessons on Tuesdays and gymnastics club on Sunday morning. Alice has Brownies on Thursdays. Today's date has 'Bella's party' written across the whole line in silver pen surrounded by little gold stars. Stephen's column shows lots of training sessions.

Stephen comes in — big, round-faced, jovial — and Helen introduces them.

'Charlie's mum? Great to meet you. Biscuit?'

He holds out a tray of iced cookies in the shape of black cats and white ghosts.

Juliet and Helen both hesitate.

'Please do,' says Stephen, 'save me from scoffing them all on my own tonight.'

Helen looks at Juliet as if for permission and Juliet gives it by taking one of the cats. She bites into it and feels an immediate sugar rush.

'Nice to see Liam in the paper today,' says Stephen. 'I didn't used to bother with the book section but I always have a look for him now. Couldn't get on with his novel, I'm afraid. I did have a go.'

'Don't worry,' says Juliet, 'it's not everyone's cup of tea.'

'I don't read much fiction. There is one chap I like. What's his name? Sarah always gets me his latest for Christmas. Robert Harris. He's awfully good.'

'Liam does think about writing a thriller.'

'He should! Spies. Moscow rules. The honeytrap. I'd read about that. Another biscuit?'

Juliet and Helen both take one.

'I'm sorry about your mum,' says Stephen. 'I didn't really know her, but I used to see you together when I was out running and think how close you looked.'

Juliet feels a lump in her throat. 'We were close,' she says, 'I miss her.'

Charlie barrels in. He has a huge spider's web patterned across his face and is wearing a big round badge. Juliet leans down. It says, 'I survived the Tunnel of Terror.'

'What's the Tunnel of Terror?' Juliet asks.

'It's very frightening,' says Stephen. 'Can we tell your mum?' he asks Charlie. 'Is she brave enough to know about it?'

Charlie nods.

'Do you want to tell her or shall I?'

Charlie wriggles away and runs off.

Stephen laughs. 'It's just the alley between our house and next door. I rig up some curtains and lights and they have to run down it in the dark. The girls love it. Sarah got the badges made up.'

Other parents arrive. Some whisk their children straight off, some are persuaded to stay for a glass of mulled wine and a biscuit.

Dan arrives with baby Daisy and an enormous floral Cath Kidston changing bag, and hands them both straight to Helen.

'You'll have to be on wine duty then,' says Helen, as she strokes the back of Daisy's head. She opens the bag, takes out a muslin square and wipes the corner of Daisy's mouth.

Dan ladles himself a cup of wine and tops Juliet up.

Juliet searches her memory for what Liam has told her and tries to make conversation. 'So you guys met when you were pregnant? And then your kids went to the same nursery?'

'We still miss the Montessori,' says Helen. 'Freddie was so happy there.'

Dan snorts. 'We thought he was a genius. An artist. Brought home incredible paintings of planets. They must have been doing them for him.'

Helen makes a reproving face at him.

'Well, it's true. Since he went to school all we get is scribble.'

Bas arrives. He is quiet but seems pleasant, not the awful self-obsessed bore that Lucy has described. He asks how they are settling in, how Juliet finds her commute, what she does. She thinks how rare and odd it feels to talk about herself and her work in this environment where her principal function is to be Charlie's mum.

'You don't have an accent,' Juliet says.

'I have lived here for twenty years,' Bas says. 'When I go to Holland and try to speak Dutch, everyone answers in English.'

Helen asks him where Lucy is.

'Shopping,' he says.

'Something nice?' Helen chirps.

'I don't know,' Bas says.

Helen looks a bit awkward and unsure of what to say next.

96

'That's it,' says Sarah, coming in. 'All gone, all done. Well-entertained children dispatched with their party bags. Only us left. Alice and Bella are organising the boys into a show. They seem quite happy about it.'

'Beloved,' says Stephen, 'you've worked so hard.'

She walks into his arms, a tiny doll in his hulking embrace.

Juliet catches Helen's eye and they share a smile but she isn't quite sure what it means.

'Get a room,' says Dan, but that doesn't feel the right thing somehow and Helen flushes.

Sarah pours herself a glass of water from the fridge dispenser and takes off the witch's hat. They debrief the party. The face painter was brilliant, if a bit slow. The slime making was OK, but the children were a bit bored by having to do precise measurements.

'Slime?' says Juliet.

'Yes, they've all got a pot in their party bags. Though homemade is never as good as the shop-bought stuff. It's too watery.'

'That's a relief in a way,' says Juliet. 'Charlie gave slime as his present.'

'She'll love it,' says Sarah. 'Honestly, she and Alice can't get enough of the stuff.'

'The Tunnel of Terror was the highlight, surely,' says Stephen, preening.

'Actually, I think it was,' says Sarah. 'Kids love anything that makes them scream.'

'Now,' says Stephen, 'can I offer anyone a tour of our loft conversion?'

'Please say yes, someone,' says Sarah, 'but don't let him bore you with details of the planning dispute about the window dimensions.'

'Cheeky,' says Stephen.

'I'd love to see it,' says Helen.

Juliet goes, too, and they walk up the stairs, Helen carrying Daisy.

'So we've used half for a spare bedroom and half for my study,' Stephen says. 'I'll show you in there first.'

His monitor is massive and curved with an enormous keyboard, and his chair looks like top-of-the-range hi-tech office furniture.

There are various medals with different-coloured ribbons hung over the edge of a photo frame, which holds a picture of Stephen crossing a finish line.

'What are all these for?' Juliet asks.

'Marathons,' he says. He picks one out and gives it to her. 'That's the midnight marathon. Tromsø.'

'You run at midnight?'

'You finish by midnight. We need to get Liam running, then he can come with us. They're a good bunch of blokes.'

Juliet can't imagine Liam in lycra, Liam caring about electrolytes, Liam coming home and saying, 'What a good bunch of blokes,' before displaying his marathon medals in the attic, but she smiles as though she thinks it is a good idea.

There is an electric guitar on a stand in the corner of the room.

'Look, Daisy, a guitar,' says Helen. 'I didn't know you played the guitar, Stephen.'

'Not any more,' he says. 'Never much, really, if I'm honest. But I like owning it. This is good. I do use this.'

He shows them a telescope that sits under a skylight. 'I want to teach the girls, but they aren't interested yet.'

He guides them across the landing into a double bedroom with a bathroom on one side. Everything is white or pale green. Helen makes lots of appreciative noises, says that it feels just like a boutique hotel.

There is a cat curled up on the bed. 'This is Rainbow,' says Stephen, stroking her head. Rainbow rolls over onto her back. 'Look how much she loves having her tummy tickled. She's getting friendlier as winter draws in. We hardly see her in the warm weather.'

'Where's the lizard?' asks Juliet.

'What?'

'Doesn't Bella have a lizard? And stick insects?'

'Oh dear,' says Stephen, making a face. 'Bella makes things up, I'm afraid. We're not sure it's lying, exactly. More not knowing the difference between truth and make-believe.'

Helen lets out a small nervous giggle.

'It's a beautiful space,' says Juliet.

Back downstairs, Alice comes in to say that Freddie and Leo are fighting.

'Sorry,' says Helen and moves to the rescue, but then all the children are there and everyone agrees it is time to go home. The coats, hats, scarves and party favours are all handed out. Helen gives Dan the changing bag and he takes it and then puts his arm around her. Freddie punches him in the leg.

All the grown-ups look away. Then Helen says, 'It's OK to be angry but it's not OK to hit Daddy.'

Juliet has the feeling she has said this many times before.

They all tumble out of the door into the cold in a chorus of goodbyes and thank yous, and Juliet and Bas walk down the street together. The twins want Charlie to go home with them, but Bas doesn't endorse the invitation and Juliet quickly intervenes to say he can't. It suits her, she thinks, to go home with her own child rather than be pulled into impromptu playdates and sleepovers and wine.

'Are you looking forward to tomorrow?' she asks Bas.

'Tomorrow?'

'Isn't it the twins' birthday? Are you going to the Wetland Centre?'

'Ah, yes. But I'm not going to feed the geese. Not enough room in the car. I am taking them for brunch in the morning and Lucy is taking them to see birds with their friend Charlie in the afternoon.'

'What a lovely day they'll have,' says Juliet, trying not to sound surprised that they are carving up the activities. 'It was so nice to meet you at last.'

'At last?'

'Well, you know. Hearing about you from Lucy and the twins.'

He nods at her. She thinks he is going to say something else but he decides against it, and they peel off into their yellow house.

They pin the 'I survived the Tunnel of Terror' badge to the curtain in Charlie's bedroom. As Juliet scrubs the spider's web off Charlie's face in the bath, he asks if they can go to eBay.

'Where's that?' Juliet asks.

'It's a shop,' says Charlie.

'Oh, I don't think you can go there, exactly. It's an online shop. Well, an internet thing. People deliver.'

'You can buy tarantulas.'

'Gosh. Can you?'

'Can I get one?'

'I don't think so.'

'They only cost sixteen pounds.'

'It's not really about the money.'

Charlie purses his lips and does a long breath out.

'I miss Granny.'

Juliet wipes the last bit of web off his ear. 'I do, too.'

'Granny was going to get me a rabbit.'

'Was she?' This doesn't sound likely to Juliet. Maybe Charlie is picking up Bella's animal fantasy habits.

'Where is she?'

'The rabbit?'

'Granny.'

'She died, darling.'

'I know, but where is she now?'

Juliet takes a deep breath. 'Um, heaven, maybe.'

'Is heaven real?'

'Some people think so.'

'Are ghosts real?'

'Some people think so.'

'Monsters? Dinosaurs?'

'Monsters definitely aren't real. Dinosaurs used to be real but don't exist any more.'

'Unicorns?'

'Not real, but it would be nice if they were.'

'Dragons?'

Juliet has to think about that one.

Charlie wants Robin Hood for his story. He likes the way Robin throws the Sheriff's treasure down the castle toilet and then later, when he is shot and falls in the moat, manages to find the entrance to the toilet and climb up the drain to safety.

'All that poo and wee,' says Charlie, gleefully.

The next day, Juliet cleans the house when Liam and Charlie go to the Wetland Centre. They come home in high spirits.

'Daddy got bit on the bum by a magpie goose,' says Charlie, laughing. 'You should come next time, Mummy.'

On Monday, Juliet works through lunch and then runs out to Pret at 4 p.m. As she is eating her jambon-beurre in the street, she browses the window of Paperchase and has a brainwave. She goes in and buys a pack of dinosaur fridge magnets. There is a red Tyrannosaurus rex, a blue Pterodactyl and a green Stegosaurus. She can't identify the yellow and orange dinosaurs but Charlie will be able to.

She gets home late. Charlie should be in bed but he is still in his school uniform watching a wildlife programme on her iPad. There are toys and Lego all over the floor and several pizza boxes on the round table.

'He's had his tea,' Liam says, defensively. 'Lucy and the twins only just left. Guess what's happened.'

Juliet goes over to Charlie. He submits to a cuddle without taking his eyes from the screen.

'Tell me,' she says to Liam, as she starts to clear the table.

'Leave that and listen.'

He is excited. Perhaps a little bit pissed. Juliet glances into the kitchen and sees an empty wine bottle on the side. She pulls out a dining chair and sits down.

'Life is only imitating art. Bas has moved out.'

'What?'

'I know. I was imagining a secret love affair for the dullest of the dull husbands and it turns out to be true. Or might be true. He's made a bid for freedom. Lucy thinks he's been dipping his pen in the office ink.'

Juliet looks towards Charlie. 'Little elephants have big ears.'

'He's stuck into his programme. Anyway, he's heard it all over the last couple of hours. Lucy doesn't hold back, not even in front of Max and Leo.'

'And he's actually moved out?'

'Yes. He hasn't admitted there's anyone else. Just says he needs a break. Some time alone to think. Lucy

103

reckons it will be someone from work. She suspects his assistant. She's Swedish. Young. Efficient. Blonde.'

'Well, that's a turn up for the books.'

'I know. The day after the twins' birthday.'

'Bit harsh, I suppose. But I guess he didn't want to do it before.'

'It's significant, is what I mean,' says Liam. 'Parents start splitting up when their kids are six because that's the first age from which they might be able to survive alone in the wild.'

'Really?' Juliet glances over at Charlie. He is engrossed in the screen but she doesn't feel comfortable having this conversation in front of him. 'I can't imagine any of the kids we know striking out alone. Not even Bella and she's the most mature.'

'It's not literal,' says Liam, taking a swig of his wine, 'or conscious. Just something that lessens the sense of obligation. Six-year-olds are more likely to survive than babies, aren't they? You'd have to be a real cunt to leave a baby. But it becomes progressively more socially acceptable, doesn't it?'

'Does it? Look, I don't want to be all Helen about it, but could you go easy on that word around Charlie?'

'He's not listening. I thought it could be a thread in my novel. All these kids turning six. It's statistically likely that another one of the marriages will start failing.'

'Is it? Maybe we should toss a coin for it.' Liam doesn't notice her joke. *How grim*, Juliet thinks, *not only to put your neighbours in a book but to hope their relationships will break up so you can write about it.*

'Think so. Don't half of marriages end in divorce these days?'

'Jesus. Do they? Why does anyone bother?'

There is a long silence.

'Well, that is the question,' says Liam. 'Maybe I should explore it in my novel.'

Juliet pokes around in the pizza boxes, finds a left-over slice and takes a bite.

'How is Lucy?'

'Massively pissed off, which is funny when you think how much she complained about him.'

'It must be a huge shock. And moaning about someone doesn't mean you want them to leave. I bet Helen wouldn't be happy if Dan walked out.'

Juliet wonders how she would feel if Liam said he wasn't coming home. She can't imagine it.

Liam picks up the bottle. 'I might go and write for a bit, is that OK? You don't mind sorting Charlie?'

Juliet waves him upstairs and peels Charlie off the iPad by promising him an ice cream in the bath. She gets one, too, and sits and nibbles off the sugar-coated chocolate, and plays with the foam letters as Charlie splashes about. She spells out LOVE and CHARLIE.

'Did you know volcano birds don't know their mummies and daddies?' asks Charlie.

'Don't they?'

'No, they never see them.'

'What would that be like?'

She hopes he will say something loving, something about not wanting to be without her, but he puts his head on one side and concentrates. 'It would depend on your species. A human wouldn't like it but a fish wouldn't care.'

'Fair enough,' says Juliet.

'Why do mummies and daddies choose each other?'

'That's a big question,' she says. 'Because they love each other?'

'Why does Max and Leo's daddy want to live with a different lady?'

Because he was bored, she thinks. *Because Lucy wasn't very nice to him. Because he believes or has tricked himself into believing that it won't matter to the twins. Because he is doing what he wants. Because he thinks he deserves it. Maybe, according to Liam, because the fact that the twins have just turned six is somehow liberating. Or maybe he just wants to live somewhere that doesn't have Lego all over the floor.*

'I don't know, darling. Grown-ups can be funny.'

When Juliet comes out of Charlie's room after saying goodnight, she can hear Liam typing in the attic. She thinks about going up there. She often used to sit on the couch and read while her mum was at the desk. She walks up the stairs. The door is closed. The floorboards creak under her feet. The typing stops. She pauses, then opens the door.

Liam looks up. His expression is not friendly. 'What is it?'

She can't bring herself to offer him company, to say she thought he might like it if she came up and read in the corner while he wrote.

'Would you like a cup of tea?'

'No. No, thanks. I just want to get on.'

She walks back down the stairs and leans on the bannister. She feels a bit sick. Uneasy. Does she need to be? Her child is in bed. Her husband is writing his novel in the attic. All is well. All has to be well. She has work to do, anyway. She has to get her laptop out and crunch email for a couple of hours. It's not like she has time to lounge around reading.

She goes downstairs, gets the dinosaur magnets out of her bag and takes them into the kitchen. She stands by the fridge and tears the plastic with her teeth. This is such a good idea. Charlie will love them, and when he is made Star of the Week or gets his pen licence they will be able to celebrate his achievements. She picks out the red T-Rex and tries to put it on the door. It falls to the floor. She crouches down, picks it up, and tries again. Their fridge is not magnetic.

The whirl of Charlie's social life continues with never-ending Halloween celebrations. On the night itself, Juliet has to leave work early because Liam says one of them needs to go out trick or treating with Charlie, while the other stays in and hands out sweets to the children who come to the door. She's surprised that Liam is going along with all this stuff, which he would usually dismiss as consumerist or whatever it is that he is currently down on, but he throws himself into it, presumably for research purposes.

'I've had the lowdown from Sarah,' he says. 'If you want trick or treaters then you put up decorations and have a lit-up pumpkin in the window. If you don't, you'll be left alone.'

'Can't we just leave it, then?' asks Juliet.

'It's perceived as unfriendly. Everyone is curious as to whether Mrs Karigi will put one out or not.'

'I hope she doesn't,' says Juliet. 'If I was a teacher, I wouldn't want the kids in my class coming round for treats. She needs boundaries.'

'I'm taking it you'll be happiest staying in?' says Liam.

'Probably,' says Juliet. 'What do I need to buy?'

'I'll sort that,' says Liam.

She gets home just before six to see a profusion of pumpkin tea lights in their window.

Liam shows her the sweets, giant plastic packets that have been specially branded with ghosts and pumpkins and blood.

He and Charlie leave to pick up Lucy and the twins. Juliet fetches her mother's mixing bowl from the kitchen and feels a twang of grief as she empties all the sweets into it. She has never used it for its proper purpose. She turns off the lights and sits by the window. Maybe she should try to get into baking. She looks at her email and waits for the doorbell to ring.

*

Charlie is tired and cold but happy when he gets home, keen to show off his bag of loot. It is full of all the same stuff she has been giving out.

She bathes him and puts him to bed, then comes downstairs to find Liam eating a sherbet Dip Dab.

'It was surprisingly good fun,' he says.

'Did Mrs Karigi put a pumpkin out?' says Juliet.

'No.'

'Good for her.'

It is only when she goes to blow out the pumpkin tea lights that she realises they are not candles, but battery powered. She turns off all the little switches and puts them in a box in the cupboard under the stairs, next to her mum's ashes. They can use them again next year, if they are still here.

The next week, Juliet has to take Charlie to the Bonfire Night party at the school organised by the PTA. Liam is supposed to be doing it but that day he is asked on *Front Row* to discuss being a working-class writer, so Juliet leaves work early again and goes straight to Lucy's house where Charlie has been playing with the twins. They walk up to the school together, calling in for Helen on the way.

Sarah is collecting money at the gate, with Alice and Bella helping. She exudes both efficiency and kindness as she oversees Alice's doling out of the change and tells Bella how many tickets to tear out of the book. They look like Russian dolls, as though they have been designed to showcase three different stages of pink, blonde womanhood.

'It's like a Christmas market,' Helen says, when they get inside.

There are fairy lights everywhere and stalls with toffee apples, marshmallows and hot chocolate. The boys all charge off to the play area. Stephen is manning the hotdog stall in a blue-and-white striped apron, dispensing jokes and fried onions.

'You look the part,' Helen tells him.

'Where's the booze?' Lucy asks loudly, and Stephen points across to the other side of the playground.

Lucy goes off to get them a drink, and Juliet is wondering what to say to Helen when the boys come back wanting money for wands and lightsabers and glowsticks. Juliet takes them all over to the stall. The items are three pounds each or four for ten, so she lets them all choose something and hands over a note to pay. Then they all want a pair of luminous glasses and she can't work out the right thing to do. She doesn't want to look tight but nor like she doesn't care about the environment. She hands over another note and regrets it when she finds out the glasses have to be assembled and she can't work out how. The woman on the stall takes pity on her and fits them together. The boys run off happily. *If only*, thought Juliet, *life stayed this simple and all human beings could be so easily pleased.*

'There you go,' says Lucy, handing Juliet a plastic cup of red wine. 'It's a bit cold but it was that or a can of Stella. You can tell Sarah wasn't involved in planning the bar.'

Lucy talks about Bas a lot but no longer uses his name. She refers to him as 'my soon-to-be ex-husband' or 'his nibs' or 'that fucker'. He didn't even tell her in real life that he was moving out, she says, just set off on a business trip on Monday morning and then emailed her to say he needed a bit of time alone. 'It's like the class thinking chair, isn't it? He's put himself in time-out. I should have noticed he'd taken the big suitcase.'

He still hasn't said anything about a new relationship.

'I have no idea,' says Lucy, spitting out the words, 'why he thinks it's better to pretend to dislike me so much that he'd rather live alone, than admit he's shacking up with someone else. I bet it's someone from work. I bet she's younger. Flat bellied. No pelvic floor issues. No stretchmarks. Hasn't given birth to seven-pound twins. Could you even imagine what it would feel like to be so undamaged? I bet she wears high heels and stockings and fitted shirts with cufflinks and trendy little black suits. Bitch.'

Helen looks at Daisy, who is asleep in the buggy. Lucy goes off to get more wine.

'I understand Lucy is angry,' whispers Helen to Juliet, 'but I wish she'd moderate her language around the children. I don't want Daisy's first words to be "lying fuck".'

When the hotdogs are sold out Stephen comes over to join them.

'Settling in OK?' he asks Juliet. 'To the street? To the school? Let us know if there's anything we can do.'

'Actually,' says Juliet, 'I am after a favour. I need to borrow a drill. Do you have one?'

'I do indeed,' says Stephen, slightly puffing his chest out. 'I do indeed. What do you need it for?'

'To put up a noticeboard. I hoped I could just bang a nail in the wall but it's too big.'

'Does Liam know what to do with a drill?'

Lucy sniggers.

'Unlikely,' says Juliet. 'He's not very practical. I thought I'd do it. Is it hard?'

'There's a bit more to it than you'd think,' says Stephen. 'You need to be careful around the electrics. And make sure you get the right bit. I can talk you through it, if you like, if Liam doesn't mind. Saturday morning?'

'It's very kind,' says Juliet. 'Are you sure?'

'No problem. I love a bit of drilling.'

Lucy sniggers again, and Juliet wonders if this is what passes for wit in Magnolia Road.

Liam had asked her to get him some parkin but there is none – she wonders if it is a northern thing – so she buys him a toffee apple and a bag of marshmallows instead.

After she puts Charlie to bed – still wearing his glow glasses – she listens to *Front Row*. Liam's bit is at the end. He comes across as funny and likeable, talks about how he never even knew growing up that being a writer could be a job, that he often can't believe his luck that people ask for his opinions about literature and want to know where he gets his ideas from. He talks about the importance of access and mentoring to increase representation. 'But is it really such a problem,' says the presenter, 'in this day and age?'

Liam laughs. 'I listen to your programme a lot,' he says, 'and hardly ever hear anyone who sounds like me. You have more Americans than you do regional accents. So, what does that mean, to a kid in Leeds or Glasgow, or Cardiff or Manchester? Might they think you can only have a career in the arts if they speak like you do?'

'Point taken,' says the presenter, sounding amused.

'Not that I've anything against your accent,' says Liam. 'I married one of you people. And my son has it. "Oh Daddy," he says, in his posh voice, "look at this lovely beetle on the *grarse*." But we could do with opening things up a bit.'

When Liam gets home, Juliet congratulates him and they gossip over a bottle of wine as he fiddles with Charlie's light-up wand. Juliet tells him how Helen and Lucy were both spiteful about the absence of their own husbands as they congratulated Sarah on Stephen's performance at the hotdog stand. Then she tells him about Stephen and the drill.

'Anyway, I said yes. He seemed to think you might mind. Why, do you think?'

'Maybe he thinks I'll feel emasculated by another man drilling on my property.'

'You don't, do you?'

'Course not. My dad would. Working-class men of

his generation would probably die rather than admit they don't know what to do with a rawlplug. But, there you go. Class is a bit easier to navigate these days, as I said on t'radio tonight, when I admitted I live a very middle-class life these days. What do you want a drill for, anyway?'

'I bought a noticeboard, half cork, half magnetic. I thought it would be useful and nice for school stuff and pictures. But it's twice the size I expected and needs drilling to the wall.'

'What else happened? Come on, spill the beans.'

She tells him how they went back to Sarah's for a drink, and the chat was all about how now that Bonfire Night was over they could all start thinking about Christmas. Helen asked what advent calendars people were going for this year, chocolate or toys, because of course less sugar was the healthier option but was a toy a day really a good idea? Stephen said that when he was a boy he only ever had a paper one with religious pictures that he had to share with his sister. Lucy said she might buy herself a swanky adult advent calendar, maybe the one from Liberty. Sarah said that if Helen wanted either Playmobil or Lego she'd have to hurry as they sell out early, and that she would be doing a reverse advent calendar and buying something for the food bank every time she shops in December. That rather shut everyone up and they all agreed they'd do it, too. Then everyone accepted as an undeniable fact that nothing was as good as a real tree, though Sarah said they weren't having one this year because they were taking the girls skiing in the French Alps, and Helen said how lovely but looked like she might cry. Lucy said she'd always wanted to go skiing with the boys but Bas wasn't keen so maybe now she would give it a go, and that Bas had yet to disclose his holiday plans and she still couldn't quite believe she had become a single-parent family. Helen said that they were going to stay with Dan's parents and it would be awful, because Dan's dad was a stress machine who liked to boss his wife about and hated it when the children made any noise and only ever wanted to play chess with one of his sons and would get in a bad mood if he lost.

'Good stuff,' says Liam. 'What are we doing for Christmas?'

Juliet hesitates. She hasn't wanted to think about it, has been putting off addressing the reality of Christmas without her mother. Usually they come here, to Magnolia Road, to the house that is now theirs. Mum being on her own was always reason enough to stay in London rather than feel they should make the trip to Liam's parents up in Leeds. Maybe that will have to change now. She hopes not.

'I know,' says Liam, 'let's be good neighbours to Lucy and the twins and invite them. It can be our good deed for the year.'

Juliet takes a sip of wine. Is this Liam scouting for material for his novel or genuinely trying to be nice? She doesn't want to spend Christmas with Lucy and her boys. But maybe it would be preferable to being in Leeds, where the first person to get up turns on the telly and it stays on until the last person goes to bed. And she might feel less preoccupied with the absence of her mum if they fill the house with other people.

'That's a good idea,' she says. 'Ask her. There was a lot of chat about the varying merits of different temporary ice rinks, too. Hampton Court or Somerset House. And I said you'd go on the Winter Wonderland walk at Kew Gardens.'

'Did Helen decide which way to jump on the advent calendar?'

'Not yet. She did ask if you should let the kids eat the chocolate before breakfast and Lucy said yes and Sarah said no, make them wait until afterwards as it teaches them how to delay gratification, and I couldn't remember if we had a policy about it, and then Freddie had a tantrum because Leo broke his lightsaber and Helen left in a hurry.'

Liam laughs and Juliet feels a bit guilty at the way she blossoms under his attention, a bit disloyal to these women she hardly knows but who might be described as her new friends. But it is so rare for him to be interested in what she has to say that she can't resist.

Liam gets most of his information and inspiration direct from the source over cappuccinos at the Coffee Traveller and wine at Lucy's house. As the autumn goes on, the women tell him more and more and he keeps writing it all down. He tells Juliet he is pleased with his progress, if a bit worried that he still doesn't know where it is heading. He has no plot and hopes that one will emerge over the course of the year. *Be careful what you wish for,* thinks Juliet, *don't tempt fate.* She's not sure she wants to see novel-worthy events unfolding in Magnolia Road.

Chapter Six

The theatre is filling up and the air is sticky with sugar.

'Here we are,' says Bas, 'Row H.'

He works his way along in that strange sideways shuffle, thanking and apologising to all the people they disturb until they find their seats and settle in. Max is next to him, then Leo, then Lucy. This is the way they always sit, with the twins in the middle. It isn't a special post-break-up configuration, though it feels a bit like it. Bas helps Max take off his scarf, then tucks it into the sleeve of the coat so it won't get lost and shoves the whole bundle under the seat. Lucy is doing the same for Leo, then she hands the boys a carton of apple juice and a packet of fruit string each. They are sorted, refreshed and ready for the show to start.

Bas sneaks a look at his watch. The matinee begins at 2.30. They'd booked the tickets ages ago, apparently. Lucy had. She'd called him last week to complain about various things and then said, 'You are still going to come with us to *Stick Man*, aren't you? They've been looking forward to it for weeks.' It might even be true, though he wonders if they are a bit old. Last year they went to *Tiddler* and they all enjoyed it, even him. Bas doesn't expect to have a good time himself when he is looking after the kids but this child-friendly theatre is the nearest he comes to it. There is no interval, it doesn't last much more than an hour, and all the children are given a booster cushion that brings them up to adult height. They are penned in and have nothing to squabble about. There is almost no possibility that they can hurt themselves, get lost, drown or be abducted, and the noise is channelled into appreciative gasps and directed by the actors. Compared to the nightmare of soft play, swimming, ice skating or the dreaded Winter Wonderland, it is almost relaxing.

Lucy leans across. 'Have you turned your phone off?'

He is a bit aggravated that she still thinks it is her job to police him, but when he fishes his phone out of his pocket it is on. There is a text from Karin. *Hope all goes well*, it says. It couldn't be any more innocent, but even the thought of her makes his cock twitch and he smiles before he can stop himself. Lucy is watching him. Their eyes meet. He feels his face flush and his palms prickle. Still, he has to tell her at some point. It might as well be today. He turns his phone off and puts it back in his pocket. Lucy is still staring at him.

'When will it start, Daddy?' says Leo.

'Soon,' he says. 'In a couple of minutes.'

Bas keeps his voice steady but can feel his heart beating hard with shame. He is a law-abiding person who never does anything wrong and the sensation of being caught out is unfamiliar.

'I want it to start now.'

'It will do soon. Just be patient.'

Lucy takes Leo's hand. 'All the actors will be getting ready behind the curtain. Look, did you see it move? Maybe there is someone on the other side.'

The lights dim. Music plays. The curtain goes up.

Two men and a woman come out on the stage and dance around a bit. Max and Leo giggle along with all the other children. Bas had rather expected, without thinking about it, that Stick Man would be played by a man dressed up as a bit of wood, but instead the actors hold up the stick characters and voice them.

Stick Man explains that he lives in the Family Tree with Stick Lady Love and their Stick Children three. The happy family dance around together. They are getting ready for Christmas. But, oh no, look! There is a dog! Stick Man is in danger. Stick Man is taken away from his family. The dog drops Stick Man and he tries to escape, but a girl plays pooh sticks with him as he shouts that he needs to get back to the family tree.

Bas shifts in his chair. Did he not know the story? He does do the bedtime routine when he's home. Bath then story. He must have read *Stick Man*, he recognises the images – but maybe that was before Karin, maybe it meant nothing to him at the time so he didn't notice it.

Bas sits as Stick Man is used by a swan made out of a glove puppet to build her nest and by a little boy as the mast for his sandcastle. Back at home, his family are missing him. They are sad and lonely and can't face the thought of Christmas without their dad.

He wonders if Lucy has done it on purpose. Is it supposed to shame him into coming home? He steals a look at her. Tears are running down her face. Maybe not. Surely she wouldn't mean to do that to herself or the boys.

There was a time when the sight of Lucy in tears would have distressed him, but at this moment he feels cold towards her. He is sorry for her but it's far away, somehow. A faint noise, like a distant bell. He can hear it but it's not too difficult to ignore. And he doesn't feel sorry enough to change anything. He's not going to be difficult about money. She can carry on living in the house on Magnolia Road. He won't make her move out or sell it. She can stay there dreaming up ideas of what to do in her garden studio. That was a waste of money, but Sarah has one and talked at length about the need to have a creative space apart from the family home, so Lucy wanted one, too. So far it has only resulted in her spending time and money on furnishing it, on making it perfect, on sourcing second-hand furniture that she then spends ages painting with stupidly named paint. Sarah told her that, too, that having hobbies would fuel her creativity. It doesn't seem to have worked. Still, it's not his problem any more, what she chooses to do when the boys are at school. She can do what she likes.

Stick Man is in trouble again and Bas feels Max's small, hot hand slide into his. It never fails to move him when one of the boys reaches for his hand. It melts his

121

heart. This is what he thought being a father would feel like, though these moments are rare, and it is easy to lose sight of them in the chaos of family life. He can't imagine Karin with the boys but he supposes they'll meet one day. At the moment he doesn't want to dilute her attention away from him. He doesn't want her looking after little people, getting involved in wiping up snot or asking whether or not they need a wee. That's what it mainly is with Max and Leo. Putting on socks, doing up zips and buttons, wiping their noses and still, sometimes, their bottoms, making them go to the toilet, stopping them running into the road. They are more like goats then miniature humans.

They'll still co-parent, he and Lucy. They know how to do that well. They are like synchronised swimmers in the way they can wordlessly step into a mirrored routine to look after their boys. He's not going to abdicate responsibility. Though he's looking forward to not having to spend so much time buried under the mess of it all.

He knows it is a cliché to leave your wife for a younger woman at work but it doesn't feel that way to him. He doesn't feel like he's having a midlife crisis or going off the rails, but as though he's arranging his life as he wants it to be. Karin looks after him very well. His last assistant had been so incompetent that he almost didn't bother getting another but Karin was brilliant from the start. Sorting things out, smoothing things over, running his diary with great efficiency, drafting his emails, capturing his tone, knowing which client needed what sort of approach. She was quiet in the office, didn't get dragged into other people's personal nonsense like the last one had, and then bring him problems to sort out. She made everything better. When he had a long list of stuff for her to do, the act of briefing her made him feel calmer. He started talking to her more and more, while at the same time realising how little he had to say because she was so quick on the uptake that she seemed to read his mind. He could concentrate on the bigger picture because she was dealing with all the lower-level stuff.

'I wish you were coming with me,' he'd said to her, not really thinking it through, when they were discussing the details of his trip to New York. He had been solely thinking about work, how useful it would be to have her there in person, not over the phone in a different time zone.

'I could, you know,' she'd said, 'any time it would be useful. All my work is portable so I could come with you and pretty much still do everything I'd be doing in the office.'

She came with him on his next trip to Frankfurt and she made everything easier. All he had to do was get in the cab she ordered to pick him up from home and then she met him at the airport and looked after everything else. She told him what to do and when to do it. He felt powerful, in command, able to focus on what really mattered. He felt like the centre of her world. When they entertained clients over dinner, she came, too, and was brilliant at working out what they wanted and doing all the small talk that always made him feel a bit awkward. He liked talking about work but was less keen on the personal stuff, never knew how to respond when people talked about their wives and families. They started having dinner together alone whenever there was a free night.

It was gradual, his desire for her. He started to compare her to Lucy and Karin was always the winner. He'd outgrown Lucy. When they'd met he'd been amused by her scattiness. She'd been a terrible temp but she was charming and funny and he'd enjoyed being with her. It was good, at first, to spend time with someone so different from anyone else he knew. And he'd been very attracted to her. But now he's had enough of how forgetful she is, how easily distracted. All that staring out of the windows and burning food is irritating. She is dismissive of his work, thinks anything to do with technology is boring, makes yawning faces at her friends if anyone asks him a question. 'Don't start him off,' she says, 'we'll be here all night,' though she always wants him to drop everything to provide free tech support to her and all her friends who are too stupid to figure out how their TVs work, or that they've used up all the storage on their iPad, or how to connect to their wireless keyboards. She acts like she is the fascinating one and he is the dull boring one who is needed to bring home the money but should earn it in a more interesting way. He has put up with it for years but doesn't want to pretend to find it funny any more.

He hadn't even noticed how much Lucy annoyed him

until he started playing the comparison game. Karin is so neat. Her bag doesn't overflow with crap, she isn't always late. She's not forgetful. She doesn't like to shock people. She doesn't dismiss his concerns about Brexit or bury her head in the sand about the political situation. What he has with Karin feels grown-up. She's the woman he should be with now, not the casual girlfriend who outstayed her welcome. That's a horrible way to think about Lucy, but it's true. There was a time he was dazzled by her but those days are long gone.

Bas doesn't want to be unkind to Lucy, but it's easier to leave knowing that her pride hurts more than her heart. She doesn't love him, she hardly likes him. He realised that when he heard her giggling with Sarah and Helen after their spa day last summer. They were in the garden drinking wine and he was putting the boys to bed upstairs. The words floated through the window. 'What a joy to get a massage without having to put up with the sex afterwards,' Lucy said. He saw then that sex was a duty she performed for their marriage, like loading the dishwasher and doing the laundry. Not that she did any of it very well, or willingly. She made a huge fuss when Magalie was on holiday and she had to do a bit of ironing. She was almost proud when she ruined Leo's new Pokémon T-shirt because the overheated iron melted the transfer. 'Mummy's not made for domesticity, darling,' she said. 'Don't worry, we'll get you a new one.'

It put him off approaching her, when he found out he was another chore to be ticked off the list. He didn't want the sort of sex they had, which always started with him massaging her back until at some point she'd turn over, open her legs and deign to let him climb on top of her until he came. He never looked at her any more. He wanted to, but she always pulled his head down to her shoulder. She pretended she liked kissing his neck, but he thought she just didn't want to look at him. 'Do you want to give me a massage?' she'd said, one night in bed, after a few sex-free days had passed. 'I'm tired,' he'd said, and caught the look of relief that flashed on her face as she reached for her book.

Perhaps he'd have got over it and climbed back on at some point if it wasn't for Karin, but then they were in Paris, and they signed a big deal, and he was too full of adrenaline to think about sleep, so they walked back together from the restaurant to their hotel and when they saw the Ritz, he suggested a nightcap. So they sat with balloon glasses of cognac listening to the pianist play Sinatra, Édith Piaf and Ella Fitzgerald, and it was cheesy but he felt like every lyric was describing how he felt about Karin, that she made him feel so young, that he'd like to dance with her cheek to cheek, that he felt his heart filled with song. And he wanted to touch her face, to feel her hair against his fingers, and he knew that he must pull himself together, that he was pissed, that he mustn't misunderstand their relationship. But then she leant across the table and put her hand to his cheek and said, 'I'm getting too fond of you. I probably need to resign. Unless, of course, you're fond of me, too.' He covered her hand with his, and they sat and looked at each other and he thought how long it had been since he'd really looked at another person, really been looked at in return, and then he paid the bill, and ignored the knowing gaze of the barman, and they walked silently back to their own hotel. And in the lift, she said, 'Your place or mine?' and pressed the button for her floor, and he was thinking that they might be about to kiss when, just at the last moment, an elderly American couple got in, too, and tried to make conversation – 'Where y'all from?' – and Karin got the giggles.

Then they'd walked down the corridor to her room and he knew with every step that this wasn't a one-night stand, that it meant the end of his marriage, but he didn't want to think about that, he didn't want to think about anything except fitting himself into Karin, connecting himself to her, being inside her while staring into her eyes.

Men are supposed to leave their responsible, organised wives for mistresses who are flighty, silly and will waste all their money, but Bas feels it is the other way around for him. Karin's flat in Kentish Town is small but perfectly organised. She never asks him for anything – 'We could just stay here in the flat,' she said, when they were discussing what to do about Christmas – but he wants to take her somewhere for a sexy and luxurious Christmas break so they are going back to Paris, and this time they are staying at the Ritz. He wants to spend money on Karin, wants to buy her lipstick and perfume and jewellery and shoes. He's looking forward to being in duty free with her, getting out his credit

127

card, handing it over. He wants to drink expensive cocktails and eat fine food. He wants to feed her. He loves the way Karin eats with gusto, unlike Lucy who is always following a new regime. He could never keep up with whether or not she was eating sugar or meat or breakfast, whether fruit was in or not, whether, on her birthday and Mother's Day, he was supposed to provide expensive chocolate or whether that would be seen as unsupportive and enabling. He won't have to be caught in the crossfire of Lucy's changeability any more. He can't imagine that Karin will make him eat chia porridge one week and chorizo omelettes the next.

He is starting a new life. In Paris, they will linger over brandy and listen to the same pianist, and he will know that being with Karin is no longer an impossible dream but his new reality. And he'll be able to sing along to Édith Piaf. He has no regrets. Maybe he will in the future. But for now, he's got what he wants.

Stick Man gets what he wants, too. With the help of Santa he makes it home to the Family Tree. Applause, laughter, curtain down.

Lucy has pulled herself together and they pour out of the auditorium, jostling with all the other parents shepherding their kids. The boys want to go to the shop – they always want to go to the shop – but the queues are massive.

'We've already got the book,' Lucy says.

'I want a toy,' says Leo, 'I want a Stick Man.' He points at a collection of cuddly toys.

'I want a pencil case,' says Max. Max is smart and

has already worked out his chances of acquiring new stuff increase if he highlights the educational aspects.

'The queue is too long,' says Lucy.

Leo juts his chin out. If he kicks off it won't be silent and weepy but noisy and violent.

'Let's go to Trafalgar Square to see the living statues,' Lucy says, just in time. 'There are some good Star Wars ones, apparently. A very good Yoda, Sarah says.'

This does the trick. Bas and Lucy exchange a re-lieved look and usher the boys out of the theatre into the bright winter sun. They help them into their coats and scarves and then walk across Leicester Square. Bas holds Max's hand; Lucy has the more wriggly Leo. Bas smiles at the thought that even though he has left his wife, he is still having to do things that Sarah thinks are a good idea.

He gives the boys a pound each, and they go off to stare at Yoda and try to work out how he appears to be sitting in mid-air. Bas and Lucy stand by the steps of the National Gallery. Bas looks down at Nelson's Column, at the tourists taking photos of each other posing with the lions. Some kids are feeding the pigeons.

'I wonder what it feels like to be a living statue?' Lucy says.

This is the sort of thing he used to like about her. Her curiosity about everyone. Then he got bored of it. *Pay attention to what's under your nose*, he could have said to her, a while ago. *Focus on me, on us*.

Bas watches Lucy watching the boys with Yoda. Her nose is red, her eyes watery.

'Sarah thinks we should try counselling.' She's not looking at him, just speaking into the space in front of her as she keeps her eyes on the boys. 'She knows someone really good.'

Of course she does, Bas thinks. He wonders what constitutes a good marriage guidance counsellor. Someone who saves the marriage, he supposes, who reunites the couple, who forces the escaping partner back and relocates him firmly into the marital home. If Lucy had suggested it a few months ago he might have agreed.

'I think it's too late for that,' he says.

'How can it be too late?' Lucy says. 'You never said anything was wrong until you fucked off.'

Another thing he likes about Karin is that she doesn't swear. When she does meet the boys, she won't swear in front of them and think it's funny when they copy her.

'There's no point lying about it,' says Lucy. 'If there's someone else, you might as well tell me.'

'There is someone else,' Bas says. 'I'm sorry. It's serious.'

They stare at each other for a long moment.

'Well, you needn't be so fucking miserable about it,' Lucy says. 'You look like you're telling me you've got cancer.'

They both laugh. Bas is grateful to her for breaking the tension.

'I still care about you and the boys, obviously.'

'Obviously.' There's a bitter undercurrent but Lucy's expression is more resigned than angry.

'I mean, I'm not going to be difficult about money, or anything. Or try to take the boys off you. Or do any of that terrible stuff you hear about people doing. Like that friend of Sarah's who had to get a restraining order.'

'Well that's good of you, thank you.'

The boys are back. They want more money for the other living statues. They want to have their photos taken with Darth Vader and Luke Skywalker. Bas thinks how even at the moment of its ending, their marriage is only allowed to happen in tiny slices in between the major work of the child rearing.

'We can talk more about it later,' he says to Lucy, as he allows himself to be dragged off.

She shrugs. 'We'll need to tell people, I suppose. Let's leave it till after the festivities. Yes, Leo, in a minute, I need to turn my phone on first.'

Bas stands and occasionally hands over another pound as Lucy photographs their children with Darth and Luke and Princess Leia and Yoda.

'Family selfie,' shouts Max, and they all gather together and cuddle and smile, and he puts his arm around Lucy as she takes the photo.

'Pizza Express?' she says, and the boys cheer. Bas wants to escape but it seems a bit churlish to run off. And maybe he's delaying the moment when he has to leave them, when they go off in different directions, so they go to Pizza Express and order the same things they always do, because, as Lucy says, who wants maple gammon or beef and horseradish on a pizza just because it's nearly Christmas? Bas thinks that he has no idea what Karin would order if she were here, whether she could be lured into a festive special, whether she has a regular dish. Lucy suggests a glass of Berry Royale and, when it arrives, makes a toast to 'our lovely family' in a way that doesn't seem sarcastic, and they take lots more photos and talk a bit about family admin, that Lucy will take care of the gifts for Magalie and Mrs Karigi, and that Bas will drop into Fortnum's and send hampers to both sets of parents.

'What about us?' says Max. 'We've been really good.'

'Then you'll need to write that in a letter to Santa,' says Lucy.

Bas tells the joke about Darth Vader knowing what Luke got for Christmas because he'd felt his presence, and the boys laugh and Lucy rolls her eyes, but perhaps not quite as much as she would have done if they were still together, and, as the warmth of the purplish fizz spreads through Bas's body, he sees a bright future for him and Lucy, that they can be friends and comrades and that all will be well.

The boys have ice cream and a portion of snowball dough balls and Bas pays the bill, then walks them to the tube at Embankment. And when Max asks why he isn't coming home with them he says he has to work, and when Leo says, 'Work is stinky poo,' he laughs. And they all embrace, a family cuddle, and he gives Lucy a grateful smile and walks out of the station and turns on his phone. There are lots of messages and missed calls from Karin, who has seen the photos of them at Trafalgar Square and at Pizza Express on

Lucy's Instagram and wonders if this means he has gone back to his family and will not be coming home to her, and he texts to reassure her, but, as he walks back past the living statues – Princess Leia is looking a bit cold – he wonders why Karin was looking at Lucy's Instagram in the first place. One of the things he likes about her is she isn't always glued to her phone in the way that Lucy is, and, for the first time since he fell in love with her, he feels like she has done something less than perfect, and he thinks how strange that he started out today expecting to get a hard time from Lucy but that it is Karin who has created the problem. He pushes the thought away and walks up towards Piccadilly. His phone rings and it is Karin. She tells him she loves him and that she's sorry she overreacted, but that one of her friends is friends with Lucy and called her to ask if he'd gone back to his wife. And now she feels silly, and of course he has to spend lots of time with the boys and of course that will include Lucy, and she knows he has to smile in the photos and she's sorry and is he coming over? He says he is, and he says he understands and that he's bringing supper, and he walks to Fortnum's where the air also smells of sugar, but a more rarefied kind. He orders hampers to be sent to his parents and Lucy's and then thinks of Lucy herself and that he should send her a gift, too. Alcohol seems safe because no matter what other dietary rules she might be following she never stops drinking, so he splashes out on the wine cellar hamper.

He goes into the food hall and roams around, looking

for romantic food. Lucy always said he was unromantic. Maybe it was her fault, that she didn't bring it out in him. He buys smoked duck and quail eggs and asparagus and a chicken pie and some French cheese that he has never heard of and a slice of truffled foie gras and a bottle of Perrier-Jouët Belle Epoque because the flowery pattern on the bottle reminds him of Paris.

Bas walks back onto Piccadilly. It's dark and cold. He imagines Lucy and the boys arriving at Gunnersbury tube station and making their way to Magnolia Road. He's glad he isn't with them, doesn't have to cope with Leo kicking off on the walk home, or the struggle of bathtime, or the inevitable demands for more stories, another glass of water, a last wee before lights out. He's escaped the family tree.

He used to think that people stayed together for the sake of the children, but maybe it's the other way around and they split up because of the children. He hopes Karin doesn't want any. Two is definitely enough for him. He doesn't want the sanctity of Karin's flat invaded by noisy babies. He looks up at the Christmas lights twinkling in the dark and then flags down a cab. His new life starts here.

Chapter Seven

Lucy waits by the flower stall outside Turnham Green tube station. The stall holder is wearing a pair of fingerless gloves. Useful, no doubt. She looks down at her own gloves, which are fur-lined leather. Not real fur, of course. She isn't a monster. Bas bought them for her last Christmas. She gave him a list of ideas and he bought everything on it. He's not ungenerous, just unimaginative. That's all in the past now, Bas giving her gifts. She is still adjusting to the many ways that his decision to leave her will impact her life.

It is cold. Lucy stamps her feet and rubs her hands together. A woman dithers for ages before deciding on a small, ugly pot plant, and then a man takes no time at all to pick out a large bouquet of red roses. Where do they all come from, these winter flowers? Are they grown abroad or in hothouses? Bas will never buy her flowers again either, though that isn't a huge loss. His taste was always a bit garage forecourt. No matter which florist he went to his offerings were a bit dowdy, a bit off-brand. Carnations or, she shudders, chrysanthemums. A flower only fit for a funeral. He presented her with a pink hydrangea in a pot once. The sort of thing you would only buy if you were visiting a great-aunt in a nursing home.

The stall holder is not unattractive. He looks strong and his cheeks are ruddy. If you met him in a pub, you'd know he worked outside. Lucy has always fancied men who do physical work, who dig roads or tunnels or who swarm over scaffolding looking like they don't care if they might fall off. She likes callused hands and high-vis vests, dirty jeans and hobnail boots. *You like a bit of rough, don't you*, one such man once said to her, as he slapped her arse during sex. He didn't last long. She liked him less out of bed than she did in it.

Lucy sees Bas a few seconds before he notices her and has to admit that his new life suits him. He is carrying himself with more confidence. He has the look of man who is getting a lot of attention and who is feeling good about himself.

He kisses her on the cheek. 'Thanks for coming to meet me.'

It feels a bit rehearsed, as if he has thought about what to say and do.

'You smell nice,' she says, surprised. Bas doesn't like scent.

'I, ah, bought something new,' he says.

'Fresh. Woody. I like it. What is it?'

He looks at the ground. 'I can't remember.'

'Oh, I see,' says Lucy, losing patience. 'She bought it for you. She bought you a fancy bottle of something and you splash it on but have no idea what is. You don't

need to lie about it. I get that you're living with someone else.'

A car beeps as the lorry in front of it stops abruptly.

'Sorry,' Bas says, 'it's all a bit new to me.'

'Talking about your girlfriend with your wife? Yes,
unfamiliar territory.'

They walk up Turnham Green Terrace together. Lucy
is spoiling for a fight now but remembers the talking-to
Sarah has given her. After listening to all her grievanc-
es, Sarah very firmly said that while of course it is natural that she should feel upset and betrayed, the most
important thing is that Bas remains involved with the
boys. Lucy must help that to happen by being coop-
erative and dialling down her instincts for spite and
revenge. *You have a choice now*, Sarah said, *of how to
behave, and it is vitally important for the boys that you
make the right one.* That was how Sarah always talked
to her girls if they were on the brink of being naughty.
Make a good choice, she'd say. And they usually did.
She is always inclined to follow Sarah's advice. Though
having regular sex with Bas even though she didn't feel
like it hasn't, as Sarah promised it would, kept her marriage off the rocks.

'I don't want to be mean,' says Lucy, 'I'm glad you've
come.'

Bas is silent.

'Though I could have flogged your ticket on the black
market. Imagine only allowing two places per child for
a school nativity concert. People are up in arms! Sarah
says it's because they bunged Year One and Year Two

together and there isn't enough room. Apparently some grandparents are planning to gatecrash. There have been a lot of conversations about crowd control and whether they need bouncers.'

Lucy stops outside Côte. 'I thought we could have coffee here as the Coffee Traveller and Vinyl Sounds will be full of other parents.'

The restaurant is largely empty. They sit in the window. Lucy orders an espresso and a glass of water. Bas asks for a cup of chamomile tea. That's another change. He must be in love if she's persuaded him to drink herbal tea.

'I was consuming too much caffeine,' he says. 'I've cut down. One after breakfast and one after lunch.'

The drinks arrive.

'I've ordered the boys' presents,' he says. 'An iPad and a stormtrooper costume each, and some Lego to share. They will be delivered to you. Do I need to do anything else?'

'I'll sort stocking fillers,' says Lucy. 'What do you want to do about Christmas Day? I was thinking we should all spend it together. Sarah says it is really important for the boys to see us getting on, that we can still like each other, that we are still a family.'

Bas squeezes his teabag against the side of the cup with his spoon, then fishes it out and puts it on his saucer.

'I'll be away at Christmas.'

'What?'

'I'll be away at Christmas. I'm going away.'

'Where?'

Bas looks at her as though he is considering lying. 'Paris.'

'Paris?'

'Yes.'

'You're going to Paris for Christmas with your new girlfriend.'

'Yes.'

'We've been separated about five minutes and you've decided to spend Christmas in Paris with your new girlfriend.'

Bas stares into his cup. Lucy knows that he wants to bolt. He hates conflict. They have never been able to have satisfactory rows because he shuts down under pressure. Fuck Sarah and her advice. She gives in to the urge to try to make him fight back.

'Did you even think about how that would make me feel? What am I going to tell the boys when they ask why you aren't coming around on Christmas Day? That you've taken your new girlfriend to fucking Paris? That Daddy is off to Paris on the knob?'

'You're speaking very loudly.'

'Oh, I'm the one at fucking fault, am I? You're off to Paris and I'm off to Faultsville, is that it?'

Lucy notices that the four older women at the only other occupied table are all gaping at them. 'What do you think, ladies? He left me and his children in November and is taking his new girlfriend to Paris for Christmas. What a star of a man he is.'

The women all look down at their drinks.

Jesus fuck, thinks Lucy, *am I the only person in this restaurant who can make eye contact?*

'October,' says Bas.

'What?'

'It was October. I left you on the twenty-ninth of October. It was the day after the boys' birthday.'

'I don't think that's the most relevant thing here,' says Lucy, but something about Bas's correction of the facts is almost funny and she feels the anger ebb out of her. She looks at him. His face is bright red and his hands are white. He is so clueless she feels almost sorry for him. He is not adequate prey, really. He's not up to her weight and never was.

'Whatever,' she says, 'do what you like. It's none of my business, after all.'

Bas sneaks a look at her. 'I'm sorry. I know I'm in the wrong.'

'Why did you never take me to Paris?'

Bas looks at her. 'Would you have wanted to come?'

'Oh, forget about it,' says Lucy, feeling a thrill of magnanimity. 'The main thing is that we both behave well for the boys. Speaking of which, we should get going.'

Bas asks for the bill and when it comes he reaches for his wallet. For a moment Lucy almost feels like she should offer to go halves, even though she would still be paying with his money. They'll have to sort all that out, she supposes. Though he already said she and the boys can stay in the house.

'About money,' she says.

140

'I don't want you to be worse off,' he says. 'You won't be.'

He's not tight, that's true. And she has always noted he has more integrity and honour in financial matters than anyone else she knows.

'I'll trust you then,' she says. 'Thank you.'

Lucy makes a note to boast to Sarah later that she found something to appreciate him for, that she is working hard to establish a cordial relationship. She smiles apologetically at the old ladies as they leave the restaurant.

As they walk up Turnham Green Terrace she is assaulted by memories. Here they bought baby clothes, and there they took the boys for haircuts when they were younger because Leo would only stay still if there was an aquarium to look at. They walk by what used to be Charlotte's Bistro. They went there a lot in the early days when she still found Bas different and unusual rather than dull. Or maybe she was too easy to please and just liked drinking artisanal gins in the company of someone who appeared to hang on her every word.

As they cross the road, Bas says, 'You're right that I don't know what it is called, but she didn't buy it for me. It's hers. It's unisex. I've been wearing it, too.'

For a moment she doesn't understand and then realises he's back on his new smell.

'It's very nice,' she says.

'I don't put much on. Just a little dab.'

They arrive at the Baptist church into a sea of parents. Lucy has her two tickets ready to show but no

141

one looks at them as they follow the crowd and file into seats upstairs.

'Look,' Lucy says, pointing below, 'there they are.'

All the children are grouped together with Mrs Karigi. Max and Leo are standing in between Charlie and Freddie. Bella is on the other side of Charlie. They are all wearing tinsel crowns and the boys look tired and bored. Only Bella is ready to perform.

'Funny place, isn't it?' says Lucy. 'Feels more like a conference centre than a church. Apart from the big wooden cross. It doesn't have that churchy smell.'

She spots Sarah and Stephen, Liam, and Helen and Daisy all sitting together over on the other side. She waves. They all smile back supportively.

Bas looks at the floor again.

'Oh, for fuck's sake,' Lucy says, 'give them a wave. You're not persona non grata around here.'

Bas raises a hand and they all wave back at him.

The headteacher, Mr Watson, stands up and double claps his hands slowly. The children all stop talking and join in with the claps. *Impressive*, thinks Lucy. She should try that at home.

'Welcome, parents and carers. Welcome to our whole school family.'

Mr Watson is extremely tall and speaks precisely, enunciating each word. He is clearly used to having to make himself understood by small children. He drones on about God for a bit and Lucy starts to fidget. She hates the way having kids means you end up getting stuck being patronised by anyone who has anything to do with the wellbeing of your children. She thinks Watson intends to go on forever but then he says, 'But you want to hear your children,' as though he is announcing something very wise.

'No shit, Sherlock,' whispers Lucy to Bas, who gives her the kind of disapproving look that punctuated their marriage.

God, she is bored. She looks at the wooden cross and wonders why there isn't a body on it. Watson reminds them that, in consultation with the PTA, they have decided there should be no videoing or photographs this year.

There are murmurs of consternation from various men poised with their devices.

'That was Sarah's work,' whispers Lucy. 'After the school assembly where we couldn't see anything because the three dads in front of us were recording it on their iPads.'

'So, enjoy the present moment,' Mr Watson says, with a flourish.

Mrs Karigi strums the guitar as they all sing 'Little Donkey'. Bella is singing her heart out. Max and Charlie make a decent fist of it but Leo and Freddie clearly don't know the words. Then 'We Three Kings', which is dire, and 'O Come, All Ye Faithful', which is even worse.

'I always think this sounds a bit rude,' Lucy whispers to Bas, and he smiles though she's not sure he gets it.

'It Was On a Starry Night' comes next, which is at least happy sounding and more difficult to make a mess of, and Lucy finds herself swaying along, tears prickling in her eyes at the beauty of it all. Then it is over, probably not a moment too soon for Leo and Freddie, who look like they have had enough.

Mr Watson stands up and asks them to join in an endless round of applause. Then, as the parents are finally beginning to shuffle about and get to their feet, he asks for their attention again. 'We know you will be proud of your children and will want to tell them so, but for health and safety reasons we ask you to remain in your seats until the children have been led out by their teachers.'

Murmurs again as all the parents sit back down. It is a bit of a damp squib. Lucy watches the twins file out after Mrs Karigi and puts her gloves on ready for the outside.

Helen looks distraught to have missed out on an opportunity to coddle Freddie. She is saying something to Sarah who is literally soothing her by stroking her arm. Daisy starts to cry. Lucy catches Liam's eye and makes a face at him. He raises his eyebrows and makes a gesture with his hand suggesting a drink. Lucy makes an 'I don't know' face and turns back to Bas just as their side starts to get up. They both wave across at the others and walk down the stairs.

'It's a shame you don't get to see the boys,' says Lucy, as they hit the cold air. 'Do you have to charge off? You could come and pick them up from school with me if you like?'

'I'm sorry. I have a meeting in town.'

'Well—' she pats his arm, a nice non-sexual act of

solidarity '—come and see the boys before Paris.'

'I will. Thank you. Thank you for giving me your second ticket.'

He kisses her cheek again and she is hit once more with his scent.

Lucy watches Bas walk away. She doesn't feel like she expected she would. She feels a vague, almost maternal fondness for him. Certainly not jealous. She doesn't care that he is on his way back to someone else.

'Bas,' she calls. He is just enough in earshot that she doesn't have to shout. 'What's her name?'

'Who?'

'Who do you think? The perfume owner.'

She watches him consider his options and then decide to be honest.

'Karin. It's Karin.'

His assistant. Lucy feels a dart of aggravation, quickly superseded by a frisson of pleasure that she has been proved right. Probably Bas has no idea how to meet a woman outside the workplace.

'Well, bonnes vacances. To both of you.'

He looks agreeably surprised and grateful and heads off. She wonders if he'll stop off at the flower stall, if Karin likes chrysanthemums and carnations. Maybe she will find a way of tactfully updating his choices.

Lucy watches the parents pouring out of the church. She hopes she hasn't missed the others. No, there they are. She wants a coffee and a debrief. She is itching to tell someone about the aftershave or cologne, or whatever it is that men call perfume. Unisex indeed.

145

Maybe even a drink. It is nearly lunchtime and Christmas, after all.

Helen is still fussing that she couldn't get to Freddie to give him some water and a snack. 'I could see he was too tired and hot. I hope he got back to school OK.'

Stephen has to go back to the office, but Sarah and Liam agree to a drink and maybe an early lunch. Helen says she will join them if she can get Daisy to go to sleep by wheeling her around the green a few times. 'I'll come with you,' Sarah says. 'I could use the fresh air, if you two don't mind getting the table?'

Lucy and Liam walk off together.

'You forget, don't you, the grind of a baby. How hard it is,' says Liam.

'I've completely forgotten,' says Lucy. 'Or blocked it out. And I can't even remember what to do with one. Helen never asks me to hold Daisy. Probably frightened I'll drop her.'

Carluccio's feels very Christmassy, with panettone and green-and-red wrapped confectionery piled high. They get a table for four towards the back of the room, making sure there is space for the pram.

'Are we going to have a proper drink?' says Lucy.

'I think we should,' says Liam.

They deliberate between the Very Merry Mimosa and the Festive Bellini.

'What makes the Bellini festive?' she asks the waitress.

'It's made with pomegranate rather than peach.'

'Let's do it,' says Lucy. 'Two of those, please.'

The waitress brings the drinks on a silver tray. They look pretty; pink with pomegranate seeds floating on the top. They clink glasses.

Sarah and Helen arrive with red cheeks. Helen parks the sleeping Daisy and they both order peppermint tea. They all decide on antipasti, fritto misto, and fig and prosciutto bruschetta to share. Lucy and Liam order another Bellini each.

'Couldn't Juliet come?' asks Helen.

'She was supposed to have the morning off,' says Liam, 'but there was some crisis with a client that she had to solve.'

'Poor thing,' says Helen.

'I doubt she minded much,' says Liam. 'She has a limited tolerance for child-related activities.'

'I don't blame her,' says Lucy. 'I often wish I had an office to escape to.'

'How was it seeing Bas?' says Helen.

'Not like I thought it would be,' says Lucy, and fills them in on the unisex cologne and the trip to Paris.

'Wasn't that a bit cruel of him?' Helen asks. 'To bang on about the perfume?'

'I don't think he meant it like that,' says Lucy.

'He's literal-minded, isn't he?' suggests Sarah. 'You asked and he answered you.'

'Maybe,' says Lucy, 'and I'm glad I know. There is a bit of relief in the clarity. I mean, imagine if there wasn't someone else. If he was just unhappy and we had to schlep into counselling and talk about our feelings and make allowances.'

Liam laughs and Sarah looks stern.

'Don't disapprove of me, Sarah,' says Lucy, 'I haven't got the energy for it.'

Sarah reaches forward and pats her hand. 'I didn't mean to. Sorry. I just—'

'You think everyone's life would be improved by therapy,' says Lucy, 'I know. But it's not my bag. I followed all your advice regarding being nice to him, so let that soothe your urge to do good. Now, I've been thinking about my new single state. Should I get back on the bike? It's ten years since I was last available. Do you think sex has changed?'

Helen laughs nervously. 'I don't like the word "available" – makes you sound like a public convenience. Why be in a hurry, anyway?'

'I'm not,' says Lucy. 'More excited about the future. I think I'm having a good attitude to it. I could be moping into a Mimosa and instead I'm being brave over a Bellini.'

'I wasn't criticising,' says Helen. 'I just don't understand why you'd want to get back on the bike when you could have a nice rest.'

Lucy raises an eyebrow and Helen flushes, perhaps realising that she has given away rather a lot about herself and her marriage.

'It's great you can see it positively,' says Sarah. 'I really admire you.'

'Ta,' says Lucy. 'I'm not in a hurry exactly, but it did

occur to me that it might not be true that I don't like sex. I mean, maybe I just don't like sex with my husband.'

Heads swivel in the restaurant. Lucy giggles.

'Here's to you,' says Liam, raising his glass. 'To Lucy unleashed.'

Sarah and Helen lift their teacups.

Lucy drains her drink. 'Thanks. I can be who I want to be now. I'll need to buy some new knickers. Shall we have another Bellini?'

Chapter Eight

Christmas morning finds Juliet peeling potatoes and listening to carols on a CD that came with a book her mother gave to Charlie last year. 'Share the magic of Christmas,' it says on the front cover next to a picture of a fat Santa, some large-eared elves carrying presents, and a few grateful-looking Dickensian children. She has decided to do without her phone for a few days as social media and the news were making her miserable. This CD is all she is allowing herself to access in the way of entertainment.

Juliet can hardly believe that they were all here together with her mum last year. She had just been for her annual tests, as usual. Every year since her recovery from cancer in 2003 she went for tests in December and got the all-clear in January. There was no reason to suspect that anything would be different. There was nothing wrong with her. She looked and felt great and, as ever, made them all feel special. She had collected Charlie after his last morning at school, and Juliet and Liam had a few days of going to parties and staying out late before heading over to Magnolia Road on Christmas Eve. Charlie had been helping with the decorations and making mince pies. He was decked out in an apron and covered in flour, beaming.

She had such a knack for making things nice, her mother. Juliet found the decorations in a box under the stairs but hasn't been able to assemble them with the same festive touch. She'd tried to make an occasion of it but Liam wasn't bothered and Charlie was rough with everything, not wanting to wait until she'd put the lights on the tree, chucking tinsel around and then breaking the golden angel that she remembered from all the Christmases of her childhood. Juliet had wanted to scream at him but she restrained herself as she swept up the jagged, glittering pieces and then cried hot, angry tears as she threw them into the outside bin. And she'd underestimated how much Mum must have been involved in making sure that she got good, thoughtful presents. Last year she felt loved and appreciated on Christmas Day. This morning Charlie and Liam gave her a carrier bag from TK Maxx that contained a scarf-and-glove set, a nightshirt with 'It's Snow Joke' on the front, a box of reindeer biscuits, and a chocolate-flavoured mini panettone. They hadn't taken the price tags off.

Juliet plops the last potato into the pan and peers into the oven. She's splashed out £65 on an easy-carve, deboned bird wrapped in a smoky bacon lattice from the M&S at Kew Retail Park. 'Spend less time prepping and more time celebrating,' it says on the label. Juliet opens the fridge. Champagne and white wine, a salted caramel Yule log, a snowy profiterole stack, and a cake in the shape of a chimney with Santa's red wellies waving in the air. She had tried to keep a hold on the excess. She sidestepped the Prosecco and gold-leaf crisps as obscene only to succumb to the multi-buy offer on cherry brandy liqueurs and Irish cream chocolates. She even bought a bottle of sherry. Fancy crackers, mandarin and clove potpourri, pre-mixed mulled wine, a candle scented with frankincense and myrrh. She stumbled out of the food hall feeling like she'd gone mad and full of self-loathing, especially when she saw the box for the food bank and realised she had forgotten to do her reverse advent calendar. *I will donate the same amount of money as the whole bill to a homeless charity*, she thought, as she packed the shopping into the car.

She did it as soon as she got home. And as she scrolled through Twitter, she clicked on all the charitable initiatives that popped up on her timeline. She bought a bed for the night for a vulnerable teenager from Crisis, two care packages from Refuge, four Christmas dinners at Centrepoint, and made a donation to Beauty Banks. She signed Charlie up as a member of the Save the Children club. He'll get a magazine that will educate him about how children live in other parts of the world. None of it assuaged her guilt or made her feel better.

The last thing she did before turning off her phone and hiding it at the back of the kitchen drawer was read an article about how Christmas is a hard time for the newly bereaved.

Christmas Day. The first one without her mother. She closes the fridge and looks at the bottle of sherry sitting on the windowsill. Is it too early? The doorbell rings: their guests have arrived. She hears Liam open the door and the twins rush upstairs to find Charlie.

'Thank you so much for inviting us,' says Lucy, handing over a bottle of champagne, an expensive-looking bottle of red, and a bag from Hotel Chocolat. 'You are a life saver.'

Juliet allows herself to be embraced. 'We're very happy to have you,' she says. 'Settle in, make yourself at home.'

Liam unwraps the gold foil from the champagne, taking off the wire hood.

Lucy gets two white boxes out of her bag. 'Bas has given both the boys their own iPad, which is good as they won't squabble over mine any more, but he's forgotten or doesn't care that he's the one who knows how to do technology. He's now fucked off to Paris with his new bint, and I don't know how to set them up.'

'It's not hard,' says Liam, handing her a glass of champagne. 'I can do it.'

'You angel,' says Lucy, smiling up at him.

Juliet watches as they unpack the iPads. Lucy looks different since Bas left. There is a spark about her, a new energy.

'He also gave them a Lego model of the Death Star. Lord knows how we'll manage to put it together.'

'I'll help,' says Liam.

There is a stampede of feet on the stairs and the boys tumble in. The twins are dressed up in their new stormtrooper outfits. Charlie has taken off his Christmas jumper and put on his Darth Vader costume.

The twins snatch at the iPads.

'Hang on a minute,' says Liam.

'Say hello to Juliet,' says Lucy.

'Hello,' says Max. Leo ignores her. The only way she can tell them apart is by their behaviour. Max is friendly and chatty and Leo never says anything to grown-ups, though he whispers away to Charlie.

'Do you want a snack, boys? It's nearly an hour to lunch.'

'They can last,' says Lucy. She pulls Charlie towards her for a cuddle.

'Hello, Darth. Have you had a lovely morning? Lots of nice presents?'

'Too many,' says Charlie.

'Too many?'

'I don't know what to play with.'

Juliet shakes her head. All that effort. Or rather, all that last-minute panic buying, and she has succeeded only in overwhelming him.

'And my hamster doesn't have a battery.'

'That's sad,' said Lucy. 'Come over to our house later. We have a drawer full of different batteries.'

'I wanted a real hamster. Or a tarantula. Or a lizard. But Mummy doesn't like pets.'

'Mummy doesn't want anything else to look after,' says Juliet.

'Nearly there,' says Liam, tapping at the iPads.

'Can you fix them so they don't accidentally watch P.O.R.N.?'

'Yes, I've set up parental controls.'

'What's pron?' asks Max.

'Nothing for you to worry about,' says Liam, ruffling his hair.

'Can I have your iPad, Mummy?' Charlie asks.

'Go on, then,' says Juliet. 'Just until lunch.'

Liam takes the boys back upstairs.

'They'll be happy now,' says Lucy, 'playing *Minecraft* or watching YouTube videos made by kids not much older than they are. I don't get it, do you?'

'No,' says Juliet, 'I'm too old.'

'Charlie is just like a mini Liam, isn't he? Same face. Can I help with anything?'

'Thanks, but I'm OK,' says Juliet. 'It's mainly pre-made from M&S. Though for some reason I thought I should do the potatoes myself.'

Juliet pours a little olive oil into a roasting pan and puts it in the oven. She tips the potatoes into the colander, lets the water drain off and then shakes them. Her mother always said that a good shake at this stage was the secret weapon with roast potatoes, that it fluffed up the outsides. Juliet peers at them. They don't look at all fluffed. Maybe she hasn't boiled them for long enough. Too late now. She opens the oven door again. There is a satisfying sizzle as they land in the hot oil. She shakes the pan and puts it back in the oven. Everything is done for a while.

Juliet joins Lucy at the kitchen table and picks up her glass.

'Here's to you,' she says. 'How are you?'

It is all the opening Lucy needs and she fills Juliet in on the Bas situation, the shock of his departure, the news that he is living with someone else.

'He sent me a hamper of wine from Fortnum's. Twelve bottles. Is that a bit odd? He always thought I drank too much.'

'Maybe he's trying to be nice,' Juliet says.

'I always thought I'd be the one to leave, if anyone did. I thought he was safe. Boring but safe. Turns out you can't tell. I settled for someone I thought wouldn't leave me and now he has.'

Lucy drains her glass and Juliet tops it up.

'Do you miss him?'

'I don't know. He's very practical. I can't work the TV. Not that I watch it, really, and the boys know how. We had this Lego advent calendar with little toys to make up. Quite hard. If the boys got stuck I couldn't help them, especially not if I was hungover. That felt a bit shit. Wished I'd gone for a chocolate one.'

The CD has come to an end so Juliet presses play again. 'Jingle Bells'.

'I'm not sure I was ever in love with him,' says Lucy. 'I chose him because he adored me and was reliable. And now here I am. Abandoned. People expect me to be upset and angry and humiliated. It's as though there's a code for how an abandoned wife should behave, but I don't feel like following it. I might even be relieved. I was fed up with him and his monotone drone.'

'I'm impressed,' says Juliet. 'I hate the way modern life dictates how we should be. It's great you feel liberated.'

'Not sure I'd go that far. I'm a bit pissed off that he's escaped. I was bored, too, but having children is the one life decision you can't back out of, isn't it? You can't return them to the baby shop because it's a bit harder than you expected. Not that I want to. I adore my boys. But I thought Bas was on the same page when it came to accepting that life wouldn't be all that exciting for a while. It's a shock to find out he felt free to fuck off and have an affair. I never thought that it would happen to me, you know?'

Juliet makes a noise of assent.

'I mean, I daily expect Helen to tell us Dan has flown the coop. I can't *believe* that marriage has outlasted mine. Helen did a sweet, odd thing. I was saying that if I got on Tinder I'd have to buy some nice knickers, and she came round that night with a box of lingerie Dan had given her. It's all too small, she says. She was glad to find a good home for it. A bit mad, do you think?'

'Mad and sad,' says Juliet. 'She could exchange it, surely?'

'I bet she doesn't want to encourage him. The only thing she doesn't listen to Sarah about is the importance of sex to marriage. I get the impression it's slim pickings for poor old Dan.'

Juliet runs her fingers through the Christmas potpourri. It's pretty – red and orange leaves with gold

157

pine cones. She remembers the scented candle and gets it out of the cupboard.

'Shall I light this?' Juliet asks. She feels an urge to confide in Lucy. 'I'm no good at Christmas. My mum always did it. I bought all this stuff but it doesn't seem to add up to much.'

'Fuck, I'd forgotten about your mum,' says Lucy. 'Sorry. That sounds odd. It just feels like you've been here forever. Anyway, you're busy and important and do better things with your life than obsessing over Christmas. Have you got any matches?'

Juliet rummages in the kitchen drawer.

Lucy looks in her bag. 'I've forgotten my lighter. Here, I'll do it on the gas.'

Lucy ignites a ring and bends towards it. For a moment Juliet thinks she'll burn herself or set fire to her hair, but then the wick is lit.

'There.' Lucy sets it in the middle of the table. 'Lovely.'

They watch it burn.

Liam comes back in. 'What are we talking about?'

'Dan and Helen,' says Lucy. 'Whether or not they have sex.'

'He doesn't have the look of man who's getting laid,' says Liam.

A couple of hours later, the crackers have been pulled, half the turkey has been eaten, and the roast pota-toes have been praised, though Juliet knew they were a bit hard in the middle. Charlie and Max have eaten everything. Leo only ate the pigs in blankets and said the turkey was yucky. All the boys have a huge piece of Yule log and a profiterole, and end up with chocolate all over their faces. Liam wipes them down. They go back upstairs to play and Liam, Lucy and Juliet sit around the table drinking the Fortnum's red, eating cherry liqueurs and discussing Bas's behaviour.

'He wanted me to know he wasn't going to be difficult about money. Said I wouldn't need to take out a restraining order or anything. I think he genuinely doesn't realise that I'm the one who gets to behave badly, if I want, that it's the abandonee that gets to kick off, not the abandoner. He said I could stay in the house, like he was doing me the biggest favour in the history of the world.'

Juliet makes a sympathetic noise.

'He's so bright in some ways and so dim in others. Like he really is a genius at his work. I mean, it's excruciatingly dull but he is amazing. And then he's such a klutz at anything emotional. He sat there through *Stick Man* like a stone. Completely unaware or unmoved that he was sitting next to his own flesh-and-blood branches, off his own family tree. And then the Paris thing. That's not normal, is it? And he doesn't get how much work there is to do with the boys. He thinks I'm Marie Antoinette because we have Magalie a couple of days a week and I used to ask him to spend a tiny bit of time at the weekend looking after his own kids.'

Liam tops up the glasses. 'That's everyone, though. None of the partners who go out to work think that staying at home is also knackering. They all come home wanting their pipe and slippers. Juliet is just the same.'

'Am I?' Juliet thinks of all the times she gets back from the office and has to throw herself into domesticity before opening up her laptop for yet more work before bed. She might be offended if she wasn't so tired.

'Yes, loads of hard stares if the house is less than perfect when you come home.'

'You make me sound like Paddington.'

There is a clatter and a shout from upstairs.

Juliet gets up. 'Shall I take the boys to the park?'

'You angel,' says Lucy. 'Would you? They never stop. I can clear up.'

'You're the guest,' says Liam. 'You sit there and talk to me and I'll clear up.'

That's the answer, then, Juliet thinks, as she walks out of the kitchen. The way to get Liam to do more around the house is to invite Lucy over so he can perform for her.

It is carnage upstairs. Lego everywhere and the brand-new Pokémon Monopoly is all over the floor. Juliet ushers the boys downstairs and into their coats. She fetches the carrier bag Liam gave her that morning. She takes the tags off the scarf, wraps it around her neck and looks at herself in the hallway mirror. The pink doesn't suit her and clashes with her hair, though she might look better if her face wasn't so flushed with wine. She puts the gloves on.

Lucy appears next to her and takes one of her hands.

160

'Oh, do you like them? I helped choose. Now, be good, boys.'

Juliet closes the front door and the four of them walk up Magnolia Road.

'That's our house,' says Max.

'I know,' says Juliet. 'It's lovely. I like yellow.'

'We've got a pond but all the fish are dead.'

'That's a shame.'

'My daddy was supposed to sort it out but now he lives with another lady.'

'Oh.'

'She's younger than Mummy. Mummy says men like to go off with younger ladies.'

'Oh,' Juliet says again, thinking of her father. Every time he embarks on a new relationship, the replacement woman is at least a decade younger than the previous one.

When they get to the park, the boys run off to the playground and Juliet follows slowly. There are alone apart from a couple of dog walkers and a man pushing a crying baby in a pram. Most people must be at home, curled up on their sofas, watching TV maybe, full of turkey and Christmas pudding. If Mum were alive she would be here with her, or she might have organised them into a game of something that would be age-appropriate for Charlie and enjoyable for the rest of them. Juliet feels another little stab of despair. She has not stepped up to the plate when it comes to all the things her mother did for Charlie. She was always teaching him things in a fun way, cooking, gardening,

161

playing games. Juliet never feels she has the energy or the inclination for it.

'Mummy,' shouts Charlie. The boys are bored of the climbing frame and want to be pushed on the big swing. They jump on it together, a tangle of limbs. Juliet pushes them, looking at her gloved hands. She never wears pink. She knows it doesn't suit her. It would go well with Lucy's dark hair. She wonders if Lucy also chose the 'It's Snow Joke' nightshirt. Would she feel better or worse if Lucy had gone the whole hog and taken off the price stickers and wrapped everything up?

The boys look cute, jumbled up together, Charlie in the middle. Like an advert for something wholesome. She should take a photo. She reaches her hand towards her pocket before remembering her phone isn't in it. This is something she's learnt, that her hand twitches towards her phone whether or not it is even there. She can't say she is feeling better for her digital detox. Maybe she needs to be able to distract herself with technology. She can cope with life when she thinks of it in social media chunks. If she could post a photo of what is happening right now, she'd look happy, fulfilled and useful. She might even be able to persuade herself that she was having a good time.

She sits on a swing and watches the boys use a set of railings to get onto a wall that runs down the side. They cooperate well, giving leg-ups and pulling each other up. When they've all managed it they sit in a row, proudly.

The day is drawing on and the cold is setting in.

They don't want to leave so she bribes them with a visit to the shop, but it's shut so they head home. Turning into Magnolia Road, they see Mrs Karigi and her husband across the street. She smiles and waves at the boys, and they all look shy and then wave back.

Max says, 'Mrs Karigi's husband is called Joseph, like the father of Jesus, but he's not a carpenter. He comes from Africa. He came into school and showed us on a map.'

When Juliet opens the front door she can smell cigarette smoke. The house is empty. She pokes her head around the back door. Liam and Lucy are smoking at the stone table. Lucy is wearing Liam's coat.

'You, too?' says Juliet, more perturbed that Liam tries to hide the cigarette from her than that he is smoking it.

'Christmas, innit,' he says with a laugh, and blows out a smoke ring.

The boys charge through.

'Daddy,' says Charlie, 'we all went up on the wall.'

Liam gives Juliet a look.

'Isn't that allowed?' Juliet asks.

'It's too high,' says Liam.

'Sorry,' says Juliet. 'I was admiring what a good job they did of getting up there. Of course it's too high. Sorry,' she says again, this time to Lucy.

'Don't worry about it,' says Lucy, 'they're always trying to get up there. All the park equipment is on that safe rubber flooring, so what they really want is to play on the dangerous high thing where they might actually get hurt if they fall off. No harm done.'

The boys go off upstairs.

Juliet goes back into the kitchen. She feels sick. The dishwasher is running but the roasting tins that are too big for it are still dirty and stacked on the side. She turns on the hot tap and squirts some washing-up liquid in the bowl.

Lucy and the twins stay for the rest of the day, Liam teaching the boys the mildly rude version of 'We Three Kings of Orient Are'. When the boys don't want to be parted, Lucy says Charlie can sleep over, and he is so excited at the prospect that Juliet can't work out how to say no. She bathes him and pops him into his pyjamas and Liam takes him across the road, carrying Froggy and the battery-less hamster. Liam doesn't come back. After about an hour, Juliet gets the bottle of sherry and pours herself an enormous glass. She goes into Charlie's room and picks up all the bits of Lego and packs away the Monopoly. She doesn't even like Monopoly and Charlie is too young for it yet. It just felt like a good idea when she saw it stacked up in piles by the tills when she went to buy the hamster from Hamleys. She has missed a card. Get Out of Jail Free. She puts it back in the box.

Order restored, she goes back downstairs and pours another glass of sherry. The scented candle burnt out hours ago. She sits on the sofa and looks at the lights glinting on the tree. If Mum were here, what would they be doing now? Scrabble, maybe. Chatting.

Juliet doesn't quite know how she has ended up alone on Christmas night. She fiddles with the bristly hair that grows out of the mole on her throat. It has been bothering her for days, but her tweezers aren't in the usual place in the bathroom and she never has time to look for them. She knows she last used them to unblock the twirly thing in the dishwasher. Where are they now?

She checks the cutlery drawer and then the one beneath it, which is full of toy animals and mini-figures and stickers and elastic bands. She finds the matches but no tweezers. She briefly considers trying to burn the hair off but decides against it. Her fingers brush against her phone. She pulls it out. Why not? She can't think she has benefitted from depriving herself of it. She goes back to the sofa, turns it on, and pours another glass of sherry as she waits for her social media apps to reload. Then she gorges herself on other people's Christmases as she fiddles with the hair.

Thank God for Liam, Lucy has posted, with a photo of all three boys. *The twins are so delighted to be spending Christmas Day with their best friend Charlie that they've hardly noticed their father is even more absent than usual.*

Juliet scrolls back through the last few weeks of Lucy's life. Liam and Charlie with the geese at the Wetland Centre, Liam building the models from the Lego advent calendar, drinking in Carluccio's after the nativity concert, with Charlie and the twins at the Christmas tree stall, with Sarah and Helen in the Coffee Traveller on the last day of term.

She tops up her sherry.

Liam comes home an hour later, pissed and smelling

of smoke. 'So much good stuff,' he says. 'I'm off to write it all down.'

'Did they have the right battery for the hamster?'

'Yes, it's amazing. He's sleeping with it.'

Juliet goes to bed with her phone and the rest of the sherry, and reads up on the state of the world until she is drunk enough to go to sleep.

The days between Christmas and New Year drag on. They spend a lot of time with Lucy and the twins, though if the activity involves going in Lucy's car there isn't enough room for both of them, so Juliet usually suggests Liam goes and then feels both left out and re-lieved to have some time to herself.

One night, after everyone but her spent the day in the maze at Hampton Court, Juliet asks Liam to help her fold some laundry.

'I'm feeling a bit oppressed by it,' she says.

She pulls the heaped-up basket out from underneath the kitchen table. It is all clean, but the final stage of folding it into person-specific piles and delivering it to their respective cupboards has defeated her.

Liam picks up a towel and looks at it as though he doesn't know what to do with it.

She wonders if he is being useless on purpose so that she won't ask him again. He is wearing a pained expres-sion. Does he think it happens by magic? How did his clothes get clean before he met her? His mum, presumably.

'Teamwork makes the dream work,' she says, as she folds the last pair of Charlie's pants.

'And this is the dream, is it?'

His tone is sarcastic and she feels the rage rise in her.

What would she say if she didn't swallow it down? *Fuck off*, she'd say. *Go on, fuck off out of it. Go and find somewhere else to live, go and find someone else to patronise and take for granted. Fuck off to a bedsit somewhere and go to the fucking laundrette and see how much you like that.*

'Someone has to do it,' she says, calmly.

'I was only trying the lighten the mood,' he says, and now she feels like she is in the wrong for being touchy.

What would Sarah do? Honesty, probably.

'I don't like it when you're sarcastic.'

He shrugs. 'There's a time and a place for sarcasm,' he says, and he walks off. She hears him climbing the stairs – to the attic, no doubt, to luxuriate in his own private space.

She feels a brick-shaped block of despair in her tummy. If she was a different type of person she'd follow him and scream and shout but she doesn't even know how to do that. Tears prickle in her eyes. Sometimes she thinks that Liam not only doesn't love her but doesn't like her very much. She looks at all the piles of clothes. They should put this in the marriage vows. For better or worse, in sickness and in health, and through all the endless fucking laundry.

On New Year's Eve Lucy invites them to hers. She asks the others, too, but Sarah and Stephen are only just back from skiing, and Dan and Helen can't find a babysitter.

'That's what they claim, anyway,' Lucy says, making a face. 'Suzannah – do you know her? She's Jacob's mum – told me that all her married friends dropped her like a shitty brick after her husband walked out because they were terrified she was after their men.'

They eat a delicious lamb tagine and then Lucy lights up. She is smoking inside now, though only in the kitchen after the boys have gone to bed, and she tries to blow the smoke out of the window. When the chat turns to resolutions, Lucy says she is going to recover her sexuality and shows them the profile she has created on Tinder. 'Took me ages to do the photos and think of how to describe myself.' It's all a code, she explains. 'Fun loving' means up for sex. 'Adventurous' means up for dirty sex. She has put that she is a fervent Remainer. 'I don't want to be picky,' she says. 'I'm open to almost anything but I'm not fucking a Leaver. That's my only rule.'

'Fair enough,' says Liam.

'It's like the Argos catalogue of humanity. I haven't started swiping yet.' She is also going to give speed dating a try. Suzannah has offered to take her to a place in Richmond where the women sit around the edge of the room and the men move seats every three minutes. 'It's a brave new world,' Lucy says, raising her glass.

'And what about you, Liam?' she asks. 'Or are you too cool for resolutions?'

Liam says he wants to finish his novel.

'I keep asking him what it's about,' says Lucy. 'Go on, give us a clue, at least.'

'I can't,' says Liam. 'If I talk about it at too early a stage then it might disappear. Vanish in a puff of smoke.'

Lucy says she completely understands. Juliet does, too, but there is something inauthentic in the way Liam is saying it, perhaps because it is a lie and the real reason he can't tell Lucy about his novel is that she's in it. Juliet is reminded of those terrible bores who know the sex of their baby or what they are going to call it, but treat it like a carefully guarded state secret.

Juliet can see how much Liam is enjoying this writerly chat. He loves being flattered and listened to. Lucy is all over him, asking him about his novel and then trying to show how well read she is, asking him questions about Ted Hughes and Sylvia Plath and nodding in admiration as he quotes lengthily from their work. Then they have a ridiculous conversation about which Jane Austen character everyone in the street most resembles. Juliet can't fully follow it as she hasn't read all the books.

'Who am I?' asks Lucy.

'Mary Crawford,' says Liam.

'Naughty,' said Lucy. 'If I had a fan, I'd hit you on the arm with it. Who is Juliet?'

Liam looks at her over the table. 'Emma Woodhouse, maybe. Handsome, clever and rich. With nothing to distress or vex her.'

'I have plenty to distress and vex me, sadly,' says Juliet.

'She's more like Elinor in *Sense and Sensibility*, surely,' says Lucy to Liam, 'and you're Marianne.'

'Funny,' says Liam. 'It's true that I'm all ups and downs and Juliet is steady. She has less emotional range.'

Juliet feels like a gooseberry, a third wheel. She wonders if she is jealous, if she is right to be suspicious, though it is a cliché, surely, to start suspecting Lucy of designs on her husband just because Bas has shoved off. She doesn't want to be like Suzannah's friends.

On the way home she turns to Liam. 'Do you really think I have no emotional range?'

'I didn't say none, I said less. It's a good thing, anyway. You're my ballast.'

'That doesn't sound very romantic.'

'Life isn't, is it? It's not all balconies and daybreaks. If Romeo and Juliet hadn't died, if they'd had a baby instead, they'd be giving each other a hard time about whose turn it was to do the dishes and take out the recycling.'

'You should put that in your novel,' says Juliet.

'It's already in there,' says Liam.

Liam spends all of New Year's Day writing, though when Juliet sends Charlie upstairs to ask if he wants a cup of tea, Charlie comes back down and says Daddy is asleep on the sofa. Part of her worries he isn't writing anything at all, and part of her suspects he is scribbling thousands of words about being in love with Lucy. But Charlie is well and happy, and she decides not to waste time on negativity and resentment. That is her New Year's resolution, not that anyone asked.

Chapter Nine

Juliet tries to be enthusiastic about the New Year but she feels like the winter will never end. Mrs Karigi goes on compassionate leave at the end of January and all the children miss her. Sarah says her father has died and organises some flowers for her return.

Hooked in by the displays in the shops, Juliet comes home early to cook pancakes for tea on Shrove Tuesday. She uses a packet mix, yet still it is a disaster. She has promised Charlie he can flip the pan but the pancake isn't robust enough.

'Is it supposed to look like that, Mummy?' he says.

'I don't think so,' she says. 'Maybe the next one will be better.'

It isn't, but Charlie enjoys squirting the lemon and sprinkling the sugar.

'They don't taste too bad, if you keep your eyes shut,' says Liam.

Juliet imagines it is all happening differently in Sarah's house. Smoothly, with freshly cut fruit rather than a yellow plastic lemon. Lucy is microwaving poffertjes,

Liam says. Tiny Dutch pancakes you eat with butter and icing sugar. The best legacy of her marriage, she'd said that morning in the Coffee Traveller, is that she knows about poffertjes and chocolate sprinkles. Helen is making her pancake batter from scratch in the Vitamix. No lumps.

The next day is Valentine's Day. Juliet and Liam don't exchange gifts but Charlie comes home with a card for both of them. It has a big heart in the middle and he has written the 'E' in his name the wrong way round. Juliet attaches it to the magnetic half of the noticeboard with the red Tyrannosaurus rex.

In March, Liam goes away to teach creative writing in Yorkshire for a week. He suggests they ask Lucy to pick Charlie up from school, but Juliet likes the idea of holding the fort herself so books the week off work. She will hang out with Charlie and maybe even with the other mothers at the Coffee Traveller. She can finally discover what it is that Liam finds so fascinating. She buys some phonics flashcards and a handwriting book from the shop near work. She can help him make a bit of progress with reading after school.

The first morning she is overwhelmed by everything there is to do. Usually she leaves home at 7.15 feeling resentful that she is going out into the cold world to earn money while Liam gets to stay at home with their lovely child, but it is all such a struggle. Nothing is any easier than it was on that first day at school. The clothes, the breakfast, the teeth, the nit spray. Charlie kicks off about everything and won't get dressed by himself, refusing even to put on his socks because he says they are too crunchy. By the time Juliet bundles him into the playground she feels like she has run a marathon. The hoped-for gossipy coffee doesn't materialise. Lucy isn't there and Helen says she has to take Daisy to her baby aromatherapy class. Juliet thinks about asking Sarah, but she looks like she has things to do and offers only a brief wave before trotting off in the other direction. Juliet slinks home on her own and tidies the kitchen while listening to Radio 4. There is a feature about the negative impact of being a boy born in August and then a depressing interview about sexual harassment in the workplace, so she turns it off. *I could read a book*, she thinks, *or go for a walk*, but she has a quick look at Twitter and then accidentally wastes most of the morning trying to follow the rights and wrongs of various arguments. After lunch she listens to podcasts while cleaning out the fridge and feeling ashamed at how much food she throws away, when there are people out there who don't have enough. She never gets it right. She tries to plan healthy meals and have the groceries delivered, but so often they end up getting a takeaway instead and all the broccoli ends up in the bin. It would be better, of course, to go to the farmer's market, but that never quite happens.

Pick-up is a bit better. She bumps into Helen at the top of the road, and they walk to school together as Helen talks about how much more energy she has now that she has stopped breastfeeding, and how sensitive Freddie is and how Dan is too impatient with him. 'Why are men so bad at understanding boys?' she says. 'They've been a boy. Don't they remember what it was like?'

'I'm not sure,' says Juliet. 'Maybe they don't, now that they have all the stress of being adults to deal with.'

'Liam's great, of course,' adds Helen, 'so much better than the others at tolerating the noise and the chaos of the kids. Perhaps it's because he's a writer.'

Or because he doesn't have a proper job, thinks Juliet.

'Dan doesn't get that Freddie still needs a lot of support. He looks at Bella and doesn't understand why Freddie isn't as well behaved as she is.'

'Bella is amazing,' says Juliet. 'She's almost another species from the boys.'

'Girls are more developed at this age.'

'When does it all change? I mean, if you looked around the playground at school and had to predict which gender would end up in charge, you'd never think it would be the boys.'

'I don't know.' Helen doesn't sound interested. 'Hormones? We have all that to look forward to, I guess.'

Lucy joins them just as Mrs Karigi opens the gate. The children are all carrying models they've made out of old cereal packets, milk cartons and yoghurt pots.

'This is where we get all our rubbish back,' says Lucy.

'It's art,' says Helen, outraged.

Lucy makes a face.

Charlie runs up holding an empty tissue box. It has a splodge of green paint on the front and a yellow pipe cleaner stuck on with Sellotape.

'It's for you, Mummy. It's a handbag.'

'I love it.'

'Or maybe it's an animal.'

'It's lovely.'

'Or maybe it's just a very pretty thing. Will you take it to work?'

'I think it's a bit too good for work. I wouldn't want to lose it. Maybe I'll keep it next to my bed.'

'Good idea, Mummy.'

They go to the shop for some sweets. Juliet lets Charlie choose what he likes, but as they leave she hears the woman behind them in the queue telling her children they can only have one thing and must not be greedy or choose anything that has any plastic, as that is bad for the planet. Juliet looks down at Charlie's hoard. Fuck, it's a plastic bonanza. A box of Tic Tacs, a Flic 'n' lic, and a whistle with a lolly in it. How had she not noticed? She feels judged by the woman and manipulated by Charlie.

She has planned that they will eat supper together every night, nourishing meals that she will make from scratch, but the cauliflower cheese takes longer than she thought, and Charlie is a bit tired and possibly still too full from all the sweets by the time she dishes it up. He pokes at it suspiciously.

'You like cauliflower,' she says, but then takes a mouthful. She has put too much mustard in the sauce. It is revolting. She shovels it into the bin and makes him some toast.

The next couple of days go fairly well, though she

gives up on the phonics cards and the handwriting book straight away as he hates it so much. Bathtime is hard work until she has the brainwave of doing it before iPad time rather than afterwards, so Charlie is motivated to get through it as quickly and cooperatively as possible.

On Wednesday the children come out of school with a permission form for a class trip to the Museum of London.

'Will you come on the trip, Mummy?'

'I'll be at work, darling. Daddy might.'

'You're the only mummy who doesn't come on school trips.'

It is as though time stops. Juliet's heart constricts. She feels like everyone in the playground heard.

'I don't think that's true, Charlie,' Sarah says. 'Lots of mummies work and can't do things during the day.'

Juliet gives her a grateful smile and hurries Charlie off so that she doesn't burst into tears in front of everyone. She tries to remember if her mum used to go on trips. It wasn't such a big deal when she was little. Parents didn't have to be so involved. They came to the Christmas play and Sports Day and that was it.

Liam texts her that night to remind her that the following day is World Book Day. Charlie has to dress up as a bookish character. No superheroes or TV or film characters.

'What do you want to be for World Book Day?' Juliet asks Charlie, as she serves his fish fingers.

'Darth Vader.'

'I don't think we're allowed that.'

'Darth Vader.'

'No, we're not allowed films or superheroes.'

She is intent on holding her position and not caving in like she did with the sweets.

'The Gruffalo.'

'I don't know how we'll do that.'

'Robin Hood.'

'Or that. Though I've got a green dress, I suppose. You could have that. Why not be a pirate? You've got a blue-and-white stripy T-shirt. We could make an eye-patch.'

They make the pirate costume. Jeans, T-shirt, an eye-patch, and a headscarf made out of a black shirt they cut up. As she puts Charlie to bed, Juliet feels pleased with herself. She reads him two stories, switches on the turtle nightlight, gives him a cuddle, then turns to leave. He lets her go. She is getting good at this.

The next morning Charlie changes his mind. He doesn't want to be a pirate, he wants to be Robin Hood. He's found his plastic bow and arrow. He wants to take that.

'But we made the pirate costume,' wails Juliet.

'I want to be Robin Hood.'

He stares at her. His feet are planted on the ground. He clearly has no intention of giving way.

'We made the pirate costume.'

'I want to be Robin Hood.'

Juliet looks at the clock. She wants to scream the house down. She runs upstairs and finds the green dress. It might work. If she ties up the straps it will look a bit like a tunic. She rummages in Charlie's drawer and brings down a pair of black pyjama bottoms and a green jumper with a hedgehog on it. It's too small for him really, but her mother bought it so she has been resisting throwing it away. It's a tight fit but the right shade, and the dress will cover the hedgehog.

The tunic is too long. Deciding she doesn't like the dress anyway, Juliet fetches a pair of scissors and hacks off the bottom three inches. Charlie looks ridiculous but they are running out of time. She bundles him into his coat and pushes him out of the door and up the road. The streets are full of slightly older kids dressed up as characters from Harry Potter, with cloaks and wands and the occasional broomstick or toy owl. Lots of them have scars drawn on their foreheads and fake glasses.

The bell sounds just as they arrive. As she hustles Charlie towards the line, Juliet sees Max and Leo in their stormtrooper uniforms. There is an immaculate Robin Hood in many shades of Sherwood green wearing a peaked cap complete with a pheasant's feather. Bella has fake red plaits.

'Anne of Green Gables?' Juliet says to Sarah.

'Pippi Longstocking,' Sarah says kindly. 'Look, she's got Mr Nelson with her.'

Juliet hadn't noticed Bella is holding an enormous cuddly monkey.

Freddie is a pirate and is hitting Helen with his cutlass.

She hears Leo pipe up, 'Why is Charlie wearing a dress?'

'It's a tunic,' says Juliet. 'He's wearing a tunic.'

Mrs Karigi beckons them in. Now, she might be Anne of Green Gables. She has plaited her hair and is wearing a straw hat. Juliet watches as Charlie walks through the door, clutching his bow and arrow, one side of the dress much longer than the other.

For the first time this week the other women are going to the Coffee Traveller. They ask Juliet to come, but she says she has work to do and scuttles off back to Magnolia Road. She manages to get into the house, then collapses onto the sofa and sobs. She cries because she has just delivered her little boy to school wearing a scraggy-edged dress. She cries with frustration that she's followed the rules, when she could have ignored them like Lucy and sent him as a Star Wars character. She cries because she was so angry with Charlie that she'd wanted to whack him. She cries because she's been fucked over by her own five-year-old kid, and it reminds her of the many times in her life when she has done what some man has told her, and how is it that she can hold her own her space at work when she is such a pushover at home. She cries because she worries that Liam no longer loves her, she cries because she worries that she no longer loves him. She cries because they are stuck with each other because of Charlie. She cries because he might leave her and go and live with Lucy and make a new family, and she will only be needed to occasionally hand over money. She cries because so little about being a mother is like she thought it would be, she cries because so little of her life is like she thought it would be. She cries because she is lonely. She cries because she misses her mum. She cries because she is old. She cries because she doesn't know who she can talk to about any of these things and maybe she should get some therapy, but then she cries because she doesn't have time for therapy.

When she picks Charlie up, she is expecting to find him traumatised but he is happy. He has added a hat to his costume, which is made out of paper coloured in with green felt tip. 'You know what, Mummy, it was really good I went as Robin Hood. There were loads of pirates and only one other Robin Hood.'

She walks home with Sarah, who asks how Liam is getting on and suggests that Charlie come round for a playdate on Saturday afternoon.

'He'd love to,' says Juliet.

'He can help the girls make bunting. And you and Liam can have a couple of hours together to reconnect.'

Juliet glances sideways at Sarah. Is she suggesting they have sex? But her expression is neutral and offers no clues.

On Saturday afternoon Liam gets home. He dumps his suitcase next to the washing machine and says he'll take Charlie to the park.

'That's OK,' says Juliet. 'Sarah's having him for the afternoon. We can do whatever we like.'

Liam looks a bit put out and says he needs the exercise after being cooped up on the train, so they drop Charlie off and walk to Richmond for a drink by the river.

It is cold but sunny, and they sit outside with other wrapped-up drinkers as Liam talks about how well his week went, how much he enjoys teaching, how all the confusion he feels about his own work melts away when he is encouraging other people to do it.

'Maybe I should teach,' he says. 'At a university or something.'

'That's a good idea,' says Juliet, and they discuss how he might go about it, who he could email.

'Lots of writers do it, don't they? I'd be able to fit the novel in somewhere.'

'Long holidays,' says Juliet. 'And having more structure rather than less might be helpful.'

As Liam gets them another drink, she thinks it probably is a good idea. He is better when he has something to do, when he has a reason for leaving the house. Whether or not he'll get around to doing anything about it is another matter.

'Here's to you,' she says, chinking her wine glass against his. 'And new territory.'

As they walk back along the river, Juliet gives him an edited version of the World Book Day incident, downplaying how upset she was. He thinks it is funny. 'You should talk to Lucy about it. She's hilarious about the time she forgot about the Montessori nursery play and had to improvise two angel costumes out of fuck all.'

Back at Sarah's house, Alice has organised Charlie and Bella into a dance act. Bella is in her unicorn costume;

Charlie wears a pink dress and a sequinned crown that Alice has made for him.

'See our show, see our show,' they squeal, and Sarah, Liam and Juliet sit on the sofa and watch them perform a song called 'ABC'. 'I'm Alice, I'm Bella, I'm Charlie.'

As Juliet claps, her eyes are drawn to a piece of wall art behind them. 'And they all lived happily ever after,' it says.

The children collapse in an exhausted heap.

'Don't forget to like and subscribe!' says Alice.

'Don't forget to check out our merch!' says Bella.

Sarah must see Juliet's confusion because she explains that the girls love making fake YouTube videos, though she never lets them record anything, let alone post one.

'Will you look at my book?' Alice asks Liam, and shows him a story about Rainbow making friends with a mouse, which she has written and stapled together.

'And mine!' Bella says, holding out a folded piece of paper covered in pink love hearts. 'It's about a princess who lives in a tower and lets down her hair and the prince climbs up it.'

'You've just copied that, Bella,' says Alice, 'it's the story of Rapunzel.'

'I have not!' Bella stamps her foot.

'They're both very good,' says Liam.

Juliet wishes that Charlie had produced anything for his dad to look at, plagiarised or not.

'We made brownies,' says Sarah. 'Take a box home. We've got loads.'

As they walk out carrying the Tupperware, they bump into Stephen coming in from a run. His face is bright red. 'Just the people I wanted to see,' he says, jogging up and down on the spot. 'It's Sarah's fortieth in July. I want to throw her a party. Should I make it a surprise?'

'I don't know,' says Juliet. 'Does she like surprises?'

'I think so,' says Stephen.

'I wouldn't,' says Liam. 'I saw it go tits-up loads of times in the pub where I worked. Women like to be prepared. Dressed up. They don't like having stuff sprung on them. They want to look their best and feel ready.'

'Good point,' says Stephen, though Juliet suspects he is wondering what on earth his beautiful wife might have in common with Liam's erstwhile punters. 'And do you think she'd like a pizza oven? We're getting the garden redone. We're getting rid of the sunken trampoline because all the neighbourhood cats come and crap under it. You can get these permanent built-in pizza ovens. What do you think?'

'You won't be able to do that without her noticing,' says Juliet.

'True,' says Stephen. 'Would she like it, though? Would you like it?'

Juliet considers. 'I'm not much of a cook so I'm not a good data sample.'

'We live on takeaways,' says Liam. 'We wouldn't know what to do with a pizza oven, indoors or out.'

'I shall mull it over,' says Stephen.

'You might get a more reliable viewpoint from Lucy,' suggests Juliet.

183

'Good idea, I'll try her,' says Stephen. 'I hope we get the weather for it. I might investigate hiring one of those heaters you get on restaurant terraces.'

He looks at them eagerly.

'Great,' says Juliet.

'And a gazebo, maybe. I'll send you the date,' Stephen says, and trots happily into his house.

They head home, Charlie still singing and wearing his crown.

'Mental,' says Liam. 'Who'd want a pizza oven in their garden?'

'It's sweet, though,' says Juliet, 'the way he wants to please her.'

'Do you think they're as happy as they look?' says Liam.

'Maybe,' says Juliet. She might be happy all the time if she lived with Sarah. Or with someone as devoted to her welfare as Stephen. 'Did you see the sign on the wall?'

'I reckon it's too good to be true,' says Liam. 'I don't think anyone gets to live happily ever after.'

Juliet hurries from the tube station to school. She arrives outside Charlie's classroom breathless and sweaty and just in time for parents' evening. Liam is not there.

'They're over-running,' says a woman she half recognises.

Juliet sits down on the windowsill and tries to get her breath back. She takes out her make-up bag, quickly powders her face and squirts a bit of perfume on her wrists. She sucks a breath mint and has a look at her phone. She is waiting for her team to send her the final deck for tomorrow's client meeting. It is a big charity campaign. Before she worked with charities, she assumed without much thinking about it that all the people would be pleasant and well intentioned. A bit do-goodish, perhaps, slightly dull, but basically on the side of the angels. Now she thinks she would rather work with anyone else. They are intensely competitive with each other and only want the world to be saved if they personally will get the credit for it. Tomorrow's meeting will be tricky.

Liam saunters down the corridor.

Juliet resents his relaxed demeanour. She had to literally run to get here on time while he only has to walk around the corner and yet manages to fuck it up.

'Am I late?' he says.

'Not really,' she says, gesturing to the other woman. 'They're over-running.'

Lucy comes out of the classroom and the woman at the front of the queue goes in.

'Hello,' she says, 'how nice you're doing parents' evening together. Bas couldn't make time in his schedule.'

'How was it?' asks Liam.

'Max is a delight. Leo is a pain in the arse. I didn't learn anything new. The best thing about having twins is that I know their behaviour is not that much to do with me. If I only had Max I'd be smug, if I only had Leo I'd think I was a disaster. As it is—' Lucy shrugs '—I don't worry about it too much.'

'We'll see you shortly,' says Liam.

'Why are we seeing her shortly?' says Juliet, when Lucy is out of sight.

'When we pick up Charlie,' says Liam slowly, as though she's a bit stupid. 'He's at her house.'

'Of course he is,' says Juliet. She'd forgotten. She checks her phone again. Still nothing.

They sit side by side, looking at the paintings of the wall opposite. Some of them are daubs but there is a castle that is quite good.

'Can you see anything by Charlie?' asks Juliet, after she has looked for a while.

'No,' says Liam. He points to a colourful parrot. 'That's Bella's.'

The door opens and they stand up. Mrs Karigi welcomes them in and offers them a tiny chair each.

She has a pile of different-coloured exercise books in front of her.

'Charlie is a lovely boy and he's settled in very well.'

She opens the exercise books and shows them pages of messy scrawl.

'This is his weekend news book,' she says.

Juliet can't make out any of it. There is something that looks a bit like Star Wars. And Lego. And Daddy.

'He's working behind the benchmark at the moment,' says Mrs Karigi earnestly, 'but as a boy born in August, that's not unusual.'

'What should we do about it?' asks Juliet.

'Nothing, really. He's got lots of interests and lots of friends and that's all that really matters. He knows a

186

huge amount about the natural world. He told us all about killer whales at circle time this morning. In slightly too much detail, perhaps.'

'Oh dear,' says Juliet. 'Was it the grey whale being separated from her calf? He's obsessed with that.'

'Yes. Some of the girls were a bit distressed when he described how they didn't even bother to eat much of the calf, and how the sea was red with blood for miles around.'

'Gosh,' says Juliet, 'sorry.'

'Don't be. I love his enthusiasm. And he explained that the carcass wasn't wasted because the hagfish ate it. His vocabulary is amazing. Hagfish. Carcass. Pod. Migration.'

'That's my boy,' says Liam.

'Actually, I wanted to ask you,' says Mrs Karigi, 'if you'd come into class and talk about being a writer. We're doing a series. Assante's dad is a lawyer and Ayali's mum is a physicist, and Bella's dad is a fireman and might even bring his engine.'

As Liam agrees, Juliet looks around the classroom. There is a big photo of Bella and Max on the school council trip to the Poppy Factory next to a collage of Christmas activities. She spots Charlie in a crown or halo made from gold tinsel. There is a poster with 'THINK' in capital letters down the side. Before you speak, it says, ask yourself if it is true, helpful, interesting, necessary and kind. She should ask for a copy to put up in her office.

They say goodbye and head home.

'I don't understand,' Juliet says. 'Why tell us he's behind the benchmark if it doesn't matter?'

'Government stuff,' Liam says. 'Not her fault. Unrealistic targets set for kids. Horrendous, isn't it? That someone out there thinks it is a good idea to tell five-year-olds that they are behind the benchmark.'

'Horrible. Is there another Bella in the class, do you know?'

'Must be. The fireman's daughter.'

'Might be worth checking in with Sarah. Stephen told me Bella makes things up.'

When they get to Lucy's, the boys are all upstairs with Magalie. Lucy offers them a glass of wine but says she can't dawdle for long as she is going speed dating with Suzannah, so they decline. When Liam goes upstairs to fetch Charlie, Lucy whispers to Juliet, 'I've bought a new dress. And boots. And I had a wax. Had it all off. Agony. I've never bothered before. I feel a fool for getting swept up in it. That's what the apps do to you – you start thinking you've got to improve on yourself.'

They take Charlie home and make a fuss of him, saying how proud they are that Mrs Karigi thinks he is a lovely, helpful boy. He is a bit glum-faced through it all, and when Juliet finishes his bedtime story, he says he doesn't want to go to school tomorrow.

'Of course you do,' she says. 'You like school.'

'I don't like school,' he says. 'I hate school. It's too hard.'

Liam comes in.

'Charlie says he doesn't want to go to school.'

'Don't you, mate? Why not?'

'It's too hard.'

'Learning new things is hard,' says Liam, pulling him out of bed and onto his lap. 'Sometimes, when I have to learn a new thing, my head hurts so much I think it will fall off.'

Charlie giggles.

'But you know what, it never does. Look. My head is still here.'

Liam folds his hand over Charlie's and raps his knuckles against Liam's head.

'You'll feel better about it tomorrow morning,' Liam says, 'I promise you will. And if you really, really don't want to go, then I won't make you.'

After she has said goodnight to Charlie, Juliet heads downstairs.

'I ordered a curry,' says Liam, 'and texted Sarah. She says there isn't another Bella in the class so thanks for the tip-off and she'll sort it out. It's an ongoing issue. Bella gave Mrs Karigi a letter asking if she could have an extra weekend with Otto because she is adopted.'

'Gosh,' says Juliet. 'She must be really good at writing to be able to do that.'

Liam shrugs. 'Kids develop at different times. We mustn't make Chaz feel bad about himself.'

'Was that the right thing to do?' Juliet asks. 'To say he doesn't have to go to school? We don't want him thinking he can just opt out.'

'At least he gets a good night's sleep this way. And you said yourself all this benchmarking stuff is horrible. It's bad for anyone to be given stuff to do that is beyond them. I think we should consider homeschooling him, actually. I'm not sure the system works for him.'

Juliet feels a wave of anger. Will no one in this family do anything they don't like except her? Does Liam now want to play school with Charlie instead of getting on with ever earning any money again?

'That would be a big decision,' she says.

'Obviously. But we should think about it. Lucy and Helen are considering it. We could all club together. Be a pod.'

Over my dead body, is what she wants to say. *What a fucking stupid idea.* But she doesn't. It might be true but it certainly isn't helpful, necessary or kind.

Chapter Ten

'We're going over to Lucy's,' shouts Liam up the stairs, 'see you later.'

'Don't forget Otto,' Juliet shouts back.

She rinses the shampoo out of her hair. She is in a foul mood. It is the day of Sarah's birthday party. All the children are spending the afternoon at Lucy's house in the care of Magalie and two parents at a time. There is a rota. Liam and Lucy have the first hour. She is paired with Dan for the 5 p.m. shift.

'I've drawn the short straw, haven't I?' she said to Liam when he told her, except there were no straws to draw, and she is cross to have been allocated a job and a partner without agreeing to it beforehand. Also, it is finally their turn to have Otto the Octopus for the weekend, and she doesn't know how they will fill in the book. All the other entries are beautifully crafted essays about stimulating and educational outings as parents up the ante on each other. Otto has been to the theatre, to Legoland, to the Tower of London and spent Christmas in France, sitting on a ski lift next to a rosy-faced Bella. He's kept children company while they baked, painted, practised the violin and did capoeira. Not that Juliet couldn't organise an outing if necessary, but she doesn't know what to do about the fact that Charlie can hardly write. Still, as long as they get some nice photos of Charlie and Otto and the other kids then maybe Juliet can type out a bit of text and stick it in. Though all the other entries are written in big childish letters. Maybe some of them are faked.

Juliet wraps herself in a towel, and sits and looks at her face in the mirror as she smooths on cream. She is looking old. Too much work and too many late nights. Too much booze. Her nails sparkle. Adi was going to a nail bar as part of her bridesmaid prep, and Juliet tagged along and allowed herself to be persuaded into glitter and stars as Adi told her all about the forthcoming wedding, the dove release, the reception photobooth, the customised and engraved scented candles that each guest will be given in a super-charged version of a kid's party bag. *How lovely*, Juliet kept saying, as she wondered whether the bride and groom would actually enjoy any of it and how long the marriage would last.

Juliet feels in need of a reboot. She tried to buy something new for Sarah's party but her trip out to Kew Retail park with Charlie that morning hadn't really worked. He was restless and cross and spent the whole time nagging her to take him to see the goldfish. She managed to buy a pair of jewelled sandals from TK Maxx because the shoe section was next to the toys, but then gave in and took Charlie to see the fish, and by the time they got home she was frazzled and fed up. All week long she thinks how nice it will be to spend time with Charlie at the weekend and it is never as she hopes.

She finds a long cream shirt and puts it on over a pair of jeans. That will do. She dabs on a bit of lipstick and uses one of her mother's scarves – green with gold stars – as a hairband. There. She looks like she has made a bit of an effort. Downstairs she gets the sandals out of the box and puts them on. Her toenails are a bit scraggy. She should have stretched to a pedicure at the nail bar. The sandals look cheap, a bit young maybe. They are all younger than her, these women Liam hangs out with, better able to stay up late drinking and not see it reflected on their faces the next day. Not that either Helen or Sarah go in for late nights.

It is Lucy who preoccupies her thoughts. Liam spends a lot of time with Lucy, looking after the kids together and laughing at her stories of bad romance. He met her in town a couple of weeks ago when he'd been at a friend's book launch and offered to swing by Brasserie Zédel afterwards, where Lucy was having a date, to check she was OK. Liam had arrived home a bit drunk and told Juliet how the man had already gone when he arrived, that Lucy said he was much shorter than he'd claimed, had a really round head, and asked her if she liked being dominated before they'd even ordered a drink. 'She said she felt like an idiot, trussing herself up in torturous stockings and high heels for some nonentity.

We had a couple of drinks to cheer her up.'

As Liam told her about it, Juliet could imagine him walking down the big staircase and seeing Lucy sitting at the bar in her finery. She could see them drinking smoky, sexy cocktails together, with lots of laughter and eye contact. They got a taxi home, Liam said, because Lucy's feet hurt. Juliet could imagine that, too. Liam always said the best way to experience London was in the back of a taxi late at night. He used to quote a line to her about littering London with remembered kisses. Maybe he'd used it on Lucy as the movement of the taxi pushed them together.

Without allowing herself to think what she is doing, Juliet walks slowly up the stairs to the attic and hovers at the threshold. She knows it is a Rubicon. And yet she doesn't want to feel like she is not allowed in here. *You can have the attic as your writing room*, she'd said to Liam, in those dark days after her mum's death when they'd been discussing if they should come and live in her house. She desperately wanted to be close to her mother, to be in her space, but also hoped that taking the house over, being there, eating at her table and sleeping in her bed, would help her assimilate that she was dead. So she'd bribed Liam with a room of his own and has felt resentful ever since that he has such a large percentage of their space as his personal kingdom.

He hasn't changed much around. The sofa is still by the window where she used to read while her mother sat at the desk, looking out of the window at the trains. Liam has filled up the noticeboard with things he might want to write about. She reaches out and touches a facsimile of a ration book. Next to it is a postcard of a propaganda poster warning people to keep quiet and not trust each other. Juliet walks over to the bookcases. One shelf is full of different editions of *The Human Experiment*. French, Spanish, Dutch, German. She isn't sure which language some of them are in, can't tell the difference between the Polish, Slovakian and Bulgarian, or remember which was Chinese and which Korean. Liam had loved all that and enjoyed dealing with the queries from the different translators. 'Imagine,' he'd said, 'the Swedish translator needs to know if Jason's aunt is paternal or maternal because they are different words.' That was in the early days, when he was enamoured with his writing life and she was enthralled by her new boyfriend and it felt like a fairy tale to both of them. Liam called her Rapunzel, and said he wanted to tangle himself up in her hair and that she should never set him free.

A train rumbles by. Juliet looks out of the window and wonders how much time Liam has spent looking out of the window instead of writing. His first novel remains his only novel. He has yet to finish anything else longer than a book review or a column or an essay. He was put off by the success of his first book, then by falling in love, her pregnancy and the birth of Charlie, then by politics and global events. Brexit, Trump, whichever injustice or disaster was the news of the day on Twitter. Everything put him off. He could cope neither with admiration nor criticism. He started a book about Leeds United and the First World War but was derailed when a bookseller told him she thought novels about sport didn't work. Then he realised that his English great-grandfather had served in the British Army in Ireland in 1919. He imagined a meeting between that man and his Irish great-grandfather, and got excited about researching the War of Independence. But then there was that blogger who wrote a piece about *The Human Experiment*, saying that Liam Quinn's women exist only to give birth or get raped. Liam was so upset by that and how lots of other women agreed with her online. He found himself rebranded as a misogynist and couldn't cope. And it was true that his next novel was mainly about men, that there were a few mothers and sisters and wives but that it was the men who got all the action. So he started researching the women. What if it was a meeting between his English great-grandfather and his Irish great-grandmother instead? But that never caught fire and all he did was stare at his phone and get into fights. He'd tell Juliet he'd been writing all day, not clocking that she would know it was a lie because she could see him tweeting from the moment she was out of the door until she came home again.

He'd have periods of optimism. He'd come back from a literary festival keen to try out the routine of some writer he'd met. He'd decide to run first, or write in cafes, or at night, but he'd pretty quickly revert to sitting around all day with not much to show for it. She'd tried to encourage him to turn off the internet and write in a short burst first thing in the morning. This seemed to be the way that most writers dealt with the continual desire to procrastinate. But he didn't pay much attention to her. *If it's good enough for Zadie Smith, then surely it's good enough for you*, she'd wanted to yell at him, but of course she hadn't. She'd carried on being sweet and supportive.

Then he stopped showering and cleaning his teeth and Juliet worried he was clinically depressed. Once he forgot to pick Charlie up from nursery and of course they rang her because she was the mummy, even though it was Liam who dropped off and picked up Charlie every day.

She'd been scared then. Liam wasn't answering his phone. She raced back across town and collected Charlie and went home with a thudding heart. Liam was in bed. 'I wish I loved the human race,' he said, 'I wish I loved its silly face.' He'd been reading a book, he said, about bowerbirds and how they collect blue things and build beautiful structures to attract a mate, and then he googled them to see but what he found was a video of a bird with the blue plastic ring from a bottle top around its neck, choking it, and he couldn't bear it, he said, how humans fucked everything up, spoiled everything they touched. She parked Charlie in front of some cartoon and told him Daddy was tired out and needed a rest, and then patted Liam's shoulder as he cried. She tried to get him to go to the doctor's. 'I'm not taking any drugs,' he said. 'I don't like them.' And then out came the story of the breakdown he'd never told her about. 'They make me slow. I can't write on them,' he said. *But you're not writing now,* she wanted to say. *And does it all have to be about writing? Can't it be about me? About Charlie? About life?* All that stayed trapped in her head, of course. She was frightened of upsetting him, of pushing him further over the edge. 'I'll be fine,' he said. 'Just give me some space.' So she did and he was fine, after a while, and he accepted social media was bad for him, that he would always struggle to cope with both the kisses and punches flying in from readers. He de-activated Twitter so he would never again stumble over anyone slagging him off, and promised to stop looking at his reviews on Goodreads and Amazon as that always put him in a dreadful mood. Then he started reading writers from the north or the working class-es. John Braine, Keith Waterhouse, Alan Sillitoe. He got very into Ted Hughes, and then he visited Sylvia Plath's grave when he was teaching near there and switched al-legiance from Hughes to Plath.

Juliet looks up at Liam's Plath shelf. He read everything. The poems, the letters, her diaries. The vast numbers of words written about her. He had an idea that he would write her missing novel. She had nearly finished one, he said, when she killed herself, but it disappeared. Liam's version was going to include Plath's novel – he called it *The Lost Eden* after some-thing he found in her diaries – and also the discov-ery of it by a young male writer not hugely dissimilar to him. That kept him going for a while but then he became overwhelmed by the scale of the project, pre-occupied with whether or not, as a man, he even had the right to try to voice her. He ground to a halt again, and when he did a day at the Museum of London running creative writing workshops with their artefacts, he flipped his attention on to the Second World War. He came home talking about rationing, and wedding dresses made from parachute silk, and how people used to sleep in the Underground stations to shelter from the bombs. *Home Front* was the working title for that project, and he was reading and researching and going on tours of disused tube stations and trying to work out what the novel would actually be about, when they arrived in Magnolia Road and his new material presented itself.

Liam's laptop is open on the desk. Juliet runs a finger over the trackpad, giving herself one last chance to draw back. She is taking a risk in wanting to know. What will she do if her suspicions are confirmed and he is wrapped up in an affair with Lucy? She can't just leave. There is Charlie to consider. She might be better off staying in blissful ignorance. Is she taking the pin out of a grenade?

She taps on the trackpad and the laptop whirrs. It is password protected, of course, but she knows the password he uses for everything. Hunslet1983. She tries it. No dice. He must have changed it. What to? Something with both upper-case letters and numbers? Homefront? LostEden? MagnoliaRoad? IloveLucy? She wishes she were better with technology. She doesn't know whether he'll be able to tell if she tries lots of different passwords, how many attempts she'll get before it shuts itself down. Maybe she should stop, consider she's been saved.

But her sense that something is wrong won't go away. She knows that if Liam is up to anything, he'll be writing about it. He was always writing about her in the early days, about them. 'I'd never been in love before I met you,' he said. 'Not properly. Everything looks different.' He was doing lots of events then, and when interviewers or readers asked about the bleakness of his first book, and whether he was suggesting, as the novel seemed to, that humanity was an experiment that should be terminated, he would say that he'd fallen in love since then and that he felt differently about the world and wanted to write something more hopeful. She loved it, of course. She didn't know how much until he stopped. But she is sure that if there is anything between him and Lucy, he won't be able to resist using it as source material.

She imagines him lying in bed with Lucy. *I only wish I could do you justice. I can't stop thinking about you. I can't wait to be inside you again. I will go to my grave dreaming of fucking you.* He doesn't say any of those things to Juliet any more. All that has stopped. They have not had sex for months, not since New Year, and she is an odd combination of relieved and suspicious.

Juliet sits at the desk. There are three empty coffee cups she won't be tidying away because she doesn't want Liam to know she's been up here. She flips through the pile of notebooks. They are mostly empty. She reads a few pages from the top one. It's a collection of fragments:

Your hair is twined in all my waterfalls

I had an epiphany about HDMI cables

Robot lawnmowers

There's not an inch of you I haven't kissed

A greedy, soulless decade

A lot of trees will have to die to write a book

How can I possibly tell her?

Is Liam that 'I'? Is he writing about himself? And, if so, is she the 'her'? But maybe this is a bit of fiction. Maybe he is imagining himself as Ted Hughes or some other unfaithful man. Or writing down something he has overheard on a bus or in a cafe.

Then she sees there is a gap where their wedding photo used to hang. Liam has taken it down and it is on the floor, facing the wall.

She takes a deep breath. She is so tired. That it has come to this. That the room where she used to sit so happily with her mother has become the scene of her rootling around unsuccessfully to investigate her husband's potential crimes. She puts everything back where she found it. She has a party to go to.

Stephen opens the door when she arrives and leans in for a kiss.

'No Liam?'

'He's doing the first shift at Lucy's.'

'Good man,' he says. 'Let's get you a drink. Champagne?'

He shows her through to the garden. There is a bar

table set out along one side and a waiter behind it.

'I'm not sure I should,' says Juliet. 'I have my child-care shift to do later.'

'Have one now,' says Stephen, 'you've plenty of time to sober up.'

He picks up the glass and hands it to her.

She takes a sip. The bubbles explode against her tongue.

'Good, isn't it? Biscuity.'

Then he introduces her to two women she half recognises. They both have children in the same class as Charlie. Sandeep is a doctor, Inbal a scientist. Inbal is explaining her research, which has something to do with light. Sandeep is nodding a lot but Juliet doesn't understand much. Some of the words are quite pretty. Particles. Refractions.

Juliet smiles and nods and watches the rose-gold helium balloons bobbing in the breeze against the wall of Sarah's shed. There is no pizza oven as far as she can tell. Stephen must have decided against it. She allows the sun to warm her face. A group of men behind her are talking about marathon training and the importance of good planning. It sounds like a highly technical business. Electrolytes, nipple plasters, gel belts. One of them says he is allergic to caffeine so can't use something or other. Another talks about how his hay fever crucified him in New York last year but that Piriton makes him sleepy. Stephen joins them, and is talking in a low voice about having learnt his lesson about needing a shit when there are only Portaloos with long queues. Juliet can only hear snatches of it but it sounds funny. 'There was a pyramid of shit that was higher than the seat . . . I had to hold on to a hook on the back of the door . . . I said to the woman who was next in the queue, "Most of that was not me . . ."' Laughter from the other men. Stephen says he's popped a couple of Imodium since then and it does the trick.

Dan and Helen are over the other side. Dan is drinking from a bottle of beer. Helen is holding Daisy, who must be too young for the kids' gathering at Lucy's house. Juliet is relieved she won't have to look after her.

Mrs Karigi comes in with her husband. She hasn't grown with the baby as lots of women do, but still looks like herself with a vast balloon attached to her front. If she were an actress wearing a pregnancy prosthetic, she'd look unrealistic. Watching her tickle Daisy under the chin, Juliet feels a fierce protectiveness over her. She wants everything to go well for them, for their happiness to endure.

Inbal asks Sandeep about her job and Sandeep is amusing about the daily challenges of being a GP.

'Isn't it odd living in the community?' asks Juliet. 'Coming to parties with your patients?'

Sandeep smiles. 'People are inclined to look a bit embarrassed when they see me. As though I might be using this as an opportunity to note down units of alcohol consumed.' She holds up her own flute, bubbles sparkling in the sunlight. 'I'm not of course.'

Juliet casts around for something else to ask. She doesn't want to have to talk about herself, about what she does for a living, to discuss brand awareness or reputation management, or justify herself by wheeling out the charity projects she gets her brands to sponsor so that everyone can feel a little bit better about themselves.

And there in that moment, something changes.

'A doctor,' someone shouts from the house. 'Where's Sandeep?'

She hands Juliet her glass. 'This happens.'

Sandeep moves quickly into the house.

Concern sweeps through the guests. Eyes widen. Mouths open. It is like a wave. Juliet watches it break. Their faces change. The expressions of polite enjoyment are gone. Accident. The word is whispered, then reverberates. Accident. Time bends. Particles. Refractions. Juliet sees Stephen come out through the patio doors and look around. His usually ruddy face is ghost-white. Who is he looking for? Sandeep? Does he not know she has already gone? And then his eyes meet hers. He holds her gaze. And in that moment, Juliet understands that whatever has happened, has happened to her.

Chapter Eleven

Juliet looks at Charlie's face, the curve of his chin, the way his eyelashes rest against the plumpness of his cheek. His freckles. His button nose. She used to sing that to him when he was a baby. *Who's got a button nose? Ten tiny little toes? And a sticky-out ear?* As he got older he'd ask for it in his clipped, bird-like voice. 'Button nose. Sing button nose.' He liked interrupting, 'I do not have a sticky-out ear.' 'No, you don't,' she'd say. 'You are perfect. Practically perfect in every way.'

His face still is. If she squints and leans closer, she can almost imagine they are at home together, that he is sleeping in his own bed and she has crept in to watch him as she often does when she gets home late from work. She has to try hard to ignore the surroundings; the machines, the monitors, the bandage around his head and the drip in his arm. Perhaps it is not possible to imagine all this away. Everything is so white, so bright. It is odd to be living her darkest hours in such a glare.

Juliet stretches out her hand and touches Charlie's

cheek. She feels the warmth of him against her fingers. Vital signs, isn't that what they call it? She wants multiple reassurances that Charlie is still alive. She watches the rise and fall of his chest, the lines on the monitor tracking his heartbeat. With all that evidence, she still seeks the comfort of his warmth.

She looks down at her feet, at the sandals she bought that morning. It feels like another lifetime – another universe – when she put them on, when she cared that her toes were unpainted. The last few hours have blurred into a sequence of fast-paced images, flashes. She tries to piece it all together. She can see herself standing at the party, champagne in hand, listening to Inbal and Sandeep, watching the rose-gold balloons bob in the breeze. Then Stephen coming towards her, as the party fell into a sudden hush. 'There's been an accident,' he said, and he took her arm and guided her through the shocked faces and then they ran to Lucy's, her sandals slapping against the pavement, Stephen by her side.

More people outside the house. A sea of faces. 'We're waiting for the ambulance,' someone said, 'he's in the garden.' And she pushed the open front door and walked through the kitchen and saw Sandeep over by the shed, kneeling at the head of a small white-clad body. A rush of relief: that wasn't her child. But there was Liam, standing by Sandeep. And then she saw Max, Leo and Freddie, off to the side with Lucy and a cluster of other children. Max and Leo in their stormtrooper uniforms, Freddie in Charlie's Darth Vader suit. The truth hit her like a punch in the gut.

Another step forward and she saw the red stain at the neck of the stormtrooper uniform, Otto the Octopus on the grass nearby. Charlie. His eyes were closed. Sandeep was holding his head in her hands, her thumbs by his ears.

Juliet ran the last few steps towards him.

Liam stretched out an arm to stop her. 'Don't touch him,' he said, 'we're not allowed to touch him.'

'The ambulance is on its way,' said Sandeep. She sounded different to how she did at the party. Professional and focused. 'He fell off the shed. We can't risk moving his head or his neck. I'm making a splint with my hands. You can come close. Talk to him. But be very careful.'

Juliet shook off Liam's arm and knelt on the grass. She whispered to Charlie. 'Mummy's here.'

Her lips hovered by his ear. She could smell his shampoo, the grass, hear a child crying, a distant train, a plane overhead. She looked up. The sky was so blue, the vapour trail coming from the plane so white. She thought of all the times Charlie had asked her about the stripes in the sky and how she had never been able to explain and had always meant to look it up and never had. 'I'll find out about the planes,' she whispered to him. 'I will find out and I will tell you all about it.' She could smell something else. What was it? Of course. Blood. The red at his neck was blood.

Sirens heralded the arrival of a man and a woman in green overalls. They put a metal stretcher on the ground next to Charlie and unclipped it into two halves.

The man said to Sandeep, 'I'll take over now.' They put bright-orange foam blocks either side of Charlie's head, and taped them together across his forehead and under his chin. 'Ready to roll?' said the man. 'And roll,' and they eased him to the left and then the right and then Charlie was on the stretcher, which they fastened back together. They lifted him up. They were gentle and fast. Juliet felt tears rise in her at their tender efficiency. As she stood up her knees buckled beneath her. She had to grab on to Sandeep.

'I'm sorry,' she said.

'Don't worry,' said Sandeep, 'you've had a shock. You'll be OK.'

Juliet took a breath. Otto looked forlorn, adrift on the bloody grass. She knew Charlie would not want her to leave him there, so she picked him up, and she and Liam followed the little procession into the house. At the doorway she stopped, looked back into the garden. She didn't know why but she wanted to imprint it onto her brain, the scene where Charlie had been playing. She saw Sandeep's son run to her and Sandeep hold her bloody hands up in the air out of the way as her son threw his arms around her middle. Juliet turned away and carried on walking, watching the paramedic's blonde ponytail bounce against her back.

'Come on then, Mum, jump in,' the paramedic said. 'There's only room for one. Dad can follow on.'

For a moment Juliet thought Liam would argue, would claim the right, as the primary carer, to be with

Charlie in the ambulance rather than the one delegated to bring up the rear. But he didn't, just nodded at her. She could hardly bring herself to look at him, and kept her eyes on Charlie as the woman closed the door and her colleague started the engine and drove them up Magnolia Road.

She held Charlie's hand as they sped through the streets, sirens wailing. The driver was on the radio. Juliet heard him say 'trauma call' and that Charlie was five and was unconscious and unresponsive after a fall from a height. She heard him give numbers. Heart rate, respiratory rate. She didn't know what any of it meant. Couldn't remember even what an adult pulse was supposed to be, though she could feel the thud of her own heart in her chest.

'Is BP blood pressure?' she said to the woman.

'Yes,' the paramedic said. 'I wouldn't worry about any of that. Just focus on the lad.'

Juliet heard the hint of a Yorkshire accent, almost asked her where she came from, almost heard herself saying, 'My husband is from Leeds,' as if they were doing small talk back at the party.

Instead she looked down at Charlie, his face white against the orange of the foam blocks, blood smeared across his cheek. As the ambulance lurched around a bend she thought back to the only other time she'd been in one, with her mum. There were no sirens and flashing lights then. Her mum was in pain and confused and embarrassed and, as it turned out, very poorly, but it was not an emergency. Not like this.

'Is he dying?' Juliet blurted out to the paramedic. 'Is he going to die?'

'He's still with us,' said the paramedic. 'Focus on that. He's still with us.'

She had to. She wouldn't be able to stay upright if she allowed herself to think Charlie might die, that this could be their last journey together, that she might have to return to Magnolia Road without him. Juliet thought of all the cars pulling over to let them go by. It had happened to her countless times, all part of city life; the jolt of the siren, the need to get out of the way to let the ambulance through. Sometimes a flicker of curiosity about who was inside, or a tiny transmission of goodwill, a hope for their wellbeing, and then the moment of divergence was over and life resumed. That was going on all around her. All those people would move out into the traffic and carry on. A tiny inconvenience, that was all.

Juliet closed her eyes. Could she be having a dream? She opened them again. She took her hand from Charlie's and pinched herself hard on the arm. It hurt. She didn't wake up. She saw Charlie lying there. It was all true. Juliet curled her fingers back into Charlie's, felt the rasp of his nails against her palm. Too long because he hated having them cut and she had to be on really good form to insist.

'We're nearly there,' said the paramedic, patting her on the shoulder.

At the hospital there was a welcoming committee, six or seven people in different-coloured uniforms. A man in blue was directing everyone. Juliet followed them through sliding doors. There was a sign to the right that said 'Children', but they turned to the left and went through the door marked 'Resuscitation'.

'Mum?' said a nurse. 'Stand next to me.'

They wheeled Charlie next to a bed, brought the stretcher up to the right height and then whisked him across. A tall woman removed the orange blocks and hunched over Charlie, supporting his head and neck either side with her hands, just as Sandeep had, while a short woman undid all the straps over his body.

The paramedic took the stretcher and nodded to Juliet as she left.

The woman kept her hands around Charlie's head as they cut off the stormtrooper uniform and all his other clothes.

'He's drenched in blood,' said Juliet, her voice cracking.

'Even the smallest scalp wounds lead to a lot of blood, and they often look worse than they are,' the nurse said. 'I know it looks distressing, but it doesn't necessarily mean anything.'

Liam arrived. He put his arm around Juliet. 'What's going on?'

'We're doing a primary survey,' said the nurse, 'finding out what we need to do to help him.'

'Will he be OK?'

'We don't know what he needs yet. We're finding out. We'll do everything we can.'

They stood next to the nurse, watching the activity

around their son. *All those impressive, knowledgeable people devoted to one small boy*, thought Juliet.

'I rang Mam on the way,' Liam said. 'She sends her love.'

Juliet was hit with another bolt of grief. If only her mum were here, she thought, and filled up with longing for her. *If Mum were here, we wouldn't have moved to Magnolia Road and Charlie would not have met the twins and would not have fallen off the shed, and we'd all be at home in the flat right now and none of this would have happened*. She imagined this other universe, her mother on the phone. 'There was an ambulance in the street, earlier,' she'd say. 'A poor little boy fell off a shed.' Juliet would make sympathetic noises but not really give it much thought, because you can't survive modern life if you care about what happens to everyone.

But maybe no one had to fall off the shed. Maybe she and Liam have altered the course of the action by moving into the street. Maybe they are the bringers of disaster, and in the alternative universe nothing bad has happened and Stephen is still pouring out champagne and talking about marathons, and her mother is up in her study or sitting in the garden reading a book, undisturbed by sirens.

The man in blue appeared to be arguing with the tall woman, who said, 'I'd rather get the tube in now.'

'What's going on?' said Liam again.

'They're discussing whether to intubate him for the scan,' said the nurse, 'so they can put him on a ventilator. As a precaution.'

'Why don't they know?' said Liam. 'Shouldn't they know?'

'It's not a clear-cut decision, I'm afraid,' said the nurse, 'but the anaesthetist wants to be on the safe side so that's what they're doing.'

Juliet watches them put a tube down Charlie's throat. She can feel the tension in Liam, the stiffness in his body. He is rigid; the arm across her shoulders is like a metal bar.

'What does that mean?' Liam asked the nurse, pointing at a huge whiteboard covered with numbers and letters.

'It's things we may need to know, calculated to Charlie's age.'

'And that?'

Liam pointed to a mass of grey tubes on the ceilings.

'That's an X-ray machine,' said the nurse.

It looked a bit like an octopus. Juliet was almost surprised to see she was still holding Otto. He was muddy and bloodstained. She felt another spasm of pain. She might collapse. Or throw up. She still couldn't believe the direction this day had taken, that only a few hours ago she'd been fretting about Charlie's handwriting. She squeezed Otto. *What adventures you are having*, she thought. *What a lot you will have to put in your scrapbook.*

'What happened?' she said, turning to Liam.

'What?'

'What happened? Why was he on the shed?'

'I don't know.' Liam took his arm from Juliet's

shoulder and looked at the floor. 'I was in the house. Alice and Bella wanted me to help with the books they were making. I heard screams and ran outside. That was the first I knew of it.'

'Was no one with them, out in the garden? Where was Lucy? Where was Magalie?'

'I don't know, Ju. I don't know what happened. Magalie was supposed to be outside. I don't know why she wasn't.'

Why won't he meet her eye? Where was he? Maybe locked together with Lucy, stealing a moment, hidden away in the bathroom or the playroom when he should have been looking after Charlie. Tongue in her mouth, hands in her hair, other bits of him in bits of her. If that turned out to be true, she thought, she would kill him, she would stab him to death with one of her mother's kitchen knives.

The man in blue came over. He spoke clearly and slowly. 'My name is Damian,' he said. 'I'm the consultant looking after your son. He is stable. He's not deteriorating. We've put him on a ventilator to give him extra support and keep him safe as we investigate further.'

'Thank you,' said Juliet.

'Will he be all right?' asked Liam.

'There's not much more I can tell you at the moment. We're taking him for a scan now. When we have CT pictures we will have more accurate information.'

The nurse walked Juliet and Liam to a waiting room and gave them instant coffee in polystyrene cups. 'We've a few forms to fill in,' she said, and she asked them questions about Charlie, about where they lived and where he went to school and did they have a social worker.

'No, we don't,' said Juliet.

'We're not a risk to our child,' said Liam, raising his voice and sitting up straighter in the chair.

Juliet put her hand on his arm.

'We ask these questions of all parents whose children have injuries,' the nurse said. 'Can you tell me what happened?'

'He fell off the shed in our neighbour's garden,' said Juliet. 'We don't know how he got up on it. My husband was there but indoors. I was up the road, at the birthday party of another neighbour.' It felt like confessing that she was a bad mother. *I was out enjoying myself while my son was in danger. I was out drinking biscuity champagne and feeling the sun on my face as my son was falling through the sky.*

She thought of all the other mothers. Any woman ever whose child had gone missing or got hurt. She'd seen them on the news. Now she knew what it felt like.

Liam looked at his phone. Sent a couple of texts.

'We should put something on Facebook,' said Liam. 'Lots of people are asking. It would be better to do one update than lots of replies.'

'Whatever you think,' said Juliet. She bit into the rim of the polystyrene cup and examined her toothmarks. Was Liam really looking at books with Alice and Bella? Did it even matter, really? Maybe she should

215

offer a deal, a pact, to God or the Devil, whichever one listened. As long as Charlie lived, she wouldn't mind about Liam and Lucy. All she wanted was for Charlie not to die. If she could have that, she would put up with anything else. And if Charlie did die, not that she could even allow herself that thought, then she wouldn't care about anything anyway. Nothing would matter. Liam could do what he wanted with whoever he liked. The bond between them would be severed. The bonds between everything would be severed.

She thought of her mother. All the forms for the funeral, for the crematorium, picking up the death certificate and going to the town hall and sitting in the same room as all the new parents waiting to register births. It was hard and cruel and much too soon, but it did still feel in the natural order of things. She wouldn't, she couldn't, do that for Charlie. *I'm not fucking doing it*, she whispered to the God she didn't believe in. *Don't think you can make me do that again.*

Liam tapped away for a bit, then asked her if she'd like to have a look before he posted. She took the phone from him and scanned the screen. He thanked everyone for their concern. Referred to what happened as an accident that was nobody's fault. Explained that they were waiting for the results of the scan. It was good, well expressed. She handed it back and nodded. She could see he wanted some words of praise. *Fuck you*, she thought. *You were supposed to be keeping our child safe. The one thing you had to do, your sole responsibility in this*

*relationship. I do everything else. I earn the money, I keep
everything clean, I buy the groceries, I pick up the fucking
empty toilet rolls. All you had to do was keep Charlie safe
and you failed.*

Juliet reached into her bag for her phone. Lots of
missed calls and notifications. She flicked onto Facebook and read Liam's post again. She had no emotional
response to it. It was as if she was reading over the draft
of a press release at work. Everyone wrote press releas-
es these days. It was no longer only companies and gov-
ernments who did it. She glanced at the replies. Love,
thoughts and prayers, 'I can't imagine what you must be
going through's, and rows of heart emojis. One of their
former neighbours, a woman she never liked much,
had written a long message about how gutted she was,
how heartbroken, how upset. Three minutes later she'd
posted a video of a skateboarding hamster. *Because we
all need to laugh*, she wrote. Two minutes after that she
celebrated 'wine o'clock' with a photo of a large glass
of rosé and a caption which read, *How much do I need
this???!!!!!!!!* Juliet counted. Three question marks and
eight exclamation marks. She couldn't work out if the
woman was suggesting she was watching the hamster
and drinking the wine because of her distress at what
had happened to Charlie, or whether she had forgotten
all about him. There were ice cubes in the wine. Juliet
imagined her over on the other side of town, shedding
crocodile tears for Charlie as she crunched down on her
booze-soaked ice cubes. Then she watched the video of
the hamster. Charlie would love it. Why didn't she let

him have a hamster? Or even a lizard? They couldn't be that hard to look after. If he got better, he could have whatever he wanted.

Juliet watched the minutes tick by on the big digital clock on the wall. Time had bent and warped. They hadn't been in the little room for long but it felt like a million years since she was looking at the goldfish with Charlie this morning. Why had she been so grudging about it? And why had she not gone downstairs when Liam said they were leaving? Why did she not race down to sweep Charlie up, press him against her, smell him, shower him with love? Had she even told him she loved him that morning? Or was she too busy being cross and feeling sorry for herself? If only she had lingered, loitered, dawdled, gloried in his enjoyment every time he caught a glimpse of gold through the green of the pond.

The doctor came back in. As Juliet stood up, she searched his face for clues.

'We know what the situation is inside the head now. And it is good news. There is no bleeding, no evidence of damage to the brain. We don't see anything sinister. There is no need for an operation. OK?'

He left a long pause, looking into their eyes in turn as though assessing whether they had taken in the information. Juliet felt her knees give way. She sat back down in the chair.

'Now, this is going to sound much worse than it is. We can see where he has hit his head. He has a crack in his skull at the back.' Damian traced his own finger across the back of his head. 'It is in a good position. We don't need to do anything about it. We hope it will heal on its own. Just like a broken finger might.'

Another pause. Juliet looked down at her own little finger. *He has cracked his head open but it will heal just like a broken finger.*

'It's a small crack and the plates of the skull haven't moved. We've bandaged him up. We think that will be enough.'

'He's going to be OK?' said Liam.

'We think so.' Damian nodded at them again. Long slow nods. 'And the wound in his scalp isn't too deep. It will need to be closed with a few stitches by one of the team upstairs but that can be done later.'

'Has he woken up?' Juliet asked.

'He's still on the ventilator, and we'll keep him on it as we move him up to paediatric intensive care. You can see him there. They will make the decision about when to bring him round.' He looked at his watch. 'They'll probably wait until tomorrow.'

'Thank you,' said Juliet. She felt numb. Her voice sounded like it belonged to someone else. 'Thank you.'

As the door closed behind Damian, Juliet looked up at Liam. 'Am I taking this in? Is Charlie going to be OK? Is that what he said?'

'Yes.'

'I think I might be sick.'

Liam knelt down next to her, put his arm around her.

'It's the relief. You'll be OK. He'll be OK. Everything is going to be OK.'

The nurse took them from the waiting room to intensive care. They walked past other children to the bottom of the ward where Charlie was surrounded by monitors and machines. He looked tiny in the enormous bed, his eyes shut, his arms down by his sides. His head was swathed in white bandages. Juliet kissed his cheek, gently brushing her lips against the softness of his skin, inhaling him. Yes, there was blood and hospital, but she could also smell the essence of her son, her living boy. She reached for his hand. Against the brightness of the ward she noticed his fingernails were dirty as well as too long. They always were, from his continual scrubbing around looking for beetles and worms to befriend. She looked at her own nails next to his. Stars and glitter and dirt, all mixed up together.

She sat back in the chair, weak again at the enormity of it all, and closed her eyes, had a vision of yet another universe where she was sobbing and wailing and holding on to Charlie's body, unable to let go while there was warmth and while he still smelt like her boy, and impossible to allow him to be taken away from her to be put in the ground. *Thank God*, she thought, as she held his hand, *thank God or whoever that I didn't have to do that, that I didn't have to cope with making decisions about what to do with his no longer breathing body.* She felt Liam put his arm around her. They had touched each other more in the last two or three hours than in

220

as many months. She pressed Charlie's fingers in her left hand and reached her right hand to rest on Liam's knee. *This is my family,* she thought. *I am holding Charlie and Liam is holding me and we are all still alive.*

Chapter Twelve

'This is what we were like when he was a baby,' says Liam.

'What?'

'We just used to sit and watch him breathe. Do you remember?'

Juliet nods. She thinks back to the maternity ward. Charlie asleep in a plastic cot while they stared at him, monitoring the air going in and out of his tiny nostrils. A miracle. Ten fingers, ten toes. A stub of umbilical cord. She'd never thought much about how babies grow but there was a time early in the pregnancy when it all felt impossible. Surely it was too much to ask that a baby could assemble itself inside her and come out in anything like the right shape. How did it know where to put its arms and legs? Wouldn't it be too easy for it to have a limb sticking out of its head, or a toe where the nose was supposed to be? Then there were scans. She saw his heartbeat, saw everything was in the right place. And tests, because, at the grand old age of thirty-nine she was deemed a geriatric mother. They went to a meeting and sat holding hands in a room full of other hand-holding couples.

'Do you remember that meeting?' she says. 'About the abnormalities?'

'We decided we'd love our baby no matter what.' Liam squeezes Juliet's hand. 'And we do.'

'Yes, we do,' says Juliet, and gives him a little squeeze back. 'I was thinking of him in that plastic cot. How relieved we were that he had arrived safely. What a miracle he was.'

'And his balls. Do you remember, when he was born, he had massive balls?'

'Yes, and the nurse said it was a normal thing.'

'Those massive bollocks,' says Liam, 'I'd never seen anything like it.'

They sit and watch Charlie. After a while Liam asks Juliet if she'd like a coffee.

'If you don't mind getting it. I don't want to leave him.'

'I could do with a stretch.'

Liam stands, pats her on the shoulder, and leans over Charlie. 'I'll see you shortly, mate.'

Juliet watches him walk down the length of the ward. She always loved this view of him, his long legs, the arch of his back. The night they met, it was as he walked away from her that she felt the first shiver of attraction. She used to be so much in love with him. And he with her. He told her he loved her when she realised she was pregnant, through all the scans, and as she grew big with Charlie. 'I want to marry you,' Liam said,

'I want to cherish you.' And he had, and he looked after her, told her just to lie on the sofa as he kept cooking the steak and spinach that was all she wanted to eat.

And Juliet loved Liam and wanted the baby they had made together, but the reality of it was a shock. About halfway through the labour, she'd decided she was too old, really, to be pushing a baby out of herself. Her body wasn't fit enough for the task at hand. She couldn't do it. She didn't know then that the inadequacy she felt when they told her she was failing to deliver the baby was only the start.

She was euphoric after the birth. Her mum came, bringing Froggy and the blue blanket with stars. Later she wondered if she'd still been high on the drugs. In the days that followed she felt ill and old. Nothing she'd thought about motherhood turned out to be true. She'd imagined herself smiling and peaceful, like some sort of secular version of the Virgin Mary, holding her babe in her arms and glorying in him. She'd imagined her and Liam cooing at each other over his head, like they had over the buying of Babygros. All their loving preparations turned out to be inadequate.

She loved Charlie, that wasn't the problem, but the love didn't seem to help her look after him. She felt cack-handed and useless. She was broken and bruised. And tired. She was so tired. She feared she'd do something stupid, like let the bath overflow or burn their block of flats down. She lost any sense of herself as a competent person. Liam had been better able to cope at the beginning, certainly, more able to tolerate the erratic sleep, less unnerved by the crying. He'd rock Charlie in his arms and sing him the songs that he'd been brought up on by his Irish aunts.

They had a Moses basket and a cot but Charlie wouldn't sleep in either of them. He would doze on Juliet's chest or in the pram but he needed to be wheeled around outside first. Liam would do that. He'd take him out and then bring him back when he'd dropped off, and they'd park him right inside the front door. When he cried in the night, Juliet would wake, her breasts tingling. She'd feed him sitting on the sofa in the dark. Then Liam bought the turtle nightlight, which showered stars over the walls and ceiling. Sometimes she'd reach up and tweak the curtain just enough so that the streetlight would let her see Charlie's little face, his tiny hands. When he was finished, she'd carry him into their bed. He'd sleep on her chest, splayed out like Froggy. She'd doze, too. Though not too much. If she moved, he'd wake. And she was scared of rolling over and squashing him if she let herself sleep too deeply. They tried everything. They played him classical music and white noise, but nothing would get him to sleep without Juliet except being pushed around the block first.

'It's a literal pram in the hall,' Liam said one night, when he came back from the sleep run. 'Who said that?'

Juliet shook her head. She was slumped on the sofa, so tired she couldn't speak, hoping Liam might bring her a cup of tea.

Liam had his phone out and was googling. 'Cyril

225

Connolly,' he said. '"There is no more sombre enemy of good art than the pram in the hall." Well, he had that right.'

Juliet closed her eyes. What a detached way to put it. From an era when men weren't expected to have much to do with the physical reality of small humans. *It's not the pram in the hall that's the problem,* she imagined saying to Mr Connolly, *but the baby refusing to make its way out of your vagina, and then never wanting to let go of your tit.*

Liam was still talking about how he wasn't getting any writing done, about how he couldn't concentrate or focus. Something about the presence of Charlie, he said, was a barrier to thought, to clarity. He'd been thinking, he said, about what a colossal gamble it was, what a gargantuan experiment, to have a baby, and how different it was for men now, that his father and all the generations before him didn't expect their lives to change when they had a child, but that now men still needed to earn money, and would be judged on their ability to do so, but also had to be involved in the granular actions of child rearing.

'Make me a cup of tea, would you?' Juliet asked, finally.

Liam stopped talking. There was some expression she couldn't fathom on his face. 'Of course, my love,' he said, and he did it, but afterwards she wondered if that tiny moment was important. It was the first time she'd put her own comfort before his writing. It was the first time she'd stopped him, the first time that anything else had been more important to her than listening to him.

At least Liam was at home most of the time, so they did it together. She had no idea how people coped alone or when their partners went back to work after a stingy allocation of parental leave. She longed for some friends who might understand. Both she and Liam had turned up their noses at the notion of choosing to socialise with other expectant couples, but sometimes, watching big groups of people with tiny babies out for Sunday lunch, she regretted it.

One day, when Liam had gone off to do an event, she went to a mothers' drop-in. All the other women looked like they knew what they were doing. They bounced and breastfed their babies with an almost casual competence, as they chatted to each other about what their partners did. Juliet sat there for a few minutes. Charlie was asleep in the pram and she dreaded the moment when he would wake up and need attention. She didn't want to have to tend to him in front of the other women and then be exposed as a rubbish mother. She'd looked at her phone, done a fake little jump as though in receipt of important news and then hurried out, running the pram over someone's toes as she left. On the way home it had started to rain. Of course, she'd forgotten the rain cover so they both got wet as she trudged back to the flat. Not that she cared about herself. It didn't matter about her, only that the rain was falling on his unprotected face, that she was failing him again. She often felt sorry for Charlie, thought how much better it would be for him to belong to some other woman, who would take him to baby yoga and rhyme times and teach him sign language and not resent breastfeeding him.

When she went back to work, she developed a radar for women like her. She'd be at the park or the supermarket and would spot the other mothers who didn't know what they were doing because they didn't put in the hard graft from Monday to Friday. They were as clumsy as she was, dropping sippy cups and staring at their querulous child in a bemused way before trying to shove a rice cake into it. She was always forgetting tissues and would look at Charlie's dripping nose not knowing what to do. She just wasn't gifted at children, she thought. She had no natural ability.

Her mother was exactly that, a natural. She soothed and calmed them all and knew what to do if Charlie was crying or had a rash. It was she who had potty trained him, bribing him with raisins. Charlie grew from a baby to a toddler to a boy. He cut his first tooth and took his first steps and delighted them all when he started to speak. Juliet felt better able to cope then. She liked fostering his interests in the stars and planets and the natural world. She encouraged him to tell her about what he learnt, like the volcano birds, how the mummy bird lays an egg in the side of the volcano and that the heat hatches the egg. The chick never sees its parent and can fly within an hour. And the killer whales. How the mummy grey whale fought for hours to not be separated from her calf.

Not all their conversations were as pleasing. 'I don't love you, Mummy,' Charlie would say. Juliet never knew how to respond. She didn't want to negate his feelings – she'd read enough childcare articles to know it was a bad idea. She tried to stay calm. She didn't want to overreact. She tried reassurance; 'Well, I love you and I always will.' She tried honesty: 'That's a hurtful thing to say and it makes me feel sad.' Sometimes, when it was late, after a difficult day at work, she wanted to say, 'Well, fuck you then.' She never did. She had all these angry conversation in her head but the words never escaped into the air.

Fuck you, she'd have liked to say to Liam in the face of his extreme obsession with himself and his writing. Fuck you to everyone at work, to needy arrogant clients, and colleagues who were so ambitious they couldn't see straight. Fuck you to everyone and everything that got in her way. Fuck you to Charlie. *I nearly fucking died getting you out of my body*, she might have screamed. *I nearly fucking died giving birth to you.*

She never said it, never did anything, remained calm and in control. She's glad about that now, as she sits holding Charlie's grubby hand and looking at his bandaged head. It seems mad, all that worry. How was she ever anything other than amazed at his existence? How did she allow herself to waste so much time and energy on caring about anything else? She had allowed her distress at the state of the world, her worry for less privileged children, to distract her from securing the welfare of this one small boy. She had been complacent about Charlie's safety because she thought he was one of the lucky ones. She'd decided he was robust. She'd been more preoccupied about not spoiling him, about how to raise him with an awareness of his good fortune.

She will do better, she pledges. Do better at expecting less from all of them, at only caring about love. As long as Charlie lives, as long as he wakes up tomorrow as they anticipate, she will never complain about anything ever again.

'I love you so much,' she whispers into his ear, 'so very much.'

She remembers kneeling on the ground next to him earlier, the intensity of the sky above. She gets her phone out, googles, reads. 'OK, Charlie. The stripes behind planes are called contrails. They are line-shaped clouds. Made of ice crystals.' She reads a bit further but is quickly into air pollution and global warming, neither of which seem appropriate subjects for Charlie's bedside. 'There are lots of sad things you'll have to know about in this world, my love,' she whispers, 'but not yet, not yet.'

Liam comes back with a bag from Pret. 'The canteen was shut. I walked up to the station.' He hands her a coffee. 'And I called Lucy. She sends big love to you and Chaz. And she's worked out what happened.'

Juliet shifts in her seat. 'Go on.'

'She was upstairs getting more colouring pencils and Magalie was in the kitchen fetching some juice so only the kids were there, but Max says that Freddie was bossing them all around. He made Charlie swap costumes with him and then said he had the force and that they had to obey him. Then he threw Otto on the roof and Charlie wanted to rescue him.'

'Yes, he would, I suppose,' says Juliet. 'But how did he get up?'

'He went into the shed and climbed up on Lucy's desk and then out onto the windowsill. He reached Otto from there, but then he fell backwards. Lucy wonders if he might have tripped over the trousers of that uniform. The legs are quite long and wide.'

'That makes sense,' says Juliet, with a shiver. 'Poor little chap.'

'There was chaos after we left. Magalie was upset. All the kids were crying. Helen went full-on hysterical and Dan slapped her face, and Sarah told him off and took Helen and the children home with her. The enchilada van turned up for the party and the men didn't understand why they were being sent away, and Stephen was trying to pay them and tell them it wasn't their fault but the party was over.'

'I feel sorry for Magalie.'

'I told Lucy to tell her not to worry. If anyone should feel bad, it's me. I'm his dad.'

Juliet has a sip of her coffee. She likes this about Liam. She noticed it early on, his sense of justice and fairness. She loves him for not trying to blame anyone else.

'And should you call Helen?'

'I sent her a text. Told her the doctors were cautiously optimistic.'

'I feel sorry for her, too.'

'So do I,' says Liam, squeezing her hand, 'and Dan. I wouldn't like to be either of them right now.'

'Funny, isn't it?' says Juliet. 'That we can be here, in hospital, and still feel lucky.'

'That's because we are,' says Liam. 'And look—' he hands Juliet a paper bag '—I got Charlie something for when he's better.'

It is a gingerbread man with an iced smile and Smarties for coat buttons.

'They didn't have anything animal-shaped but I thought he'd like this fellow.'

'He'll adore it,' she says and knows it is true, and thinks that whatever else Liam may be, he is kind and a good father who loves his son, and she may have lost sight of that.

Hours pass. They chat to Charlie about his friends and his toys. They talk about everything funny he has ever said and everything nice that has happened to him over the course of his five years. They reminisce about rock pooling at the seaside and how he always wanted to keep the little crabs as pets, and the time they found the starfish, and the ladybird cake Juliet bought Charlie from the bakery at Sainsbury's that he loved so much he refused to eat it, and so it sat on a shelf of the fridge and he visited it every day until the cream went off and Juliet had to throw it away.

In the silences, Juliet counts his freckles. By 1 a.m., all the other parents have gone home. Juliet nods off on Liam's shoulder. She dreams that she is in the sea and

Charlie is on a lilo floating away from her. *It was just a dream*, she thinks, when she comes to with a start, but then takes in the big bed, the monitors, and realises it is all true.

'Listen,' says the nurse, kindly. 'Why don't you pop home for a few hours? Nothing is going to happen here.'

'What do you think, Ju?' asks Liam. 'We could lie down for a bit. Have a shower.'

'That's a good idea,' says the nurse. 'You can come back in the morning. As early as you like. Bring him some pyjamas and some clothes. And his teddy and blankie.'

'Can I leave Otto with him?'

The nurse looks down at the muddy and bloodstained octopus. 'Might be better to take him home and give him a wash.'

The house is different. So much has happened since Juliet last closed the door behind her. She feels like she has stumbled into a film set. She looks around for evidence to root her to this place. Froggy is on the sofa. She picks him up. As usual, he smells a bit grim because Charlie wipes his nose on him.

'Let's give you a rinse, shall we, Froggy?'

She puts him in the washing machine with Otto and sinks down on the floor to watch as water floods into the machine and the toys begin to rotate. She can see her own reflection. She is unrecognisable from that woman who looked in the mirror earlier today and made herself ready to go into the world. Tired, yes, but she knows things. She has learnt how crackable life is, like Charlie's skull. *Just like a finger,* she thinks, *it will mend just like a broken finger.*

She looks up at the noticeboard. Bought by her, put up by Stephen. She never got round to sourcing a family planner. The Valentine's Day card Charlie made for her and Liam is still up there. She looks at the 'E' written the wrong way around and is filled with a desire to protect her child from anyone who wants him to be any more than he is. *Fuck benchmarking,* she thinks. *Charlie's life is going to be full of love. We must love one another and die. Who said that? Liam will know.*

Once again she is watching minutes on a digital display. Thirty-six minutes left on this cycle. Maybe she should just sit here. She rarely does nothing for thirty-six minutes. She is always busy, always rushing, always nagging Charlie, Liam, herself. There is never any space. She wants life to be different, though she doesn't know how. She wants to be happy, but she's not sure she knows how to do that either. But it must be possible for them. She misses her mother but here they are, in her lovely house.

She remembers the first time she saw it. She was at university when her parents split up, and came to stay with her mother at Christmas.

'I think I can be happy here,' Mum said, showing her around. 'And you must consider it your home, too. Would you like the attic room? Or the one next to me?'

'Don't waste the attic on me,' said Juliet, neither wanting nor expecting to live with her mother again. 'I can bunk down anywhere. You should use it as a study.'

They went out for a walk that took in Kew Bridge and Chiswick Bridge, and her mother pointed out the exotic-looking Egyptian geese that had escaped from Kew Gardens. 'Yes,' she said. 'I can make a life here.'

And she had. Juliet never moved in with her, but she visited a lot and brought Liam over not long after they got together. He said Magnolia Road was like a street full of doll's houses. He was new to London then, couldn't believe how tiny and expensive everything was. He'd look in estate agent windows and exclaim, 'How much? For one bedroom? You'd get a mansion in Leeds for that.' Juliet had taken him on the walk between the two bridges. It felt like a gift, as though she was letting him into a secret. She showed him which houses were worth a discreet, sideways peer as you walked by – 'look at the piano in that one' – and pointed out the allotments on the other side. They sat outside the pub, and he said that even the pigeons were plump and posh and had an entitled air about them.

Juliet brought Charlie to stay when he was six weeks old. It was late September and the sun shone. They did the two bridges walk every day, trundling Charlie along in his pram, and then they would sit on the bench near the pub and Juliet would feed him and then watch her mother cuddle him. She felt like she was travelling back in time to her own childhood. This must have been what it was like when she was a baby. What a thing it was to be so loved.

When Charlie reached the age where he was mobile

235

but not sensible, the river was a bit of a threat, so they would sit in the garden or go to the park so he could clamber on the climbing frame and be pushed on the swing. And then her mother's illness dropped a bomb on them all.

'Do you think you'll move into Magnolia Road when I'm gone?' she said one day, after the oncologist had said there was nothing more to be done. They were sitting on the riverside bench. She could go no further, by then. There was no more walking between the bridges but she liked to make it to the bench, have a rest and then potter back slowly.

'What do you think we should do?' Juliet asked.

'Your decision, darling. I like to imagine you there. Charlie playing in the garden. But don't be sentimental about it. Do whatever is right for you. Sell it if you like. They're worth quite a lot these days. I'm glad my divorce bolthole has turned into a nest egg for you.'

Juliet stroked her mother's hand. Her skin was paper-thin.

'I wish you weren't going so soon,' she said.

'We're all still alive, for now. Could be worse, darling. It could always be worse.'

Which was true and sad and cheering all the same, and turned out to be prescient because not long after that, when Juliet went to pick her mum up for one of their gentle strolls, there was no answer at the door. She used her own key and found her mother collapsed at the top of the stairs, white-faced and surrounded by an awful smell. She'd been there all night.

'Can't get up,' she whispered. Juliet phoned an ambulance.

'So embarrassed, darling,' her mother said, as the ambulance men held her up so Juliet could clean her and get her into a new pair of pyjamas. They all got into the ambulance and Juliet's mother left Magnolia Road for the last time.

It was quick at the end. Merciful, even. After the bright lights of the busy hospital, the hospice was a calm and pleasant haven. All the people who worked there were angelic compared to everyone Juliet had to deal with in her normal life. *If only time could stop,* she'd think, as she watched one of the staff massage her mother's hands with lavender oil or gently wash her hair using an inflatable basin. *If only we could all stay here.* But time continued its relentless march and then one day Juliet arrived and instead of waving her through, the receptionist asked her to wait. She knew then.

She spent the rest of the morning just sitting in the room next to her mother's body. A hospice worker called Jean offered to call Liam but Juliet wanted to be alone, to not have to think about anyone but herself and her mum. She said goodbye and thank you. She held her hand and wondered if she would feel her body start to cool, but Jean said that wouldn't happen for twelve hours. She didn't want to leave but didn't want Jean to have to tell her to go, so at lunchtime she gave her mother a last kiss on the forehead and walked out into the July sunshine knowing that her life had changed.

237

And that night, when Charlie was in bed, Liam had said, 'Shall we do something to take your mind off it?' She thought he was suggesting a film or a game of Scrabble but he meant sex, and she couldn't believe he might think she wanted to chase orgasms with her mother cooling in a mortuary, but couldn't work out how to say no and so endured a comfortless comfort fuck. It was the first time she had ever unwillingly had sex with him, but it set the tone for the next few months until all that stopped.

She looks up at the magnetic knife rack, remembering her rage and despair at the hospital. All that has dissipated. These knives will only ever be used for cooking. Maybe she can do more of that in the future. Bake, even. Use her mother's mixing bowl for its proper purpose.

Liam comes in. 'Shall we go to bed and try to get a couple of hours' kip?'

Juliet nods at the washing machine. 'Froggy and Otto are in there. Twenty-four minutes to go, and then they can go in the dryer so we can take them tomorrow.'

Liam sits down next to her. She feels the warmth of him against the side of her body; his reflection joins hers in the washing machine. This is what Charlie will look like when he is older, if he gets to grow up. Which he will. *We don't anticipate further problems*, that was what the intensive care doctor said, as he deftly sewed up Charlie's wound, *we don't anticipate further problems*.

Liam catches her eye in the reflection. 'Are you doing OK?'

'Yes. Still can't believe it all.'

'Nor me. Listen—' he takes her hand '—I've been thinking. I want to tell you something. Confess it, really.'

She feels a twinge. Here it is. He is taking the plunge. He has figured out that this is the best time, when she is so bound up with Charlie that she will have no energy to smash anything or even be angry. She wants to get in first. To have a bit of pride. To not be a total dupe.

'Are you having an affair with Lucy?'

'God, no.' He turns his head and looks her full in the face. 'Is that what you've been thinking? Is that why you've been so distant?'

'I did wonder.'

'Sweetheart.' He puts his arms around her. 'It's only ever been you.'

'But you don't seem to love me any more. Or like me. Or want to have sex with me. Why haven't we been having sex?'

Her voice breaks on a sob. She'd thought she had no tears left but more come.

'I didn't think you wanted to. You didn't look like you were enjoying it. I felt like something on your to-do list being ticked off. Lucy always says that sex with Bas was a chore. And Helen doesn't talk about it much but I think she feels the same. I didn't want it to be like that with us.'

'I have never felt like that,' says Juliet. 'It was only after Mum died that I didn't want to. I couldn't stop thinking about her.'

'Sweetheart.'

She cries as Liam holds her, great racking sobs for Charlie and for her mother. *I should have done this the night Mum died*, she thinks. *I should have said, I don't want sex, I just want you to hold me while I cry my eyes out like a kid.* Gradually, the sobbing abates. Liam's T-shirt is wet with her tears and snot. He lifts himself up from the floor, gets a piece of kitchen roll, sits back down with her and mops her face. She wants to be reassured again. 'So you're not secretly in love with Lucy?'

'I really like Lucy. But you are my love.'

They sit huddled together. Juliet watches Froggy and Otto bash against the washing machine door. Her mind is a jumble. All these months she has wasted on jealousy and suspicion.

But he does have something to tell her. What is it? Images flash into her head of the many and various crimes of men, as told to her by friends or read about in the news. Not serial killing or anything truly gruesome like that. Not an affair. He can't have been caught doing something dodgy at work – embezzling or insider trading – because he hasn't got a job. Plagiarism? He hasn't written anything for ages so he can't be accusing of stealing it from someone else. Gambling? Please let him not have found a way to put her mother's house on the horses.

'Go on, then. Tell me.'

'I'm ashamed.'

'Just tell me. Nothing matters compared to Charlie. We can deal with anything else.'

Liam looks at the floor and then meets Juliet's eye

240

in the washing machine door again. 'I just can't—' He stops, tries again. 'I just can't—'

'It's OK,' says Juliet, 'tell me.'

'I just can't write this fucking novel.'

Relief floods through Juliet. 'Is that it?'

'I can't do it. All those unfinished books and I still can't do it. Every time I'm at an event and someone asks how I wrote my novel, I want to say, I don't fucking know. I mean, I must have done it because it exists but I don't know how. I can't remember and I can't imagine ever being able to do it again.'

He runs his hand through his hair.

'I did try. I started writing all about Helen's Vitamix and Sarah's dishwasher and Lucy's au pair, but then I got a bit fond of them all. I didn't want to make bad things happen to them. Lucy is really nice to Magalie. She doesn't exploit her. And so what if Stephen likes marathons and gadgets? I was writing him as a massive cunt and then thought I'd fallen into that trap of making all rich people bad and, you know what, I quite like him.'

'So do I,' says Juliet, 'I like them all. I'm glad you're not going to write a spiteful book about them.'

Liam sighs. 'I lack the chip of ice in the heart, maybe.'

'I much prefer you without the chip of ice.'

'Do you? I was supposed to have nearly finished the novel now, but I've got fuck all. It dissolved in my hands like tissue paper in the rain. There's nothing salvageable. A prologue and some notes about various absurdities of modern life. And then I tried to do something else. About London. How I moved down here in 2012 and everything was golden, and how just a few short years later it all turned to shit. But I couldn't make that work either. Because I don't understand it myself, maybe. And why would anyone care about me and what I think? Maybe as a white man I should just shut up. We've had the stage for long enough. I should just make way.'

'You are in a pickle, aren't you?' says Juliet. 'Does it offend you if I say it doesn't really matter?'

'I didn't want to let you down. You shouldn't be with a failure.'

'You're not a failure. Why do you think that? You wrote one good book. That's more than most people manage. There's loads of other stuff you can do. And there's Charlie. You're great with him. And children need looking after, don't they? Sarah and Lucy and Helen all accept it as their job.'

'You never seem to think that's enough.'

Juliet considers this. 'Listen, I don't care if you never write another book. But I do care about you being in a continual bad mood about it. Is that OK to say?'

They sit. Liam strokes her cheek.

'The thing about real life,' Juliet says, 'is that it's messy. It doesn't behave. People are flawed, much more so than in books. And bad things happen. It's so easy to get sucked in. We both do that. I think you spend too much time on the internet winding yourself up. But we have to find a way to be optimistic about the world. You can give up on writing but you can't give up on life, and you can't give up on working out how to live in this unjust world because we've got Charlie, and we're going to need to help him figure it all out.'

The spin cycle stops. Juliet stands up, takes Froggy and Otto out of the washing machine and puts them in the tumble dryer. 'I'll tell you what we need,' she says, as she presses the button.

'What?'

'We need to get a cleaner. I'm fed up with coming home from work and the house being a mess. I can't clean as well as everything else.'

'I thought you liked it. You're always going on about how relaxing and therapeutic it is.'

'I'm making the most of it, you fucking idiot. Of course I don't want to come home from work and start cleaning up.'

'Sorry. I had no idea it was such a thing.'

Juliet stares at him and they both laugh.

'This is exhilarating, isn't it?' says Liam, getting up from the floor and stretching his arms above his head. 'Extreme honesty. Anything else? Give it to me.'

'I was upset you forgot my birthday.'

'But you said you didn't want to do anything.'

'I didn't really mean it. I said I didn't want anything for Christmas, but I didn't expect you to get Lucy to choose me a scarf from M&S and not even wrap it up. And the "It's Snow Joke" nightshirt. If you ever buy me punning clothes again, I'm leaving home.'

'Fair point. Though Charlie picked the nightshirt. He thought you'd like it.'

'Well, I might have done if I'd known that. But he thinks my life would be improved by a tarantula. He's five.'

'Got it. Less moaning and moping. More cleaning. No more shit presents. Anything else?'

Juliet takes a deep breath. 'You turned our wedding photo around. You faced it to the wall.'

She feels her face crumple.

'Oh, sweetheart. Not because I don't love you. It was distracting, to have us there, radiating happiness and innocence when I was trying to write. I meant to bring it downstairs. I'm sorry.'

Juliet thinks of how much meaning she ascribed to that one misunderstood action. 'And I didn't expect you to colonise Mum's study so completely. Or to rebrand it.'

'Rebrand it?'

'Saying that "study" was a twattish word.'

Liam frowns. 'It wasn't the wrong word for your mum. It just didn't feel right for me, that I could be the sort of person who has a study. You've got to remember where I come from, Ju. I'd only ever encountered studies in books before I met you.'

'I'm sorry,' says Juliet, 'I never thought of it like that. It felt like you were slagging Mum off.'

'Well, I can be a defensive, chippy fucker,' Liam says, 'but I want to be better. I want to love you like you deserve. Is there anything else?'

'You know, I don't think there is,' says Juliet slowly. 'Be in a good mood, be a good dad, and don't fuck anyone who isn't me. That's all I want.'

He holds his arms out to her and she collapses into him. They stand and sway. She feels all the tension drain out of her. All the injuries. Charlie's birth. Mum's death. Taking everything on herself. She could just let it all go. Put it all down. 'We must love one another and die. Who said that?'

'Auden. Though he said, "We must love one another or die."'

'That, too.'

Juliet looks up at Liam. 'Do you know what else we need?'

'What?'

'Something to take our minds off it.'

She reaches up her hand to his cheek, lifts her mouth to be kissed.

The next morning they are sitting in the canteen. They have been sent away from Charlie's bedside while the medical staff extubate him. They wanted to be there, but a new nurse, a tall, black man, explained it was better and safer for Charlie if they waited in the canteen. He has promised to come and get them as soon as Charlie is awake. Juliet is holding Froggy and Otto and the blue blanket with stars that her mother had brought to the hospital on the day of his birth. Liam has the bag with Charlie's clothes, pyjamas and toothbrush that they packed together that morning, choosing his favourite things to create an enjoyable jumble of Star Wars and animals.

'I love you,' says Liam, 'I'm sorry that you ever thought I didn't.'

'I love you, too,' says Juliet, tilting her paper cup against his. 'Here's to us. And our boy.'

Then Liam grips Juliet's arm. The nurse is there, over by the door. They both stand up. Time stops, judders, starts again. They watch a smile break across the nurse's face as he raises his hand and gives them a huge thumbs-up.

Charlie is groggy but very much himself, and Juliet thinks her heart might burst with love. She kisses his cheek.

'Look,' she says, 'look who came to see you.'

She tucks his blanket around him, and nestles Froggy and Otto in the crook of each arm.

'All right, mate,' says Liam, and gently pats his shoulder, 'all right, Chaz. Are we pleased to see you.'

'Sleepy,' Charlie says, 'don't forget to check out our merch,' and he cuddles Froggy to him and closes his eyes.

'He'll spend most of today napping,' says the nurse. 'We'll want to keep an eye on him for twenty-four hours but then you can take him home.'

Juliet and Liam sit at his bedside again, watching Charlie sleep. He looks so different from the night before, now that the tube has gone and his arms are no longer down by his sides but wrapped around his favourite toys.

'Look at him,' whispers Liam.

'He's a miracle,' Juliet whispers back.

'I feel like I let him down.'

'We've both been letting him down. But we can be different.'

'It feels like a second chance,' Liam says.

'It is a second chance,' says Juliet.

'It feels like we've dodged a bullet.'

'We have dodged a bullet,' says Juliet.

'We could be happy,' says Liam. 'Why don't we try to be happy?'

He reaches for Juliet's hand and they sit, cuddled up next to their sleeping son, waiting and hoping.

Chapter Thirteen

When she remembers the first week of Charlie's convalescence in later life, Juliet looks back on it as a period of pure happiness. On Tuesday morning Lucy comes to pick them all up from the hospital in her huge 4x4. It's the first time Juliet has been in it, and as she slides into the luxury of the front seat she sees what Liam means about the feeling of being above everyone. Liam sits in the back with Charlie, who is a bit fractious and upset, though the doctors say there should be no lasting damage from his fall.

'Have you got lots of instructions?' says Lucy. 'What does he need?'

'To be kept quiet, mainly. His stiches will dissolve in forty-eight hours and can't get wet before that. We've got to keep the bandage around his head and keep him off school for a week or two. And take him straight to hospital if he vomits. Apart from that, fingers crossed, all will be well.'

'A big shock for you,' says Lucy. 'When do you have to go back to work?'

'I've said I need the rest of the week off. I don't want to leave him.'

'Don't blame you.'

Juliet feels a ripple through her body. They are becoming gentler now, these waves, easing off as the danger recedes and normal life resumes. But she still experiences them like electric shocks that start in her belly, as an image of Charlie on the grass or in the ambulance or the resuscitation room flashes in front of her eyes. She takes a deep breath and listens to Liam singing 'The Bonny Shoals of Herring' to Charlie. It soothes her, too, though her heart is still banging in her chest.

'He's so good with him, isn't he?' Lucy says, in a low voice. 'There's something really moving about hearing a man sing to a child.'

'There is,' says Juliet, and thinks how little credit she has been giving Liam for the loving care he offers their son. She has been focusing on what he doesn't do, rather than what he does. Maybe the rest isn't important.

'Liam has a good voice,' says Lucy, 'so that helps, but I even miss overhearing Bas croaking his way through Dutch nursery rhymes at bedtime.'

'How is he?' Juliet asks.

'Fine, I think. Presumably content in his love nest. We've settled into a good routine. He picks the boys up from school on Thursdays and takes them to the park and then to Café Rouge for tea. And he usually has them on Sundays. It all works. He's going to take them to Holland in the summer holidays.'

'That's good,' says Juliet, looking out of the window

as Lucy turns onto Chiswick High Road. The familiar territory looks new. She has never noticed before how beautiful the flower stall is.

'Nearly home,' says Liam to Charlie as they swing into Magnolia Road.

As they approach the house, Juliet sees something tied to their wheelie bin. A profusion of rose-gold helium balloons. She feels a lump in her throat.

'They're from the party,' Lucy says. 'Sarah and the girls did them this morning before school. They wanted to welcome Charlie home.'

And as they all get out of Lucy's car, as Juliet watches Liam lift Charlie into his arms, and she gets out her key and puts it into the lock, she realises that her mother's house has become their home.

That afternoon, there is a knock on the door. It's Sarah and the girls.

'They've made Charlie some cards and pictures.'

'Come in,' says Juliet. 'He's asleep at the moment, but when he wakes up he'd love to see you.'

They all go through to the sitting room and the girls perch on the sofa. Alice shows Juliet the Brownie doll that is hers for a week for doing a good deed.

'What did you do?' asks Juliet.

'A cup fell out of a buggy and the mummy didn't notice, and I ran after her with it.'

'That's a really good deed.'

'And I got a merit in my Grade One recorder exam. That's the second-best mark.'

'Well done.'

'Shall I play Charlie a song? I can do "The Bare Necessities". Or do you know a song called "The Yellow Submarine"?'

'I think the recorder might be a bit much for his head. Maybe just sit and do chatting when he wakes up.'

Bella is wearing a gold leotard. 'I'm going to be a villager in the Year One assembly.'

'What's it about?' asks Juliet.

'It's the story of Noah.'

Juliet can't see how things are going to end well for Bella the villager. She catches Sarah's eye and they share a little smile.

'I have to say, "Noah opened the doors and the animals chattered, cheeped, cawed and roared, and they went off to their new homes."'

'I'm sure you'll do it beautifully,' says Juliet.

'Mummy stuck it on the fridge to remind us to practise.'

'That's a good idea.'

'If Charlie comes back to school in time, he will be a villager, too, but he doesn't have anything to say. He just has to stand next to me.'

'That sounds sensible. Maybe if he isn't quite well enough for school, I could bring him to the assembly and we could watch together.'

Bella nods her approval. 'Did Charlie grow in your tummy?'

'Yes, he did.'

'Mrs Karigi is growing a baby. She can't be our

teacher any more because she has to stay at home and wait for the baby to come out of her vagina.'

Juliet isn't sure how to respond.

'When will Charlie be able to play with me again?'

'As soon as he wakes up.'

'I brought him Starlight to cuddle,' says Bella, holding out her purple unicorn. 'Do you like her?'

'She's lovely. I love her golden horn and purple toes.'

'Hooves,' says Bella. 'They're called hooves, not toes.'

'So they are,' says Juliet, 'thanks for putting me right.'

'I've made Charlie a card,' says Alice. 'That's me and that's him.'

There are two stick men with big toothy smiles and a love heart between them.

'It shows I love him.'

'That's so kind.'

'I made him a rainbow,' says Bella, 'because that's a sign of hope. God sent it to Noah to promise that he would never drown people again.'

'That was nice of him.'

'And I brought him Hermione's wand,' says Alice, 'but he'll have to be careful. It cost thirty pounds.'

'Wake up, Mr Wand,' says Bella.

'It's plastic, Bella,' says Alice, rolling her eyes.

When Liam calls down that Charlie is awake, Sarah reminds the girls to be careful and they skip up the stairs.

'They're so lovely,' Juliet says to Sarah.

'They really adore Charlie,' Sarah says, holding out

the Tupperware she is carrying. 'We brought you some brownies and flapjacks.'

Juliet opens it. Lots of tiny squares with a smattering of icing sugar.

'How pretty. Let's make a cup of tea and have one.'

As she fills the kettle, Juliet feels an instinct to be honest. 'I always feel so intimidated by your baking. By everything, really.'

'Do you?' Sarah laughs. 'I feel bad about myself when I look out of the window and see you heading off to work. You look so purposeful. And smart. Like you have a life beyond this street.'

'I do, I suppose,' Juliet says, getting a plate out of the cupboard. 'Not that it seemed important, when Charlie was in hospital.'

'And now?'

'Not comparatively. I want to change my life. I don't know how yet.'

The kettle clicks. Juliet makes the tea and they go back into the sitting room.

'Lovely Get Well cards,' says Sarah, pausing by the mantelpiece.

'I think half the street has sent something,' says Juliet. 'His favourite is that fat tarantula from Mrs Karigi. She knows him very well.'

She bites into a brownie. 'This is delicious. A bit like fudge.'

'That's the secret to a good brownie,' says Sarah, 'crispy on the top and gooey in the middle.'

'Are they hard to make?'

'I'll give you the recipe,' Sarah says. 'I like that photo of you and Liam. Your wedding day?'

'Yes. We didn't bother with a photographer, but Mum took a few and had that in her study. Liam brought it down here.'

'You look really happy.'

'We were.' Juliet touches her temples. 'And I had no grey hair then.'

'Sign of wisdom,' Sarah says, curling her legs up underneath herself on the sofa.

'Can I ask you something?'

Sarah nods.

'You and Stephen seem happy. Are you? What's your secret?'

'I don't really believe in happiness.'

'Don't you? What about that sign on your wall?' Juliet says. 'About living happily ever after?'

'Oh, that,' says Sarah. 'A present from Stephen's mum. She's always gifting us fridge magnets and coasters full of wisdom. I hide them away until she visits. But the girls like that sign.' Sarah makes a face. 'The funny thing is, she's not a cheerful woman and most definitely does not look on the bright side herself.'

Juliet laughs. 'So if you don't believe in happiness, what do you believe in?'

'Meaning and purpose, that's what I look for. And to try to enjoy the moment, the process. Stephen and I both have our demons to battle, but we try to take life one day at a time. We have couples' therapy, which helps.'

254

'Really?'

'Yes.'

'Did something go wrong? To make you go?'

'We weren't paying attention to each other. The grind of co-parenting can take the shine off friendship, let alone romance. It's easy to use up all your cuddle energy on small children and have none left for each other.'

Juliet wonders if cuddle energy is something Sarah has learnt about on her course. She resists the urge to cringe at the expression. 'So, the therapy?'

'Just once a month to keep us on track, and we go out to dinner every fortnight and don't talk about the kids.'

'As simple as that?'

'Simple but not easy. I'll tell you the big secret, if you like, in confidence. It's not something I talk about but I'll tell you if you'll keep it to yourself.'

'Of course I will,' says Juliet.

'I have a grim relationship in my past.' Sarah's eyes darken. 'I've got actual scars. It gives me a sense of perspective. Stephen gets on my nerves sometimes – that's marriage – but I know he'd never hurt me. He's not cruel. I'm safe. That's a big thing.'

Juliet is overwhelmed by the thought that anyone could ever want to harm helpful, kind, tiny Sarah.

'Thank you for telling me that. And about cuddle energy. I will think on, as Liam would say.'

'And you're still grieving your mum, aren't you?' Sarah says. 'That's a big thing. You've had a lot going on.'

'I suppose I have. I've yet to do anything with Mum's ashes. I can't decide where to scatter them.'

'It's nearly a year, isn't it? Probably good to let them go.'

Juliet relaxes back onto the sofa. She can hear the sound of the girls singing 'Yellow Submarine' upstairs. Though they have changed the words of the chorus: 'We didn't like the colour so we painted it green.'

'Yes,' she says, 'I think you're right.'

That night, Lucy comes over with a lasagne when Charlie is in bed. Juliet puts it in the oven and Liam opens a bottle of wine. Lucy asks after Charlie and then says, 'I'm struggling with the etiquette of when it's OK to make everything about me again.'

Juliet laughs. 'Go for it.'

'Magalie is leaving.'

'Oh no.'

'I did know she was coming to the end of her course and that she wanted to go back to France, but I'd blocked it out of my mind.'

'What will you do?' asks Liam.

'I don't know.' Lucy shrugs. 'I'm paralysed by the horror of it. She'll be gone in a month. She really loves and understands the boys and it all works so well, her fitting us in around college. And I like her so much. She's fun but also responsible. Remembers things like trips and the dentist and what forms need taking into school. I can't do all the Mum stuff on my own. I hate the way it takes over and you don't feel you have any identity outside the care and feeding of children. I don't know what I'll do without her.'

Juliet allows her eyes to meet Liam's. She wonders if he, too, is thinking that Lucy is more upset about Magalie leaving than she was about Bas.

There is another knock. Juliet opens the door. She is so used to seeing Helen with her children that she almost doesn't recognise her alone. She holds the door open, but Helen shakes her head. 'I won't come in,' she says in a low, shaky voice. 'I just wanted to say how glad I am that Charlie is home and to bring you this.' She holds out a bundle of black material and Juliet realises it is the Darth Vader costume.

'I didn't wash it because I couldn't find the instructions. I didn't want to melt the rubber bits. How do you do it?'

'I don't think we ever have,' says Juliet. 'I'm afraid I can't give you back the stormtrooper uniform. They had to cut it off at the hospital.'

Helen's face falls. 'I can't bear it,' she cries. 'I'm so sorry. I can't bear that it was Freddie's fault.'

'Hey,' says Juliet. She steps out of the house, pulls Helen towards the low wall, sits her down and puts an arm around her. 'Hey, don't feel bad. They're children. It could easily have been the other way around.'

'It couldn't, though,' sobs Helen. 'Charlie is so sweet and kind. Everyone loves him. He's not difficult like Freddie. I don't know what to do about him. Dan thinks there's something wrong, that he needs to see someone.'

Juliet holds Helen as she cries, feeling the sobs move

through her body. *This is what it must have been like for Liam holding me the other night*, she thinks. What power there is in being allowed to cry, or being the one who is present for someone else in their sadness.

After a while, Helen lifts her tear-stained face. 'I'm sorry,' she sniffs, wiping her nose with her sleeve.

'Don't be,' says Juliet. 'We all need a good wail. What do school say about Freddie?'

'Just that he's a bit boisterous sometimes. At her last parents' evening, Mrs Karigi said he struggles on wet play days when he can't let off steam outside. And Sarah knows a child psychologist who says that most kids would be better off running around at this age rather than being forced to sit still and do formal learning.'

'That sounds about right,' says Juliet. 'Charlie has started saying he hates school because it's too hard.' She wants to share the clarity she felt at Charlie's bedside. 'Listen, Freddie is six years old. He's a lovely boy. They're all delightful, our children. It doesn't matter that Bella tells lies and Leo won't talk and Charlie can't write and Freddie is a bit jealous. They'll grow out of all that. We just need to love them.'

'I think it's my fault,' says Helen. 'Happy mum, happy baby. That's what they say.'

'They can all fuck off,' says Juliet, giving Helen's shoulder a squeeze.

'I think it's true, though. I'm so anxious all the time. Terrified that we're messing Freddie up, that we've ruined him. And tired. And Dan hates work. Though

258

he's got an interview for a new job. That might cheer him up, if he gets it.'

Juliet pats Helen's knee. 'Well, if you want unsolicited advice – and you can tell *me* to fuck off, if you like – I think you should look after yourselves, you and Dan, before worrying about diagnosing Freddie. Sarah was extolling the virtues of couples' therapy to me earlier. Why don't you give it a go?'

'I don't know if he would,' Helen sniffs.

'Ask him,' says Juliet. 'Explain that you think life could be improved. Tell him you want him to feel better.'

'What he really wants is to move back to Leicester. He hates London.'

'Does he? Well, you could consider it, couldn't you?'

'I don't know—' Helen shudders '—I don't want to leave here, the street, you guys.'

'Maybe you could say that you'll give it some proper thought if he agrees to the therapy. Now, come inside and have some lasagne and a glass of wine.'

'Are you sure? I thought you'd never want to talk to me again.'

'Come on.'

When Juliet ushers Helen into the sitting room, Lucy jumps up, hugs away her awkwardness, offers the armchair and sits on the floor next to her. Liam fetches another glass and then serves the lasagne, and they all chat and eat and Liam talks about when Charlie was in hospital, but gently, downplaying the terror and making a story out of how the doctor used his first name, as though he'd been on a training course about approachability. Then Lucy says, 'I don't think Helen has heard *my* big news yet,' and fills her in on Magalie's departure.

Helen sympathises and Lucy says she won't be able to go on dates any more, though maybe that doesn't matter as the last person she matched with invited her to play indoor crazy golf and then immediately sent her a photo of his penis, 'A dick pic, as the young people say, but I can't bring myself to use that expression.' And when Helen says she must go, that Dan will be wondering where she is, Juliet says she must take him some lasagne and packs up a generous portion, and they wave her off into the night and Lucy agrees to a last glass of wine, as she might as well enjoy herself now, in these last weeks before Magalie goes back to France and she is never again able to escape from her own house after dark.

The rest of the week passes pleasantly. Liam bans himself from the news and Juliet promises not to even look at her work email and they concentrate on each other and Charlie, who is subdued and needs a lot of cuddling and reassurance. They spend most of their time in the garden, on a blanket, surrounded by Charlie's toys – Froggy, Hammy the hamster, the animals from Noah's Ark – as Liam reads *The Lion, the Witch and the Wardrobe*, pausing every few minutes to let the trains go by. Charlie likes Juliet to lie down so he can put his head on her tummy, so she does and strokes his hair and thinks about wardrobes and the lure of magical lands as she looks up at the sky and the contrails of the planes. She has explained them to Charlie and heard him pass on his new knowledge to Alice and Bella and be immediately educated about global warming by Alice, who has learnt all about it at school and told Stephen that they mustn't go on holiday any more.

At the end of every school day, some combination of the Magnolia Wives and offspring drop in to offer food and company. All the children – including Freddie – treat Charlie with a grave and gentle courtesy that belie their years. Charlie plays Lego with Max and Leo, and watches a programme about a transparent squid who lives in the dark depths of the ocean with Freddie, and sings and dresses up with Alice and Bella and, with Sarah's supervision, helps them make bunting squares. Juliet gives them all of her mother's scarves that are in colours she will never wear, and likes the thought that they will form part of something that is brought out every year and becomes a little piece of the history of the street.

Juliet and Liam chat to the mothers in the garden and get updates on the new class teacher, Mrs Belton, who seems to know her stuff, though she is neither as sweet nor as beautiful as Mrs Karigi. 'We can probably start calling her Amy now she's a neighbour and not the kids' teacher any more,' says Lucy.

'I asked Mrs Belton about Freddie,' whispers Helen to Juliet in the kitchen. 'She said she doesn't see much to worry about and that I should just make sure he gets lots of exercise and fresh air.'

Alice and Bella bring Liam more of their literary endeavours to look at. They have written a book about Charlie's accident.

'This is wonderful,' says Liam. 'Look, Ju.'

Juliet sits on the sofa between the girls and braces herself for that punching feeling in her tummy, but it never comes. Alice turns the pages. 'There you are,' she says, pointing to a figure with bright orange hair, 'and there's Charlie on the ground. We used red crayon for the blood. And here he is at the hospital, and Bella did this page.'

Juliet reads, 'And then I crided and crided until he woke up.' Alice turns to the last page, which shows Charlie, bandage on his head, sitting on the wall outside the house next to his balloons, waving, with a speech bubble saying, 'I am better.'

'It's amazing,' says Juliet, and then has a brainwave. 'I wonder if you could do a shorter version in Otto's scrapbook, and take him back to school for us?'

Juliet has remembered her bedside promise that Charlie can have whatever pet he wants, and Lucy offers to drive them over to Pets at Home. 'I'm staying in the car, though,' she says. 'I am not a pet person.'

Juliet feels excited as they walk in but the reality soon hits. This is not a toy shop packed with cute, furry things. The hamsters and degus look too much like rats, and the bearded dragons are terrifying in their unblinking scaliness. They need live locusts to eat and she can't cope with the thought of that. The corn snake looks less threatening but feeds on a diet of frozen mice.

'I don't think I can bear it,' Juliet whispers to Liam, as Charlie stares entranced at the rabbit enclosure. 'I know I said he could have what he likes but I wasn't fully briefed. I don't want mice in the freezer. And I don't like the smell of this place. I hate that animal pong.'

'Well,' says Liam, 'he doesn't need to own things, does he? Just because he likes them. When we go to the Wetland Centre, he's not allowed to bring the geese home.'

'True,' says Juliet, watching Charlie, whose face is lit up with glee. 'But look how much he loves them. Will he be upset, when we don't get anything?'

Liam puts his arm around her. 'Maybe. But it's good that he can't just point at what he wants and then sit back as we provide it for him.'

'I suppose it is.'

Juliet watches as Liam goes up to Charlie. She can't hear what he is saying but it all looks very amiable. She leaves them to it and walks over to the gift area, where she finds a sticker book of reptiles. As she is paying, Liam and Charlie walk up holding hands.

'Charlie has decided he's quite happy to leave all the animals here,' says Liam. 'He understands that the cages and tanks and food would be harder to sort out in our house. And we're going to come over once a week after school and visit.'

'That's lovely,' says Juliet, and hands Charlie the sticker book. 'Look, loads of interesting creatures. Isn't it exciting?'

'It's not as good as a real pet, Mummy, is it?' says Charlie. 'And you can't make things exciting just by saying they are.'

'That's my boy,' says Liam, patting Charlie's shoulder, 'he's nobody's fool,' and Juliet laughs and they all troop out, back to Lucy's car.

Lucy drops them off at the park, and Juliet holds Charlie on her lap on the swing as Liam gently pushes them. They did this when he was a baby; he is too big for it now, really. It is only because of the fall that this is happening.

It feels like a little gift, to be reminded of those early days, her holding Charlie and Liam looking after them. An old lady with a small yappy dog points at his bandage and says, 'What happened to you, young man?', and Charlie says, rather proudly, 'I fell off a shed and nearly died.'

That night, when Charlie is in bed, Juliet takes over Lucy's lasagne dish. She knocks and walks in, as Lucy is always telling her to do, but as she gets to the kitchen she sees a man sitting at the table with his head in his hands.

Juliet tries to reverse out before she is spotted, but the man looks up. It is Bas and he has been crying.

'Sorry,' Juliet says. 'Just bringing this back.'

She puts the dish on the counter.

'Lucy's just gone upstairs,' Bas says. 'One of the boys called out.'

'I'll catch up with her later.'

She goes home and tells Liam. 'What do you think it means?'

'Something gone wrong with his company? Or his girlfriend? I'm sure Lucy will come over and tell us the minute he goes.'

Lucy never materialises, but the next morning she texts Juliet to suggest she join her and Helen for coffee.

'Do you mind?' Juliet asks Liam.

'You go,' says Liam. 'Though you'll miss Aslan getting the better of the witch. Bring me back a cappuccino and all the news.'

When Juliet gets to the Coffee Traveller, she finds Lucy and Helen at the long table at the front. Daisy is sitting in her buggy, giggling and smiling.

'Big news,' says Lucy. 'Can you guess? Bas has come back.'

'Wow,' says Juliet. 'That's a surprise.'

'I know. Turns out his new woman was still secretly in love with her ex and seeing him on the side. Bas walked in on them together at the flat last week. He was distraught.'

'And he just came straight back?' asks Helen. 'And you let him?'

'He's been staying in a hotel the last few days. I'm not sure he was going to tell me, but when he brought the boys home last night he looked like shit and I got it all out of him. I don't think it had occurred to him he could come back but I thought, why not?'

'You look really happy about it,' says Juliet.

'To be honest, being single wasn't anywhere near as nice as I thought it would be. I didn't want to admit it, but I'd been feeling nostalgic for my dear old dull, respectful husband.' She sips her coffee. 'I went on some horrible dates.'

'I thought you enjoyed them,' said Helen.

'Oh, you know.' Lucy grimaces. 'I was trying to make the best of it. Didn't want to be an object of pity. But it was all much more tawdry than I'd imagined. I'm not cut out for modern sex. That awful thing where they try to hold your head down. I thought men had grown out of that. And all the effort you feel you need to go to. So liberating to think I'll never need to bother with my bikini line ever again.'

'Lucy,' says Helen, gesturing to Daisy.

'She doesn't understand,' says Lucy.

'Still,' says Helen.

'Fine, I'll save my more grown-up reflections for another time. The thing is, it is extremely tiring being a single parent, putting in the hard yards alone, feeling like the buck stops with you. I know I used to moan about Bas not doing anything, but it was only after he left that I realised that wasn't actually true. So he stayed last night and he's bringing back the big suitcase later today. And we've agreed he'll try not to talk about politics all the time and I can smoke

266

indoors, but only in the kitchen with the windows open.'

'Are the boys pleased?'

'Delighted. Well, Max is. Leo didn't say anything. And so is Sarah. I told her this morning on the way to school. She was dashing off to college after. She said she thought Bas only went off with the Swede because she listened to his problems. She thinks he might not be neurotypical anyway.'

'What does that mean?' asks Helen.

'I'm not sure. She's sending me a link to an article. It was something she found out on her course. She said that if I spent less time expecting Bas to conform to stereotypical notions of romance we'd be a lot happier, that unrealistic expectations are the curse of modern life.'

'She really is learning some stuff on that course,' says Juliet.

Lucy nods and laughs. 'We'll be the most psychologically healthy street in the world when she's through with us.'

Lucy and Helen head off to Kew together, and Juliet has a sudden urge to see the river and sit on the bench where she spent so much time with her mother. Maybe she can take some photos of Egyptian geese to show Charlie. She heads down the alleyway next to the pub and emerges on the riverbank. There is someone on her bench. As she gets closer she sees it is Mrs Karigi. Amy. Sitting as Juliet used to, with her fingers splayed across her bump.

'May I join you?'

'Please do,' she says, shifting along. 'How's Charlie?'

'On the mend. Still tired and a bit weepy. We're keeping him off school for another week, at least. And he might not go back before the summer holidays. He adored your tarantula card.'

'He's a lovely boy.'

'Do you know what you're having?' asks Juliet.

'No,' says Amy. 'We decided not to find out, which feels a bit silly now. Still, we'll know soon enough. Is it normal to doubt it will ever happen?'

'Completely. It feels impossible but then, suddenly, they are there. Real. In your arms.' Juliet stops, overwhelmed by this act of creating another human being that is both ordinary and miraculous. Should she tell her, this woman she hardly knows, not to worry if she feels mad and exhausted and useless? But what if she doesn't, and wonders why Juliet felt the need to spread fear and confusion?

'Will you have help?' Juliet asks, compromising.

'Joseph will be around a lot. And my mum is coming up. Dad died in January, and he said to me before that it would be good for her to have a baby to love and worry about.'

'I'm sorry about your dad,' says Juliet. 'My mum died almost a year ago. It's such a big thing to lose a parent.'

'I still can't quite believe it,' says Amy.

'That's what I kept thinking. Though I've stopped that now. I was so cross that everyone kept telling me

268

it would take a year, but that does seem to be about the time I needed to think it was real, to accept that Mum is dead.'

Juliet tries it again inside her head. *My mother is dead. Mum is dead.*

There is a silence. Juliet looks out at the river, remembering sitting on this bench with Charlie when he was younger. 'People in boats,' he used to say, pointing. She worries that she has overshared. She has felt emotionally incontinent since Charlie's accident but she likes it. She wants to spend more of her life talking about things that matter.

'I'd better get back to Charlie,' she says. 'We'd love to help, when the baby is born. It can be nice to have someone wheel them around outside for a bit so that you can have a shower and a moment to yourself.'

'Thank you,' says Amy. 'And thanks for telling me about your mum. It's useful for me to know that it won't always seem like a bad dream.'

Juliet smiles. 'I have been thinking more – but this is very recent – about how lucky I was to have her, rather than being stuck in despair that she's gone. So that's something.'

Juliet is walking through the front door when she remembers Liam asked her for a coffee. She finds him and Charlie in the garden playing a game with the Lego mini figures.

'I'm sorry. I forgot your cappuccino. Would you like me to go back and get you one?'

'And why would I need coffee when I am rich in love?' says Liam.

'Don't be soppy, Daddy,' says Charlie, and Juliet thinks how cross she would have been just a short time ago if Liam had forgotten anything she'd asked him to do, and joins them on the blanket.

'Chaz doesn't believe I have the force,' says Liam.

'Don't you?' asks Juliet.

'No,' says Charlie. 'I'm nearly six, Mummy, I don't believe in the force any more.'

Over their Chinese takeaway that night, Juliet asks Liam what he thinks they should do about the ashes.

Charlie's eyes open wide. 'You said Granny was in heaven.'

'Well, she sort of is,' says Juliet, 'but her ashes are in a box in the cupboard under the stairs, and Sarah thinks it is time we did something with them.'

'How did she get turned into ash?'

Juliet stops eating her piece of prawn toast and looks at Liam, who raises his eyebrows and bravely jumps in. 'Well,' he says, 'after they die, people used to be buried in the ground, but mostly now they are cremated because it is more environmentally friendly.'

'What is cremated?' Charlie asks.

'Burnt,' Liam says.

'Burnt?' says Charlie. 'All of Granny got burnt?'

'Yes.'

'Her toes?'

'Yes.'

'Her knees?'

'Yes.'

'Even Granny's teeth?'

'Yes.'

Juliet pushes away the spare ribs. 'And now we need to decide what to do. We could scatter the ashes on the river, maybe. Or at Kew Gardens, if we're allowed.'

'Maybe we could bury her in the garden,' says Liam. 'With a new tree. Would you like that?'

'Yes,' says Charlie. 'With lots of flowers. Then bees and butterflies will come.'

When Charlie is in bed, Juliet lies on the sofa with her feet on Liam's lap as he researches trees on the internet. 'We don't want anything that will grow too big, or need a lot of work,' he says. 'And how will we actually decant the ashes? Feels a bit too relaxed to just snip a hole in the bag.' He taps away. 'Jesus, did you know you can get cremation jewellery? It's twenty per cent off at the moment if you fancy an angel wings pendant. It has a little cannister you fill up with the "cremains". What a horrible word. Fuck, there's a whole world out there of people having the ashes of their pets turned into ornaments.' He reads out a thank you comment from a woman who has had her dearly beloved fur baby made into a Christmas bauble. 'And poetry. There's some godawful religious rhyming stuff. Listen to this.'

He is interrupted by a knock at the door and Lucy walks in carrying a bottle of wine.

'Well, he's back. The big suitcase is unpacked. We all

had supper together, and he put the boys to bed and sang his funny Dutch songs to them. And now he's doing some work at the kitchen table and you'd think the last few months had never happened.'

'So, all's well that ends well then?' Liam says.

'Pretty much,' says Lucy. 'Excellent timing really, with Magalie leaving. I'm not good at being on my own.'

'Aren't you angry with him?' Juliet asks. 'I'm not saying you should be. I'm really impressed that you're not. I just don't quite understand.'

Lucy shrugs. 'Can't be arsed. And Sarah's theory is that he only left because I was mean to him. I was unsympathetic, she says. About Brexit. About the extent to which he felt cut off and betrayed. So, I've apologised for that and he's apologised for deserting me for the efficient but ultimately unfaithful Swede, and we are giving it another go.'

'Interesting,' says Liam. 'Things are always less about sex than we think, aren't they?'

'I don't know,' says Lucy. 'I mean, things aren't *not* about sex. Being with other men made me think favourably about Bas. I've a new bedroom theory, anyway, which I tried out to great effect last night. Would you like to hear it?'

'Yes, please,' says Juliet.

'Sex is like playing games with the kids. You're never really in the mood but as you'll end up doing it anyway, you might as well approach it with a positive attitude and then you can be pleasantly surprised at what a good time you have.'

'That's the most romantic thing I've ever heard,' says Liam.

'Yes, well, we can't all be love's young dream. I think it's worth a mindset change, as Sarah would say. There's a lot to be said for lying safely in the arms of someone who loves you.'

'Better the devil you know?' asks Juliet.

'Exactly that,' agrees Lucy. 'There's no shortage of horror stories from the other women at speed dating, I can tell you. It seems almost immature to care about a bit of infidelity when there are so many worse things that men can do. And trying to get a new one is full of pitfalls. Everyone comes with baggage. Older men are still living with their wives and younger ones won't wear condoms. Suzannah was ghosted recently. Had the most amazing night with this guy who just disappeared on her.'

'How is she?' asks Juliet.

'She says she's lowered her expectations to the point where she'd be over the moon with someone who can spell, and asks her a question about herself that isn't whether she likes having threesomes or can immediately send nude pics.'

'Poor Suzannah,' says Juliet.

'I know,' says Lucy, 'it is exhausting, and you start to doubt men as a whole, which is depressing as the mother of boys.'

'You won't miss the freedom?' asks Juliet.

'Don't think so,' says Lucy. 'I didn't feel very free when I was teetering on a bar stool with no pubic hair making up stories about my non-existent sexual kinks to impress an accountant I didn't even fancy. I get a lot of financial and emotional freedom from Bas. And we've got the boys to raise. That's the important thing. Marriage vows mean fuck all to me, but you can't break the unspoken vows you made to look after your kids, can you? So, on balance, I'm glad to have him back.'

'I like it,' says Liam. 'The "my husband is slightly less of a cunt than most other men" philosophy. You should have it put on a fridge magnet.'

'I'd make a fortune,' says Lucy. 'Maybe I could manufacture a whole range of merch from my shed. Bags, fridge magnets, cushions.'

Juliet laughs. 'Then Stephen's mum could buy it all for Sarah.'

'Speaking of Sarah,' says Lucy. 'She's worried she's been telling us all what to do. She had feedback from her tutor this morning that she needs to listen more. That she moves too quickly into advice giving. He made her do a visualisation where she had to imagine herself as a massive ear covered in ears.'

'Typical man,' says Juliet, reaching for her phone. 'Trying to put a wise woman down. I think she's wonderful. And I'm going to tell her so. I don't want her to stop giving me advice. It's all so good.'

Later, in bed, Juliet lies spooned into Liam as he twines his fingers into her hair. 'Rapunzel, Rapunzel,' he whispers. 'Your hair is twined in all my waterfalls. Are you enjoying lying in the arms of a man who loves you?'

'I am,' says Juliet, glorying in the sensation of her skin against his, the warmth and the smell of him, the feel of his damaged finger stroking her cheek.

The next morning Charlie gets into bed with them.

'Mummy,' he says, with hints of suspicious outrage. 'Why haven't you got your pyjamas on?'

'Because I was so warm in the night,' says Juliet, 'that I took them off.'

On Sunday afternoon, Juliet sits in the garden at one end of the stone table, crunching through her email in preparation for going back to work the next day. So much of it can just be deleted. Lots of what she would have needed to do something about if she'd seen it at the time is irrelevant a few days later.

Liam and Charlie are playing at the other end. Liam had told Charlie that Granny thought the stone table looked like it came from Narnia, and then helped him bring down all his cuddly toys from his bedroom and arrange them on it. Now they are making up conversations between them about Aslan and the White Witch.

Charlie looks up and sees her watching them. 'You can play, too, Mummy.'

'I've got to do this instead,' says Juliet. 'I'm enjoying being near you, though. It's a lovely game.'

'Do you have to go back to work tomorrow?'

'I do, sweetheart.'

'Why?'

'I need to earn money so we can pay for things.'

'What like?'

'Food. Clothes. Toys. Books.'

'Why can't Daddy earn money?'

Liam looks up anxiously and then smiles at her.

'Daddy does get paid for journalism and teaching,' says Juliet, 'and he might write another book one day. But his job for now is mainly to look after you, and my job is mainly to get the money we need. I have loved being at home with you this week, though.'

Later, squeaky clean in his Star Wars pyjamas, after Liam has bathed him, Charlie brings Juliet's laptop to her. He has decorated it with stickers from the reptile book. 'Look, this is an anaconda, this is a rainbow boa, and this is a glass lizard.'

She looks down at the three snakes. She'd rather have pictures on her laptop than creatures in her house.

'I love it.'

'It's so you don't get lonely at work.'

'Thank you, my darling.'

'I was going to give you the baby leopard tortoise but he's my favourite. I wanted to keep him for my own book.'

'That's OK. You've been more than generous. You are such a kind boy.'

Juliet cuddles Charlie to her, and then tips him slightly forward so she can part his wet hair with her fingers and check the wound on the back of his head. It is healing nicely. She wonders if his scar will last forever, although it will be hidden from view unless someone looks very closely. Will Charlie, as a grown man in

276

the barber's chair or in bed with a lover, ever be asked what happened? What will he say?

It is all so many years away. Juliet hugs her boy again, rubs her nose against his cheek, and decides that she won't be peeling the stickers off her laptop this time.

Chapter Fourteen

It feels like a group effort, in the end, organised in the last couple of weeks of the school term as Charlie recovers and the summer holidays start. It is Helen who suggests they plant a magnolia tree and Bas who, at Sports Day, contributes the knowledge that they shouldn't put the ashes in with the roots. 'Human remains have a high alkaline and sodium content, which discourage plant growth,' he says in his precise way. 'Isn't he wonderful?' says Lucy, clapping as Max wins the egg and spoon race. 'He knows everything.'

Lucy drives them to the garden centre and helps choose, agreeing with Liam that they can't go for something with an awful or tacky name, and throwing her support behind the sweetheart variety that has pale pink petals, which are a darker shade on the inside. 'There's a metaphor in there somewhere,' says Liam. 'Though I can't see what it is.'

Charlie wants to invite his friends. Juliet calls Sarah to see what she thinks. 'How sweet. It's probably quite good for the children to be introduced to death in this gentle way, as long as you don't mind being used as a teachable moment.' Helen is up for it and Lucy says yes, as long as it is in the afternoon as the twins have their tae kwon do assessment in the morning.

Liam borrows a spade from Stephen, and he and Charlie dig the hole together the day before, following Stephen's instructions to make it slightly bigger than the plant pot.

The morning dawns grey and cold. Liam takes Charlie to the park and Juliet tidies up, though now that Sarah's wonderful cleaner is coming to them one morning a week, she only has to deal with mess, not with dirt. After lunch, Juliet makes walnut brownies, measuring all the ingredients into her mother's mixing bowl and getting Charlie to do the stirring. She scrapes the batter into a tray, smooths over the top, and slides it into the oven. She has made a few batches now and is getting the hang of it.

'Ready?' calls Liam from the sitting room.

He has retrieved the cardboard box from under the stairs and brought the serpentine vase down from the attic. They decided against buying a scatter tube or a biodegradable urn but felt in need of slightly more cere-mony than the bag, so came up with this plan to use an emotionally significant temporary decanter. Juliet likes that knowing the vase once held her mother's ashes will prompt a moment of remembrance every time she fills it with flowers.

'Do you want to hold or snip?' says Liam, offering Juliet the scissors.

'I'll do it,' says Charlie. 'Let me do it.'

'I think you'll have to leave this to us, mate,' says Liam. 'We don't want any spillages.'

Liam lifts the bag and Juliet cuts across the bottom corner. They all watch as the ashes pour into the vase. They are a reddish colour, like powdered granite.

'Would there be more if Granny was a taller person?' says Charlie.

'I don't know,' says Juliet. 'Probably.'

Lucy, Bas and the boys arrive first, the twins still wearing their tae kwon do uniforms and proudly brandishing their yellow belts. Then Sarah with the girls – Stephen is doing a half-marathon that has been in the diary for ages – and Helen and Dan with Freddie and Daisy. The adults crowd into the kitchen and the kids go off with Charlie.

'I want,' says Daisy, struggling in Helen's arms.

'OK,' says Helen, wiping her nose, then putting her down. 'Go with your brother.'

Daisy toddles off.

'She's getting so pretty,' says Lucy.

'And very independent,' says Helen. 'I don't have to worry about Freddie being rough with her any more. She gives as good as she gets.'

Juliet assumes Charlie has taken the children upstairs to his bedroom, but when she goes to call them down she finds them in the sitting room, clustered around the vase.

'We're cuddling Granny,' says Charlie, and she can

see from his expression he knows he is being naughty. She looks more closely at Daisy. Is that . . . ? Yes, Daisy has a fistful of ashes and has rubbed them into her face, mingling them with her snot.

Juliet swoops in and picks her up, just as Dan is coming out of the kitchen. She'd rather tell Helen but blurts out, 'I'm so sorry but the kids have been in the ashes. She's got them all over her face.'

Dan laughs. 'Don't worry.' He holds out his arms for Daisy. 'Let's sort you out, poppet.'

'We'd better get on with it,' says Liam. 'Looks like rain.'

It starts to spit as soon as they get into the garden. Everyone gathers in a circle around the hole and Liam helps Charlie to lift the tree in. Each of the children use Charlie's toy shovel to throw in some earth. Then all the grown-ups use Stephen's spade and Liam hands Juliet the vase.

She looks at these people, their friends, with their sombre respectful faces, and then at the pink petals of the tree. A huge drop of rain falls on her nose as she starts to speak. 'Thanks so much, everyone, for coming to be with us and to witness this scattering, of my mum and Charlie's grandmother, Charlotte. She loved this street and she loved this garden, so it feels like a fitting thing to leave her here. And for there now to be a magnolia tree in Magnolia Road.'

Juliet bends over so that there is no chance of a rogue gust of wind blowing cremains into the faces of any more guests, and sprinkles a symbolic amount of ash around the base of the tree and then the rest into the longer grass at the back of the garden. The rain is falling fast now and she can hear a train approaching. 'Liam was going to read a poem, but in view of the weather, let's call it a day.'

The children run inside and Freddie says, 'What's that yucky smell?' and Juliet realises she has forgotten about the brownies and says 'Fuck' really loudly and then, 'I'm so sorry. I don't have anything to feed you now,' and everyone says it doesn't matter and Juliet offers more tea. Then Bella's high-pitched voice echoes around the house – 'My granny isn't dead. We're moving to Sunset to live with her and I will have a pony' – and Helen says, 'That's not true, Bella, don't tell lies,' and Bella bursts into tears and stamps her foot and says, 'I am not lying.'

The kettle clicks into the silence and then Sarah says, slowly, calmly, 'It isn't a concrete plan. Just something we're discussing. Stephen worries about his mum and likes the idea of the girls growing up in the country. In Somerset. And you wouldn't have a pony, Bella, but there is a riding school nearby.'

'Oh,' says Helen, in a sad little voice, and Dan reaches his arm around her and says, 'Good idea. We're thinking about it, too, aren't we, love? Give London the slip. Go back to Leicester.'

And Helen looks up at him and smiles, and Juliet thinks maybe their marriage does stand a chance, and Liam says, 'Well, we're not going anywhere given we've just buried my mother-in-law in the garden,' and Dan laughs and Daisy says 'Fuck' and then they all laugh, even Helen. Liam opens the fridge and asks if anyone would like a proper drink, and offers Dan a can of lager, and then Bas and Lucy take one, too, and Alice rounds up all the younger children and marches them off to play in Charlie's bedroom, and Juliet stands in the kitchen and listens to the chat and watches the magnolia tree in the downpour and feels grateful to Bas, because what if they didn't know about the soil thing and the tree died and it felt like a curse or an omen. There was nothing elegant or moving about her mother's last ceremony but she wouldn't have it any other way.

Sarah comes up to stand next to her and looks out at the deluge and says, 'My mother-in-law gave me a mug that says, "Life isn't about waiting for the storm to pass, it's learning to dance in the rain."'

Juliet laughs. 'Are you going to enjoy living with her?'

'I doubt it will happen. Stephen likes to have ideas on the boil, but I don't think he really wants to leave London.'

They stay in the kitchen all afternoon as the rain lashes down outside. Lucy encourages Bas to explain some of his attempts to Brexit-proof his business, and Dan tells them how much he likes his new job and shares some of the humiliating things that his old boss used to do when they were behind on their sales targets. Liam says his dad told him that every boss is either a mug or a cunt and you have to work out which. Juliet giggles as she watches the others not quite know how to respond to this and looks at Liam, leaning against the side of the fridge, can of lager in his hand, and thinks how much she loves him. Then he talks about the part-time role as writer in residence in a young offenders' institute that he'll start in September, and how Juliet is going to take Fridays off so that she can be home for Charlie whilst he does it. Sarah says she hopes they'll get better weather for the street party and that the bunting is all sewn together, and Lucy says she is looking forward to the hymn singing when they are all squiffy at the end of the night, and that Brian has offered to print out the words of 'Dear Lord and Father of Mankind' as no one can ever remember past the first two lines. Then she asks Liam to read the poem, so he does. And then Stephen arrives and tells them he ran a new personal best at the half-marathon. They all congratulate him, and then he says he has just bumped into Joseph Karigi, and that after a long labour Amy is safely delivered of a baby girl and they are both doing well. All the women ask what the baby is called and how much she weighs, but Stephen doesn't know. Lucy says, 'You're such a bloke, Stephen. Men never ask the right questions,' and Stephen says, 'I was busy telling him about my new PB. He was very impressed. I remembered to find out if it was a boy or girl, at least,' and Sarah says, 'Leave my husband alone,' and Liam pats him on the back and they all laugh. It might be the lager, or the poetry, or the conjunction of life and death, or even the rain, but they all hug each other and everyone cries.

Epilogue

The sun has shone on the residents of Magnolia Road all day, but the air is turning chilly now and it is getting dark. The bunting flaps in the breeze. All the men are at home with the children. Juliet and Helen sit on a hay bale and Sarah and Lucy stand talking to Joseph, who has little Elizabeth Wangari Karigi in a sling on his chest. She won't sleep in her cot, he says, she needs to be walked around.

'I hope the hymn singing won't disturb you all,' says Sarah.

'Don't worry,' says Joseph. 'We're not on any sort of schedule. Amy sings to the baby all the time.'

'She's adorable,' says Lucy, as Joseph heads off up the street, 'but I wouldn't have a baby again, would you?'

'I miss it,' says Helen. 'The physical closeness. And you don't stop worrying, do you? You think it will get easier as they get older but it just changes.'

'Sandeep says her eldest won't hold her hand in the street any more,' says Sarah.

'Wait until they get to big school,' says Lucy.

'Suzannah's boy told her there's a girl in his class who takes cocaine. Then he wanted to know what fingering is.'

'Don't,' says Helen. 'I don't want to think about all that yet.'

'Pimples,' says Lucy, 'wet dreams, tattoos, gap years.'

'Stop,' cries Helen, 'I mean it.'

Lucy makes an apologetic face, and Juliet puts her arm around Helen and gives her a squeeze.

'I thought Suzannah's new boyfriend seemed very nice,' says Sarah.

'Yes,' agrees Lucy, 'let's hope he doesn't turn out to be too good to be true. She deserves a bit of a break.'

Juliet looks up to see the light in their attic go on. They share the room now. One of Charlie's birthday presents, along with his uniform for Beavers, is a little white desk to go in the corner. Liam has started writing again, just something for Charlie and the other children, he says. It's called *The Amazing Adventures of Charlie Quinn* and is about a boy who can time-travel and talk to animals and who wants to save the world.

'Ladies,' she says, getting up, 'I love you, but I'm tired and cold.'

'Aren't you staying for the hymns?' says Sarah.

'I'm knackered. I'll see if Liam wants to come out for a bit.'

Juliet walks through their gate and down the narrow passage to the garden. She can just make out the magnolia tree in the shadows, behind the stone table. Charlie likes playing by it. 'Look,' he'll say, 'a butterfly has just landed on Granny.'

'Goodnight, Mum,' Juliet whispers, and walks in through the back door.

Juliet pokes her head around Charlie's door. He is fast asleep, his arms around Froggy. She looks at the badge on his curtain; 'I survived the Tunnel of Terror.' Every night it prompts her to remember the ambulance, the hospital, reminds her to give thanks for the continued existence of her son, of them all.

Up in the attic, Liam is at the desk writing in a notebook. Juliet kisses the top of his head and then flops onto the sofa. She looks over at the serpentine vase on the windowsill. 'I often think about Mum,' she says, 'but I only talk to her if I've been drinking.'

'I'm sure that's very normal,' says Liam, putting down his pen. 'Our rational secular beliefs don't hold up in the presence of alcohol. Or tragedy.'

'I sort of prayed. Over Charlie. Or threatened. Did you?'

'Yes.' Liam gets up and comes over to the sofa. 'I promised I'd be a better person. Less obsessed with myself.'

Juliet nestles into the crook of his arm, rests her hand on his chest. 'You can have a turn at the party if you like. I've had enough.'

'I'm happy here,' Liam says.

And he intertwines his fingers with hers, and they sit together as outside in the street the singing begins.

Acknowledgements

I'm grateful, as ever, for the support of my wondrous agent Jo Unwin and all at JULA. This is my fourth book with my editor Francesca Main and I continue to regard our relationship as one of the great privileges of my life. If Liam had Jo and Francesca in his corner he might not be in such a mess. I'm thrilled to be published by Francesca's new imprint Phoenix, grateful to all her colleagues at Orion and Hachette, and delighted to include them in the credits.

For practical, moral, writerly or research support: Grace Alexander, Alison Barrow, Claire de Boursac, Marion Bowyer, Roberta Boyce, Geoff Caddick, Sara Collins, Esther Connor, Jo Dawson, Kate Dimbleby, Caroline Dinham, Janine Giovanni, KK, Sophie Kirkham, Sara Lister, Fiona Lockhart, Julie Lovell, Ashleigh McLellan and Philip Molyneux, Sandeep Mahal, Bonnie Meloche, Wyl Menmuir, Sanja Oakley, Julia Samuel, Jane Shemlit, Nina Stibbe, Sophie Seamark, Jennie Stoddart-Scott, Clare Tyndall and Kit de Waal.

For help with the medical bits: Keir Shiels, Liz O'Riordan, Julie Swain, Inbal Brickner-Braun and Geraldine and Julie Latchem-Hastings. Any mistakes are mine.

Thanks to John, Lizzie, Alice and Annie Waterhouse for hospitality and enduring friendship.

Thanks to my parents, Kevin and Margaret Mintern, for everything and to Ada Buitenhuis-Rentzenbrink for being a dream mother-in-law.

Thanks to Erwyn for inspiration and dishwasher wrangling. Thanks to Matt for graciously giving me permission to make creative use of some of his belongings and expressions and for discussing the plot with me and being my accountability partner. He is very disappointed that Charlie never gets a tarantula. Or a tortoise. Or a kitten. He also says that if I don't acknowledge the contributions of Arabella the cat and Reepicheep the lizard he will leave home.

Credits

Phoenix would like to thank everyone at Orion who worked on the publication of *Everyone Is Still Alive*.

Agent
Jo Unwin

Editor
Francesca Main

Copy-editor
Claire Gatzen

Proofreader
Donna Hillyer

Marketing
Cait Davies

Production
Claire Keep
Fiona McIntosh

Editorial Management
Clarissa Sutherland
Kate Moreton
Charlie Panayiotou
Jane Hughes
Claire Boyle
Jake Alderson

Design
Lucie Stericker
Debbie Holmes
Joanna Ridley
Nick May
Clare Sivell
Helen Ewing

Publicity
Leanne Oliver

Audio

Paul Stark

Amber Bates

Contracts

Anne Goddard

Paul Bulos

Jake Alderson

Finance

Jennifer Muchan

Jasdip Nandra

Rabale Mustafa

Ibukun Ademefun

Levancia Clarendon

Tom Costello

Sales

Jen Wilson

Victoria Laws

Esther Waters

Lucy Brem

Frances Doyle

Ben Goddard

Georgina Cutler

Jack Hallam

Ellie Kyrke-Smith

Inês Figuiera

Barbara Ronan

Andrew Hally

Dominic Smith

Deborah Deyong

Lauren Buck

Maggy Park

Linda McGregor

Sinead White

Jemimah James

Rachael Jones

Jack Dennison

Nigel Andrews

Ian Williamson

Julia Benson

Declan Kyle

Robert Mackenzie

Imogen Clarke

Megan Smith

Charlotte Clay

Rebecca Cobbold

Operations

Jo Jacobs

Sharon Willis

Lisa Pryde

Rights

Susan Howe

Richard King

Krystyna Kujawinska

Jessica Purdue

Louise Henderson